Plague of Darkness

Daniel G. Keohane

Other Road Press
www.otherroadpress.com

Plague of Darkness

ISBN 10: 0-9837329-4-9
ISBN 13: 978-0-9837329-4-5

Published in October 2014
by Other Road Press, Princeton MA

For information, please contact:
www.otherroadpress.com

Cover Design by Elderlemon Design

Printed in the United States of America

Other Novels
by Daniel G. Keohane

Margaret's Ark
Solomon's Grave

as G. Daniel Gunn

Destroyer of Worlds

Short Story Collections

Christmas Trees and Monkeys

i

Daniel G. Keohane

For Linda

Many, many thanks to everyone over the years who's been a part of making this story what it is today. My wife Linda, first reader extraordinaire who never lets me get away with anything, as well as Mark Lowell, Fran Bellerive and Marty Holman. Karen Heath of St. Francis Episcopal Church, invaluable and generous with information on how things work in her denomination. Chantra Prum for sitting with me to work out the *Khmer* (language of Cambodia) translations throughout the manuscript, and Joe and Sharon DiFranza for bringing us together. Rev. Dr. Clayton Morris, from the main offices of the Episcopal Church in New York City, who was kind enough to answer my strange questions one day over the phone. Special shout out, wherever you are, to the people of the *Olive Branch* and *Borders* bookstores, where I spent many lunches working on early drafts of this novel. Alas, both bookstores are no longer with us. Life moves on. Dave Long who had some very good personal comments on an early draft of where the story could go, and the late Jim Hicks, who provided insight into ham radio operation and lingo. Mom & Dad, as always, for everything. Andrew, Amanda and Audrey for making me the proud papa that I am. And, of course, I thank God for giving me the ability, and opportunity, to string words together like I do sometimes.

I hope you all enjoy the story.

Plague of Darkness

Daniel G. Keohane

Paul,
hope you enjoy the book
and merry Christmas,

Dan Keohane
Dec '14

Daniel G. Keohane

Then the Lord said to Moses, "Stretch out your hand toward the sky so that darkness will spread over Egypt – darkness that can be felt." So Moses stretched out his hand toward the sky, and total darkness covered all Egypt for three days. No one could see anyone else or leave his place for three days. Yet all the Israelites had light in the places where they lived."
– Exodus 10:21-23, NIV

Out of the Darkness

An hour before her world was swallowed by the Darkness, a football sailed by Gem Davidson's window. It dropped from sight and landed with a *thap* in someone's hands. Her brother Eliot and his buddy Carl, tossing the ball around while they waited for the Patriots' preseason kick-off at one o'clock. She was surprised Mrs. Watts, her new neighbor, hadn't stormed outside and yelled at them to get off her grass, since she and her husband owned most of the property between Gem's house and the church.

Not a church, she corrected herself. It always looked like any other house in the neighborhood, but *inside* it used to be different. Though she'd never been a part of Saint Gerard's congregation, Gem missed waking up to their music every Sunday morning. She'd lay in bed, listening to the tinny organ and off-key voices.

At this point she assumed the place was gutted with holes in every wall. Gem hadn't been over there since the ceremony last December, when the Episcopal bishop closed the church and kicked God out. After peeking inside the front doors for a few minutes that night, Gem had risked one last excursion to the downstairs meeting hall while everyone was busy upstairs – a way of saying goodbye to her secret hidey-hole and the closest she'd ever come to attending the church, herself.

A sad smile worked across her face as she sat watching the football sail past the window again. That night Paul Giroux – he, of the electric blue eyes which made her legs weak whenever she passed him in school – had caught her peeking through the front church doors and spoken to her as he, and three others, carried out the altar. He'd explained that Saint Gerard's was being *deconsecrated*. It didn't make a whole lot of sense then, and still didn't. You couldn't simply un-make a church, could you? Well, obviously you could, because they did.

Still, every weekend since December, Mister and Mrs. Watts, the architect and his wife who'd bought the place, dragged out more broken pieces, brought in fresh lumber and smiled and waved when they saw Gem – at least *Mister* Watts did. His wife had long ago perfected that neighbor-hating glare of hers. So far the woman hadn't made any issue of Eliot's incessant games of catch between their homes, but it was only a matter of time. In any case, Gem never waved back.

The sound of saws and hammers was absent these past few weeks. On a rare night last Thursday when Gem's mother actually sat with the rest of the family for supper, Deanna Davidson mentioned seeing a moving van in front of the house next door.

Gem leaned forward, rested her chin on her hand and stared out the window. Her on-again, mostly off-again boyfriend Matt was vacationing with his family, and her best friend Audrey was competing in a summer swim league. A beautiful Saturday with nothing to do. She should go to Salisbury Beach alone, work on her tan. Her new driver's license was burning a hole in her pocket, may as well use it. She wondered – a flicker of consideration she tried to snuff out completely – if Paul Giroux was doing anything. He'd been saying *hi* to her in the halls more often during school, and he'd actually invited her during that infamous snowy night in December to visit the new church in Westminster. Gem tried not to read anything into that. He would've picked something a bit more romantic than going to church if he'd been asking her on a date.

She got up from her chair and wandered downstairs. The house was quiet. After mowing the lawn, Dad had disappeared into the attic to play with his ham radio. Right now he was probably deep in conversation with some fellow hammer in Germany. Those disembodied voices snatched from the air were her Dad's real family. She and her brother were afterthoughts, blinked into focus whenever he deigned to come downstairs and see what the "locals" were up to. Her mother said she was going out. As always, she never said where. Didn't matter, nothing new.

Gem eventually settled on the front porch. Not much of a tan to be gotten here. Eliot appeared on her left, running back to catch a long pass. He noticed her, said, "Hey." She ignored him.

An ugly tan Volvo squealed to a stop in front of the church. Gem recognized the car before the tall, red-headed woman stepped out from the driver's seat.

Mrs. Lindu was back.

Reverend Joyce Lindu and her daughter Rebecca used to live next door until they closed the place up. She'd been the pastor and still was a priest, as far as Gem knew, over at the new digs in Westminster, just not in charge anymore. There'd been a *Mister* Lindu for a while but he'd split. *Good riddance*, in Gem's opinion. She assumed living in a tiny corner of a house that was used mostly by other people wasn't for him. Not to mention Ray Lindu was a complete dick. Thinking of him sent a stab of fear through her, so she focused on Joyce, who was laying one of her priestly sash-doohickies around her neck and looking up at the Watts' house.

Gem stood and stepped off the porch. She only intended to take a few steps and pretend to watch the boys. Except she didn't stop. Her heart beat faster as she passed Eliot, ignoring his questioning glance. In her head she screamed, *Go back, go back!* but kept on walking. Passing the front of the Watts' house, Gem remembered she wasn't wearing any sneakers. Her white socks were going to turn green from the lawn. She wondered briefly if Joyce had come back to reopen the church, then realized how stupid that thought was. Probably just visiting, and here was Gem waltzing into the middle of it. Too late to turn back, though. She was standing in the Watts' driveway, the pavement hot under her socks. Joyce gave her a wide smile.

"Gem!" She closed the distance between them and wrapped her in a long-armed hug. "How are you?"

"I – " she began, a bit flustered by the affection. "I'm OK, I guess. Are you back to open it up again? As a church I mean?" Her face burned. Why did she say something so stupid? Why the hell did she care, anyway?

Joyce looked at her for a moment without speaking, laid a hand briefly on the girl's cheek. The touch was cool, affectionate. Her silence, of course, could have indicated scorn or pity. "No," she whispered, "I'm sorry."

Gem looked down in embarrassment and watched her socks melt into the hot driveway.

"You seem upset about that," Joyce added. "Having second thoughts now about all those invitations?" She said it with a laugh, but the words hurt. Over the years, the

Davidsons had been invited over, sometimes just for a visit, other times to attend service. The former was accepted, at least a couple of times. Though Gem and Rebecca were six years apart they got along okay. Bec even baby-sat her a couple of times, eons ago. Never the latter, though. Her parents weren't church people and after Gem's brother was born, Joyce stopped asking. Tired of rejection, most likely.

She stuffed her hands into the pockets of her jeans. "No. I wasn't. I mean, it's just that, I don't know, it all was kind of weird. Closing up for good like that."

Joyce laid a hand on Gem's shoulder and gently nudged her around to face the house. "Closing a parish is always tough. But it was for the best. Everyone's adjusted to the new place. Have you met the Watts?"

"No." Gem didn't mean to say the word so harshly. "I'm sorry. I should go home."

To Gem's horror, Joyce led her along the walk towards the front door. "Come inside with me. I'm getting the *grand tour*, then giving the home an official blessing. I haven't been inside myself since the deconsecration ceremony."

Gem held back. She didn't want to be rude and pull away, but no way did she want to get *any* closer. "I really should go."

"Reverend Lindu!"

Oh, no.

Mrs. Watts held open the screen door. Her husband loomed a couple of steps behind her, just inside and smiling as always. Unlike Mister Watts, who was tall and lanky, his wife was short and Chinese, or some kind of Asian. Pretty for her age, though Gem would never admit it. Their eyes briefly met before the woman turned her attention to the priest.

If Gem didn't leave now Joyce would try to introduce them.

God, please, get me out of this!

"Seyha, have you met your neighbor? Seyha Watts, this is Gem Davidson from next door."

Part of her knew that Joyce was fulfilling some sisterly-love requirement, but Gem really, really wanted to punch her in the mouth. That was probably some kind of sin, since she was a priest, or *minister*, whatever they called themselves.

"Gem," Joyce said, "meet Seyha Watts. Seyha, would it be possible –"

No, no, no no!

"– if Gem joins us? I think she'd find it fascinating."

Maybe one punch would only be a *minor* sin, nothing to keep her out of heaven.

Mrs. Watts didn't seem to care much for the idea. After a pause she said, "Well, of course," and glared at Gem. "I mean, it's changed quite a bit since you've been here last. The *upstairs*, too."

Gem's heart skipped a beat. She *knew*. Of *course* she did. That final night, when Gem had been standing in the hall downstairs, surrounded by coffee urns and cookie trays the sudden clomping of boots from upstairs had given her barely enough warning to clamber back outside before everyone poured into the room. Nothing like seeing someone's leg scurrying through the cellar window to prove your neighbor had stopped by for a visit.

It was time to go, no question.

"That's OK," she said, taking a step sideways. "You guys go on without me. Maybe another time."

Her neighbor looked pleased. "Well, if you must. I'm sure we'll have a house-warming party for everyone soon, so you can see it at a more appropriate time."

Joyce moved her gaze from speaker to speaker, raising one eyebrow as if to say, *Last chance*. Ten seconds earlier

Gem was ready to run home and hide under the bed, but Mrs. Watts' gleeful acceptance of her answer felt like an insult. She wasn't good enough to step inside their shiny new house.

Joyce lowered her eyebrow and said, "Very nice seeing you again, Gem," then stepped towards the house, leaving her behind.

This is what you wanted wasn't it? Get out *of here.*

No, what she wanted now was to irritate her snotty new neighbor.

Joyce stepped inside the open door. Gem trotted a step behind, keeping her eyes on Mrs. Watts. When it looked like she was going to close the door on her, Gem shouted, "Actually, maybe I *will* join you. Just for a little while. See what you've done with the place."

At the door, they both avoided eye contact, but Mrs. Watts' tightened expression gave the girl the first bit of pleasure in an otherwise boring day.

* * *

The amazement on Reverend Lindu's face when she got her first look inside almost made the hassles of the past year worth it. Seyha would have preferred giving her the grand tour without the *Girl Next Door* glaring at them – she'd been glaring all year, in fact. And for what? Taking her playhouse away? One afternoon prior to the closing, when she'd walked through the house with the appraiser, Seyha had noticed the lingering presence of a candle. None was found, but when she opened one of the stained glass panels for fresh air she caught a glimpse of Gem Davidson running like a madwoman across their respective backyards. It was the last time she'd found any sign of the girl having been inside the house until the night of the ceremony,

13

when Bill discovered a melting pile of snow under the basement window and footprints in the snow outside leading next door. She made him change the locks as soon as they passed papers. Little Miss Davidson never returned.

Until now.

Just ignore her, she told herself.

Bill ushered them in with a wave. Joyce gave him a hug and introduced the girl. He smiled and shook her hand, pleased to finally meet her in person (his words). At least he hadn't *hugged* her. Seyha wouldn't have put that past him. Bill was an interminable hugger.

He said, "You ready for the tour?"

Joyce nodded, still looking around the foyer and sneaking a peek beyond. Bill began to recount, with too much detail in Seyha's opinion, how they'd redone the entranceway into a small foyer, leaving the basement door but adding a new wall to separate the former church hall. He pointed out one of the two original pews he'd refinished, sounding like a child showing off artwork to a parent. Seyha supposed that wasn't far from the truth. Joyce had been Bill's pastor here. *Only* Bill's. Seyha stopped attending with him after only a few trial runs. He knew enough of Seyha's background – the fact that she'd lost her family very young, been raised in a Catholic-run orphanage in Cambodia before coming to the United States as a teenager – to assume her reluctance related somehow to that time. She never dissuaded him of this, only of ever talking about it. The past was gone. It had no place in the present, in their life.

Seyha took Joyce's arm and said, "Bill, let's keep to the big stuff. Reverend Lindu doesn't need all this detail, yet. If ever."

"Please, call me Joyce."

Seyha ushered her into the Great Room. The kid

followed behind like a stray dog, gratefully keeping any comments to herself.

Just ignore her.

The floor plan in this part of the house – once the church-proper – remained open, the demarcation of living and dining area defined by changes in the flooring instead of walls. The living area was covered with thick, white carpeting. A couch and two matching chairs took up most of the space, forming a U that faced the windows until the new entertainment center arrived next week.

Joyce stared up at the ceiling. Seyha said, "As you can see, we kept the full height of the room. A cathedral ceiling – literally!"

"That's Sey's favorite sound bite," Bill said, "for when the reporter comes. The paper wants to write a piece on the house."

Joyce smiled. "That's great. Couldn't ask for better publicity for your construction business." She waved her arms around the living area. "This is incredible. This is *beautiful.*"

They walked toward the far end, a step-high raised hardwood floor with dining table and chairs, then a short hallway and the bedrooms beyond.

The entire left hand wall facing the Davidson house was the most striking feature of the room. Half of the original, full-height stained glass windows remained. Every other had been replaced with clear, double-pane casements. The mixture of natural and filtered light played across the room like shallow water, draping the otherwise bare walls with soft patterns of color.

"Down the hall," Bill said, "we've retained the full bath and your daughter's old room as a guest room, but as you can see," he waved towards the far end, "we've moved the kitchen up front here, and used its old location to expand the master suite."

"You turned the altar into a *kitchen*...?"

They hadn't noticed Gem wandering past until now. Her arms lifted slightly as if warding off some unseen attacker. When she turned to face them, her stunned expression was directed at Seyha. "You made it into a kitchen?"

Bill stepped between them, pretending not to notice her anger. "Sure did! As you can see, we didn't completely seal off the Great Room from the chancel end of the building." The small, modern kitchen was visible through a large rectangular opening in the wall in front of them. He gestured to the right. "The actual entrance to the kitchen faces the bedroom hallway."

When it looked like Gem was about to say something else, Seyha gave the minister's arm a slight tug. "Joyce, come see the rest of the house. There's so much to show you. Then you could perform the blessing before Bill drags you back to look at all his new trim."

As they walked towards the hallway, Bill said, "Coming, Gem?"

The girl shook her head and looked back into the kitchen. Seyha stifled an urge to slap her.

*   *   *

The Watts had done a wonderful job with the renovations. The most surprising aspect – a pleasant surprise, Joyce decided – was how well she'd taken being inside the house again. All during Bill's excited comments, she'd felt oddly detached. This wasn't home anymore. Perhaps the past year living with Bec in their new apartment had been more therapeutic than she realized. Time away, time to forget. Begin a new life somewhere else.

She opened the ceremony book, and said, "The Lord be with you." Her sweeping gestures included the Watts' sullen neighbor. Gem was sitting with her stocking feet curled under her on the couch. She looked so bored with the proceedings, Joyce wondered why she bothered to stay.

Bill and Seyha replied, "And also with you."

"Let us pray."

She nodded to Bill, who struck a match and lit the long white candle held in Seyha's hands. Joyce read from the *Book of Occasional Services,* the same one used in the ceremony last December. "Almighty and everlasting God, grant this home the grace of your presence, that you may be known to the inhabitants of this dwelling, and the defenders of this household; through Jesus Christ our Lord, who with you and the Holy Spirit lives and reigns, one God, forever and ever. Amen."

"Amen," replied the couple.

Someone whispered behind her. Joyce turned.

No one besides Gem was there. Outside, her brother continued his eternal game of toss in the side yard. Must have been *his* voice, carried through the open casements. She turned back to the couple, laid down the book and lifted her Bible, opening it to a bookmarked passage. She read aloud a story from *Genesis,* of Abraham and the three visitors. In the corner of her eye, Gem Davidson watched them with a slow-growing interest.

Joyce's right ear itched. She reached up to scratch it and noticed Bill doing the same. She finished the passage. Gem looked suddenly over her shoulder. A look of worry creased her forehead, then she turned back and slumped onto the cushions. The girl's eyes kept returning to the back of the couch, as if expecting something to leap up behind her.

Joyce focused on Seyha and Bill, laying the Bible onto the dining table and taking up the smaller ceremony book again. "Let the mighty power of the Holy God be present in this place, to banish –"

"*Sometimes enn sssh...*"

The whisper was behind her, closer and clearer. Her surprise showed as only a pause in her reading, minimal enough she hoped no one noticed. "...from it every unclean spirit, to cleanse it from every residue of evil, and to make it a secure habitation for those who dwell in it."

Bill looked towards the kitchen. So did Seyha. Joyce finished, "In the name of Jesus Christ our Lord. Amen."

Realizing she'd finished, the couple looked back and muttered a distracted, "Amen."

Bill raised a hand, "Excuse me a moment, Reverend." He walked into the kitchen, looked around then returned quickly. "Sorry, thought I heard someone talking."

Joyce exhaled slowly. "I heard something, too. I think it's just the boys outside."

Seyha looked at the windows, then back to the kitchen. With a suspicious glance towards Gem, she shrugged and raised the candle higher.

"We should proceed to every room," Joyce said, "and offer a specific blessing. We'll come back to the living room for the final invocation. Sound like a plan?"

Bill and Seyha agreed and they moved into the kitchen. Gem stayed on the couch, following their progress with a slight turn of her head. Joyce gave her a wink through the opening in the wall and was heartened to see the girl blush. Gem wasn't as tough as she liked to pretend.

Joyce read, "Blessed are you, O Lord, King of the universe, for you give us food and drink to sustain our lives: Make us grateful for all your mercies, and mindful of the needs of others; though Jesus Christ our Lord. Amen."

"Amen."

"*Amen...*"

The voice was clear, and did *not* come from outside. The fine hair on the back of Joyce's neck prickled. She looked over at Gem, but the girl hadn't spoken. Joyce had a sudden mental image of Linda Blair in *The Exorcist*. The voice had been male, a tone of amusement with that one spoken word.

You heard the boys outside again. Nothing more. It *felt* like more, and the feeling wasn't helped by the fact that the kitchen suddenly darkened. The sun, dimming behind a cloud. The Watts were waiting. They apparently hadn't heard anything.

"You all right?" Bill asked.

"I'm fine. Just lost my place. Time to move down the hall?" She looked at Gem in case she'd decided to join them. The girl watched with a forced indifference, then turned her head sharply towards the front entrance.

Something was wrong.

The living room looked darker, too. Definitely just a cloud, Joyce thought nervously, moving in front of the sun.

* * *

This house was starting to give her the creeps. Gem kept hearing someone whispering, once from right beside her. She pulled her feet tighter beneath her and stared at Eliot and his friend, still tossing the football. Just before releasing it, Eliot would glance at the house. She'd never seen her attention-deficit brother stick to anything this long. Obviously, he'd seen her go inside and was waiting for her to come out, tell him about the Magical World of Watts.

This is nuts. Why am I still here?

Joyce and company were in the master bedroom by now – not a place Gem wanted to see.

She should leave. Mrs. Watts wasn't even *pretending* to like her.

She thought about the Bible passage Joyce read. Bizarre, of course. A lot of the stories in that book were. Gem tried to read a few chapters this past Spring in the school library, making sure she was tucked well out of sight in a corner. Just out of curiosity, to see why so many people kept going to church week after week. The stories were pretty repetitive and disjointed. Maybe Joyce could explain it to her.

Why bother, she thought. Gem didn't even go to church. Joyce wasn't going to take time out to explain anything to someone like her.

"Someone like you...." The words were followed by a quiet giggle, stretched out, then, *"Yea..."*

Gem bit her lip to keep from screaming. Someone was in the room. She stood up on the couch and glanced over the back again, half-expecting to see one of Eliot's buddies crouching there with a stupid grin on his face.

No one.

Things were getting a little too *Twilight Zoney* here.

The lights dimmed. Gem looked around. The lights weren't even *on*. Outside was bright and sunny. Inside, everything had an evening quality to it.

She stared at Eliot holding the football close to his chest. His buddy Carl was beside him, now. They talked and glanced surreptitiously at the house, looking like they were finally giving up and heading inside for the kick-off. They'd better not have put one of their buddies up to sneaking downstairs and spooking the neighbors, because it was also spooking her. *Bad idea, Eliot.*

Problem was, her brother was too *boring* to be that creative.

Gem got off the couch and walked towards the

window, intending to ask him before the Watts got back. Tell him to knock it off.

"*You're alone...*" the voice was behind her. Gem screamed and spun around, swinging her right arm.

No one there. Again.

Joyce ran out of the hallway and into the dining room. "Gem, what's wrong?" She still held that little black book she'd been reading. The Watts followed a pace behind.

Oh, Great. Definitely, absolutely, time to leave.

"Nothing," she said. "I'm okay."

Bill stepped past the others. His earlier smile had dropped to a scowl. "Did you hear something, too?"

The room was getting darker. Gem found it hard to focus on his face. Was she fainting? She nodded and said, "I thought I did. I don't know."

He looked out the window. "One of those boys your brother?"

Mrs. Watts stumbled forward as if pushed, turned around and covered her ears. She moaned quietly, the opposite of Gem's earlier reaction but no less startled. She stared at her husband and lowered her hands.

"Bill, who is that talking?"

Seeing the fear on the everyone's face, Gem's only thought was to get outside, fast. "Listen, things are starting to get weird, so maybe I –"

"And it's getting dark, as well," Joyce interrupted. She was looking around the room.

Mrs. Watts took a step toward Gem, her once-startled expression changing to rage. "If you think this game you're playing is funny, Miss Davidson, you're wrong." The candle in her hand had almost melted, some of the wax dripping over the round cardboard base above her fingers.

"I'm not doing anything, lady! Maybe it's you trying to scare *me*. You didn't want me here anyway!"

"Maybe I don't – "

"Sey, please..." Bill interrupted.

"No. It's true. This girl sneaks into our house more than once and then waltzes inside today, of all days, completely uninvited."

Gem tried to act casual, walking towards the couch. If she left now, it would be admitting she was responsible for what was happening. She stopped short of sitting back down, however.

Joyce's voice was quiet but stern, "Seyha, I invited her, you know that. I'm sorry for causing trouble. I really think we should finish the ceremony." She scanned the room one more time, then added, "Soon."

"*Finish...*"

Everyone jerked at the voice, and the laughter that followed. Gem screeched and finally jumped onto the couch, pulled up her feet and half-crouched. They'd *all* heard it this time. Why was it getting so *dark* in here? Mrs. Watts stared at her.

"What now, Gem? One of your friends waiting in a closet with a monster costume?"

"Sey, please."

Gem shouted, "No, you're crazy. This house is haunted!"

With an edge of uncertainty, Bill said, "There are no such things as ghosts, Gem. Let me run downstairs in case someone's hiding down there."

"No." The desperation in Joyce's voice held him back. She walked into the living room and stood in front of the coffee table. "We need to finish the ceremony." Her hands shook.

"Joyce," said Bill, "don't tell me *you* think...." But he didn't finish.

Her attempt at a smile did not hold long. "No... no, of

course not. But something feels wrong here. That wasn't a child's voice. And the room is getting noticeably darker, at least to me. I don't understand what's happening, but the only thing that makes sense is to finish."

"Nothing's happening!" Mrs. Watts screamed. She no longer pretended to be angry. She looked as terrified as Gem felt.

"There are other concerns in the world besides ghosts." Joyce opened the book without waiting for a response and read, "The effect of righteousness will be peace..."

The light in the room faded, darker, darker, someone slowly turning a dimming switch. Gem felt claustrophobic. She had to get out of there. On the other side of the tall windows, Eliot and Carl had spread out, not yet content to go inside. The sun shone bright and cloudless over them. Except its light didn't make it through the glass. Maybe the windows were tinted. An opaque, smoky darkness spread along their edges like black frost. Gem focused on her brother. Her throat was too tight, she had no voice. Instead, she sent a mental scream for help, praying Eliot would smash through the window to rescue his big sister.

Joyce was shouting. "...and the result of righteous tranquility and trust forever."

Eliot wound back for a throw. *Look at me!* Gem pleaded.

"My people will abide in secure dwellings...."

Somewhere far away, Gem heard laughter. The darker the room, the louder the voice. Laughter running like a creek under more laughter.

God, please help me. If this is my fault, I'm sorry.

"...and in quiet resting places!"

But God didn't live here anymore, did he?

Mrs. Watts whispered, "Bill, what's going on?" The darkness had physical presence, filling up the house like dirt in a grave, wrapping around Gem's head. The only clear thing she could see was the center of the window across from her, Eliot releasing the football in a long arcing path to his friend.

Joyce screamed, "Unless the Lord builds the house, their labor is in vain who build it! Let us pray!"

Then the world was swallowed up in darkness.

First Day of Darkness

Bill Watts could see nothing in front of him. The upper half of his face was enveloped in a thick black gauze which had no weight, no substance even as it pressed snugly against his cheeks. He fumbled with his fingers to pull the mask free, but felt only his skin. There was nothing there. But there *was*. He could *feel* it covering his eyes and nose like a blindfold.

"Bill! Bill, I can't see!" Seyha's voice, next to him. He reached out, his left hand closing around an arm. Seyha screamed, tried to pull away.

"It's me! Sey, it's me."

The struggling stopped, the arm moved closer. "I can't see you," she said. "I can't see!" Seyha's familiar shape leaned against him. "Get it off me, get it off!"

"Quiet. Calm down." Bill wanted to reassure her, but could barely manage composure in his voice with so much of his own confusion and panic.

He felt Seyha's arm rise up to her face. Bill reached around her and managed to grab both of her wrists, more to not lose her than stop his wife from hurting herself. The blindness was so complete. He suddenly imagined they'd been sealed inside a box, the box filled with dirt, buried below the ground. His breath came in short gasps. His panic was growing. He needed to be rational, for Seyha's sake. The others were shouting – Gem for someone named Eliot, Joyce for Gem then for him and Seyha.

He pulled his wife against him again and shouted, "We're OK. We're here." He no longer was sure where *here* was.

Seyha shouted against his chest, "We're blind!" He felt her arms trying to reach up to her face again.

We're blind. No, that can't be true.

He said, "The lights are just out...."

Even before Gem shouted, "It's daytime!" Bill knew his statement was ludicrous. His eyes were open, he'd inadvertently poked them more than once before his hands became too occupied in holding Seyha. He purposefully moved his eyes left, right, saw nothing. Again, he couldn't shake the sensation of something covering his face. He didn't try to touch it again. It would mean letting go of Seyha.

They weren't blind, just *blinded.*

"Calm," Joyce's voice, further away now. "We have to stay calm. I'm not sure which way the entrance..." Her voice faded entirely.

"Joyce?"

"Bill!" Seyha's voice, distant though she was right in front of him. The phantom gauze crawled further along his cheeks, towards the back of his head. Creeping like foam over both ears. *No... please!*

Then she was no longer there. Bill's hands were empty. He called out, not hearing his own voice. In desperation he clawed at his face, struggling to breathe even though his mouth seemed free of the enigma. Only his eyes and ears. He could breathe, but began to gasp with a drowning man's terror. He sucked in a deep breath, screamed a loud and guttural shriek, hoping if nothing else to hear his own voice.

Silence, like his teenage days wearing oversized headphones, too lazy to get up and turn the record over. Emptiness. He was lost, buried alive in black.

He didn't dare step forward. Instead Bill bent his legs and reached down. There, the familiar texture of the carpet. He was still in the living room. Nylon fibers under his fingertips. He tried to situate himself from where he'd been before the lights went out. He reached forward, to lay hold of Seyha again or touch one of the chairs, coffee table, anything. Nothing there. If he could only get to Seyha, lay her hand down on the carpet like he was doing. Show her they weren't as lost as she must be thinking.

His body hitched with a sob. *God, help me! Help us!*

No sound. No light. Nothing but touch.

That was when the laughter returned, the same darkly amused voice they'd heard earlier. It penetrated the gauzy black air covering his ears. Very close.

Bill froze.

The whisper said, *"If you only knew."* Another chuckle. *"But you know nothing, do you? Secrets and more secrets."* The voice sounded male, but... *loose.* Not a physical voice, belonging to any person, any mouth – Stop it, he thought, this is insane!

Who are you? He shouted, but heard nothing of his own voice, not even an echo in his head. A renewed sense of claustrophobia gripped his chest, a feeling that there wasn't enough air. He ran his fingers along the carpet to reassure himself.

And felt grass.

Tall grass, which hadn't been cut in a long time. When he leaned forward the tips of a few blades tickled his nose. Bill jerked back, rubbed his hands along his face and arms, slowly lowered them again. Definitely grass.

How....

The darkness thinned. The texture of the blindfold against his face didn't change, but Bill could see a hazy detail in front of him. The scene was indistinct, viewed through a thin curtain.

His hand was in grass. Dirt under that, pushing into his nails.

That made no sense. He hadn't moved from his spot

on the rug, but now he was outside. At least he could see *something*. Bill tried one more time to pull away the dissipating mask. His nails scratched lightly across his cheeks, but found no purchase. The darkness faded to a lingering mist, a translucent veil hanging in front of him.

At least now he could see where he was. Crouched on all fours, on a familiar hillside. His brain whirled from vertigo. This is not where he had been. He'd been... where? He couldn't remember.

The periphery of his vision was stained black, like the windows a few minutes ago, but he recognized this knoll. It overlooked the town of Hillcrest, the next one over from where he.. where he *what*? He was... he had moved out after graduation, rented a small room in Hillcrest... hadn't been here long before meeting... someone. He couldn't even remember where he'd just been a moment earlier....

Someone approached, over the hill, a blurred impression sharpening as it neared the lone tree in front of him. The tree itself stood out in perfect focus, the center of all things. Now a young woman, black hair. Asian. *Cambodian*, he thought, not understanding how he knew this. Bill sat back on his haunches, ready to run if she asked what he was doing here. Having crested the hill, she knelt in the grass beside the tree. He saw her face clearly, but a cloud hovered over his memory, an inability to place her in the context of a bigger life he couldn't remember.

She rearranged a small bunch of flowers in her hand. Finished, she rose again and ran the remaining few yards towards him. Her dress flowed behind as she ran, billowed as she knelt a second time. Bill remembered.

He was married to this woman.

Seyha! he said. He could hear his voice no more than before. She laughed, catching her breath.

"I need to rest. But I beat you! Remember that!"

Was she talking to *him*? Yes. They were on a date. Their *first* date. He liked her. This shy but strong woman, ten years older than he was, who worked as secretary to his boss, Brian Naughton.

She brushed a strand of black hair from her face. He needed to say something to her. God, he thought, she's so beautiful. *Sey, can you see me?*

She shook her head. "They're going to miss us if we don't get back soon."

Her words were slightly off from the movement of her lips, as if dubbed. Maybe, Bill thought, it took longer for sound to reach him in this nightmare universe of half-memory. She smiled, reminding him how much her round face lit up his world every time this happened, and how rare it had become.

Behind him, the dark voice said, "*So rare that smile now....*" A low, guttural sound. Bill turned to see its source, and would have moaned in despair if he had a voice. Behind him was a solid black wall. More specifically there was *nothing* behind him. Nothing at all....

He looked back to Seyha, who was saying, "I don't care either." She stared at him. Was he supposed to say something? Maybe she was talking to the owner of the other voice. No, she was speaking to him. He remembered this conversation, but it was a long time ago. Then again, when was... now?

The tree beside her blurred, like a frustrated artist wiping a palm across his newly-painted creation. Seyha blurred with it. Bill tried to reach out, saw the details of his own hand smeared by a second, angry swipe.

A second later his hand came back into focus, holding Seyha's across a white tablecloth.

In this new place, everything became clear again. They were lost in some insane darkness which had swallowed their home. As ludicrous as the thought sounded in his mind, it felt truer than what must be the only rational explanation – he'd passed out for some reason during the ceremony and was now dreaming.

Sey, I have you. Hold on!

She looked down at the plate, her salmon barely touched. He saw the fear he felt reflected on her face. "I know. I'm not... I know."

An overwhelming sensation of *déjà vu* washed over him. This had happened before. The dream, but not a dream. Memory. Their first dinner date after the miscarriage. Only four years after the soft joy of that time on the hillside and already the hardness was changing her beautiful, exotic face.

Her hand in his. The engagement ring and wedding band on her finger glistened in the candlelight. It looked new. Newer, at least. They were still three months shy of their first wedding anniversary. He wanted to look around, but could not control his body. The place was instantly recognizable, however. They were in Hillcrest again, at The Cabel Grille.

Seyha, what's happening?

He would have trembled with fear if the emotion had an outlet, but his body didn't seem to notice. The hand before him - *his* hand - was calm. Bill was not in control of this body, only a passenger, a moaning spirit inhabiting the *Bill Watts* of this sad, but healing moment in their life.

"We can try again soon, though." It was his voice, but he hadn't intentionally said the words. "That's what Doctor Chen said, right?" He felt his jaw, his throat move with the words, heard the voice in his head. He sensed something behind him again, likely the same *something* from the hill. Its presence was confirmed by a tickle of breath on the nape of his neck. He tried unsuccessfully to grip Seyha's hand tighter. She didn't notice, her fingers cool and light against his palm. He could not turn his head to see the demon – that's what it was, no question, that's what it *had* to be, *There are other concerns in the world besides ghosts*, Reverend Lindu had said. He tried to scream for Seyha to run, but she only said, "I love you, Bill. Always." Looking up and into his eyes for the briefest of moments before closing them, releasing twin streams of tears down her face.

Something was different with the memory. The look in her eyes. He remembered a seemingly unfathomable sadness in this dinner. Maybe it was still there, in that brief glimpse, maybe his perspective was skewed from the insanity that was going on around him. It seemed... diminished. But he was seeing it with different eyes.

"*Always*," mocked the demon beside him, just out of sight – *no, there are no demons*, Bill thought. *Not like this*. He was just having a nightmare. All of this was a nightmare.

The voice laughed, almost kissing his ear. "*Now, Billy, listen and watch carefully. For once in your silly pious life, look... and listen.*"

Help me, someone!

"*Help me, someone!*" the voice echoed. "*OK, ready? Pay attention, there'll be a quiz later....*"

When the voice behind him spoke next, Bill understood that it was parodying something he himself must have said in this moment. With its dark cadence, it said, "*Someday, when Watts Construction is on solid ground, we can get a real house, with a real yard.*"

She looked directly at him, her face alighting on something positive. This, the healing part of his memory of this night. Hope for her to latch onto and, more importantly for Seyha and her need to be doing something, being actively focused on something aside from what she'd just been through. She gripped his hand tighter. It felt like he was holding her through gloves, never completely feeling it. "So you're going to do it? You mean it?" She looked sideways for a moment. "'Watts Construction'... Sounds plural!" She laughed. "Always has."

Even in the midst of this nightmare, Bill smiled to himself, remembering her words so clearly. *Plural.* The Watts, both of them working together. Bill and Seyha.

The demon-voice hissed, *"And someday, (giggle),"* it spoke the word "giggle," *"I promise, Watts... plural of course... and son. Or daughter. Or both!"*

For just a fraction of a moment Seyha's smile dropped, and the act clouded the sunlight which had been rising on her expression. Then the moment passed. The sun came out again. "When are you going to do it? When...."

Another swipe of the artist's palm across the picture. Instead of colors smearing, his wife was covered in black. Swipe, swipe, black and more black, over and over. Seyha was buried in layers of darkness.

Wait! he shouted. *What was that? What....*

The preternatural blindfold crawled like a thousand insects across his face. He was lost again, blinded from the world both past and present. Something grabbed him by the chest, hot hands burning. Bill screamed soundlessly.

The other voice, angry and still very close said, *"You've been blind a long time, William Watts. Time to rip that sad little heart out...."*

* * *

As soon as Joyce Lindu understood she had not gone blind, that something – as intangible as it was – covered her face, the only alternative was that she'd lost her mind. The ghostly blindfold felt like it had substance, but remained no more than vapor to her fingertips. For a few dying seconds she heard the others shouting, claiming the same condition as she. Their words offered her a macabre sort of hope.

Maybe she wasn't crazy after all.

Maybe they were dead. All of them. When the blindness seeped past her ears, blocking out all sound, she put it down as the final flickers of her dying brain, fading into nothingness.

She waited for the Light, for the warmth of the Lord's hands on her.

Nothing happened. Silence and darkness. She was deaf, blind and dead.

Joyce shuddered, and such a minute physical act shook her from a self-imposed paralysis. She could move, could still feel the touch of her fingers on her face and arms, feel the sway of the ceremonial stole across her chest. She shuffled her feet, felt the carpet scuff under her shoes. She didn't dare reach down. It would be too much like falling, like giving in to this strange half-death.

Fear smothered her in furious and increasing waves. No experience in her life could label what was happening, though the situation *was* familiar in one way. Biblical, a blindness that could be felt. One of God's plagues against Egypt. OK, maybe she *was* crazy after all and only *thought* she'd heard the others shouting.

There had been another voice, too, everyone heard it before the lights went out. It had sounded no more tangible than the gauze around her face.

Demonic. That particular word had occurred to her during the end of the ceremony, along with an urgent need to complete the blessing, drive back whatever force invaded the house. But the blessing only sped up the process and cast them into this darkness.

Joyce said, *Bill? Seyha?* She heard nothing, only the concept of having spoken in her mind.

She should be praying, asking for guidance. Everything had happened so fast.... She reluctantly knelt, bending both legs until the comforting familiarity of the carpet touched her knees through her skirt.

Jesus, help me. I don't understand what's happening, if this is your work or not. Please, let me see again, let me hear the others, let me help them. Deliver us from this nightmare.

Were the others as blind as she was? Was the whole world like this? The idea was too horrifying to consider.

Protect them – protect Gem. She's too young to face this. Please show me something, help me to see....

A soft glow danced in front of her. She turned her head and the spot moved, like the after-glow of a camera flash.

A low, throaty chuckle behind her. Joyce stumbled forward on her hands and knees, away from the voice, closed her hands around soft dirt.

Somehow she was outside.

When the afterglow expanded, the laughter faded into the distance like low-rumbling thunder. The world came into focus.

The sun shone brightly above, and it was very hot. Joyce's head was filled with a thousand sounds and smells. This was not her world. Her gaze drifted, unfocused over a million oversized leaves, large fronds, bright green with brown frayed edges. She was in a clearing bordered by four walls of trees, green magnified foliage. Heavy smell of dirt, leaves heated by the sun, headier though, older than the fresh-cut lawn smell which drifted through the Watts' open windows a few minutes ago. The air was thick and humid with odors of decay and sounds of life. Birdsong, squawks from every direction, rising and falling in volume as if competing with each other, screams that sounded *almost* human, the steady buzz of insects, some as close as her own ears.

The word *jungle* fit this place more than any other she

could come up with.

"I'm hungry."

A child's voice, barely heard over the constant soundtrack of chatter and shrieks.

Crouched like a frightened animal, Joyce turned toward the source. She hoped the voice belonged to Gem, but instead saw a much younger girl standing at the edge of an overgrown path. The girl raised a hand to scratch at her tangled hair. No more than six, maybe seven, mocha skin mottled with pale spots along her neck and bare chest. Around her waist hung a skirt, frayed at the edges like the leaves of the forest. A single leaf, unnoticed or simply ignored poked out of the nest of wild curls that made up her hair.

Where am I? Joyce said. *God, what is this? Am I asleep?*

The little girl raised both her hands and said, "Help me." Though she spoke English, a odd accent flavored her words.

Joyce didn't dare move. If she did, she'd be trapped in this illusion forever. That's what this was – an hallucination brought on by something perfectly logical. She simply didn't understand it yet. One thing Joyce was sure of, even if the reasons for such certainty weren't clear. She was *not* asleep.

The laughter returned, no longer behind but leaping tree to tree, just out of sight. "*You were always a clever one, Reverend Lindu. At least, you like to think so.*"

Joyce scanned the branches, then the tall grass in the clearing. *Who are you?* she shouted. *Where am...* but she gave up, too confusing to speak without a voice.

She looked back to where the girl had been standing but there was no one there, only a flash of skirt among the shadows of the forest, then a scream which was quickly cut off. The large leaves swayed where she'd been standing, but settled again under the heat.

Joyce was running towards the spot before making any conscious decision to do so. The ceremonial stole swayed from her shoulder, chafing the back of her neck. She entered the woods, pushed aside the fronds and the thick branches of a bush that looked like mountain laurel except for its long, pointed leaves. Twisting ahead of her was a makeshift path, closing as quickly as it had been made either by the girl, or whoever had taken her.

I'm coming, Joyce silently shouted. *Where are you?*

Sometimes the ground under her shoes was spongy and moss-covered, other times hard-packed dirt, layer upon layer of fallen leaves. She found it hard to focus on direction because every couple of seconds brought a blinding flash of sunlight through the canopy of deep green shadow. Insects swarmed around her head. She ran through them. A sharp pinch on her neck, then another on her cheek. Some of the smaller bugs she breathed in. Always, Joyce had to swat at a swarm or an oncoming branch.

The voice rumbled just out of sight, keeping pace beside her in the jungle, *"Wouldn't it be wonderful to leave the old world behind and come here, to this forgotten place? Hmmm? To run away from your memories and your failures...?"*

I'm not running away!

"No?"

Something reached out from the jungle and grabbed the top of her right foot. Joyce's momentum pushed her forward, arms out straight as if she was preparing to fly. She crashed onto the path, twisting as much as possible to avoid snapping her ankle since the foot was held fast. Her face scraped against a broken branch. Its sappy tip tore at her cheek below the right eye. She cried out, clawing at her leg as she twisted more to see what had hold of her. The muscles in her leg burned until she rolled back the other way to alleviate the strain. As she did her foot came free of the root under which it had become tangled. Just a root, no skeletal arm reaching from the jungle to drag her away.

The heat was intense, more so here in the green shade. The air was wet with it. Mosquitoes buzzed around her face, drawn by her heavy breath and sweat. Joyce touched her cheek and the fingers came away red with blood. She wiped them on her skirt. The insects swarmed as if in a feeding frenzy.

Not until Joyce rolled onto her hands and knees, carefully rolling her right foot to make sure it was still functioning, did she notice the man standing at the edge of a new clearing twenty yards or so along the path. She was about to stand, wave to him for help when recognition almost sent her flat against the ground in hiding.

No, she thought. *I will not hide. This is not real. None of it.*

Ray Lindu stood - *posed* was more accurate - with a large sack slung over one shoulder. Her ex-husband wore khaki shorts, long brown socks and button-down safari shirt unbuttoned most of the way to his belt to allow a wide view of his muscular chest. He smiled from under the wide-brimmed hat. The smile was warm and inviting, though the invitation was a lie. Always had been. He looked the part of a famous jungle explorer. Not that Ray ever had aspirations in that regard. Not that he ever *could.*

He was dead.

Joyce stood, slowly, staring across the distance like a gunslinger in some mixed-up Western.

Ray leaned back and laughed. "Oh, Joyce, you're funny," he called across the distance. "Still living in your make believe world, are you?" He leaned forward and readjusted the sack over his shoulder before continuing. "No time to talk, sweetheart, not that you seem too inclined for that anyway."

Joyce clenched her fist, fighting the sudden thrill at seeing this man after so long.

She hated herself for the feeling. Hated him all over again.

Ray turned his back to her, raising one arm briefly and calling, "See you in the jungle pages!" The sack was large and bulged at odd angles. The girl was in there, had to be. Joyce was about to shout out for Ray to stop, let her go, *something*, when a long, lithe arm, a *Caucasian* arm, fell free from the sack, drawing down one edge as the girl within reached out. Ray moved into the light of the clearing but before he was out of sight, their daughter's head and one bare arm shifted forward from the sack, exposed. Rebecca's short black hair was matted against one side. She looked dead, until the freed arm rose up weakly and her eyes widened at the sight of her mother staring back across the distance.

Becca! Joyce screamed, thrashing at another root which had suddenly, impossibly wrapped around her ankle again. *Rebecca!*

The young woman's arm was still reaching for her, mouth moving silently, as her father carried her out of the clearing and out of sight.

Joyce struggled with a mad frenzy against the root for a few more seconds, then stopped. She breathed the stifling air deep into her lungs. This was a dream, and if it was a dream then she could wake up from it. This was only a variation of the same nightmare she'd had since that final night at the house with Ray. *Just wake up.*

The forest around her had become still and very silent. No insect buzz, no chattering of animals above her or anywhere in the distance. Even the mosquitoes seemed to have fled.

The hair at the nape of her neck rose up, as if a

thunderstorm was rolling in. Then she heard it, a deep, throaty rumble that she hoped was thunder but knew was not. Joyce turned back towards the jungle behind her, her foot still held tightly. No sign of any path, nor the clearing where she'd first arrived. Only trees and hanging vines in front of more trees and vines, layers of them folding into a green darkness that thundered and rumbled with the arrival of something monstrously huge smashing its way through everything. This *something* was alive, grunting and howling as it pushed through the foliage. To the right, deep into the green, a tree fell onto the side, moved aside by something that looked like the back of a whale cruising past towards the left.

Joyce knew it would turn her way soon. It was coming for her and one thought suddenly dominated any other, though she didn't understand it.

It's found you.

The trees closest to her disappeared, enveloped in a thick blackness that poured out and enveloped them. It was neither smoke nor solid, just Darkness, an absence of *everything* that pulled in the light around it and never let go.

When it washed over her like a tsunami, Joyce was gone, too.

*   *   *

How long Gem Davidson sat on the couch, shrouded in that invisible black cotton she didn't dare guess. She could not remove whatever covered her head, and had quickly stopped trying. Still, her hands stayed flat against her face, covering her eyes, hiding from whatever monster now lurked in the black house or, worse, stood in front of her. Now and then she'd spread a couple of fingers, hoping to see something, anything, to prove she wasn't blind or crazy. Nothing.

The only saving grace with this whole situation was that if she *was* crazy, then so was everyone else. They all saw the darkness creeping in around them. Now they all, like her, were blind. At least it sounded like that during a brief moment of shouting. Were they also deaf now, like she seemed to be? Probably. Or dead. No, not that. She was alive, so maybe they were, too....

Gem kept waiting for a hand to grab her, feel someone settle onto the couch. No one came. She was alone, leaving the others to wander among the rooms, probably crawling on all fours like the blind people in that old movie *Day of the Triffids* she watched on some random cable television station a couple of weeks ago. Stupid movie. People don't just go blind like that. They don't. She closed her eyes and tightened her fingers. Then she heard it. A faint *Tick, Tick, Tick*. A clock, perhaps. Hopefully not a bomb.

The next time she spread two fingers apart, the room was no longer dark. Gem opened her fingers so wide the skin between them hurt. She could see everything, but what she saw made her whimper in confusion. The whimper made no sound, but she was too dizzy to notice, too dizzy with the realization that she was *not* where she had been. The couch she sat on was not the same couch.

It was *hers*, in her own house.

She sat up straighter, swallowed and said, *Mom? Dad?*

How come she didn't hear...? Gem cleared her throat. When she realized she couldn't hear *that*, she decided not to try to talk again. One shock at a time.

Tick, Tick, Tick.

The tall, imposing grandfather clock – one she never thought fit in with the cluttered décor of the Davidson house – counted the seconds beside the stairs. At first that was the only sound Gem could hear. Then a second joined from outside. A plane passing overhead, on its way to Logan Airport.

Gem tried to whisper, *What's going on?* but cringed at her absent voice.

The windows reflected back the interior of the living room, lighted by the single yellowed lamp in the far corner. Even so, the street light outside was visible through the glass. How long was she out... or asleep?

Gem stumbled off of the couch and ran into the kitchen, not hearing the sound of her footsteps but spurred on by the thought that she might still be at the Watts' house, unconscious or dreaming... or dead. The back screen door screeched as loudly as it always did when she pushed it open, slammed closed behind her. She heard everything except herself. *Next door,* she thought. *Everyone's probably still in there.*

She ran down the porch steps, across the grass to the Watts' house. Evening dew soaked into her socks. The windows next door were dark. No one home. But there'd been that weird black smoke creeping over the glass, burying the scene of her brother as if the windows had been spray-painted.

Eliot wasn't around now. What time was it? Early evening, dark enough for the street lights to be on, the grass wet. The sky above was still more purple than black, some semblance of dusk hanging around. How did she get out? *When* did she get out?

The window nearest the back of the house was stained-glass. Gem stepped sideways. One of the new ones, tall like the original, but clear. It reflected the lights from the street, an impression of her own house. No reflection of herself, though. She moved one way, then another... nothing. *Like a vampire,* she thought.

OK, so the whole scene in the Watts' house was a

dream. She'd fallen asleep on the couch, and was still dreaming. Bad news was Joyce Lindu hadn't come back to visit, good news was Gem could probably fly now if she tried.

She leaned forward until her forehead rested on the window, cupped her hands on either side. Nothing to see. Maybe they had drapes. When the thing standing on the opposite side of the glass lifted its lids, two glowing yellow eyes stared back at her.

Gem tripped backwards over her own feet and landed hard on the wet grass. The pain in her tailbone was sharp. She gasped, staring at the window and the eyes drifting toward the lower casement as it opened like a drawbridge. The eyes slid through the opening – or more accurately the dark head upon which they were attached pressed against the inner screen, buckling its frame and pushing it free to fall onto the flower bed below the window.

Gem forgot her pain and crab-walked backwards. Some – *thing* slinked from the house and landed with a thud onto the dented and torn screen. Gem pulled her feet away, not wanting to be too close. The creature's body glistened in the street light when the limbs uncoiled. Details were lost in the shadow cast by the house, from the moon suddenly rising on cue from the far side. Except the eyes – big and bulbous like Tolkien's *Gollum* staring around the yard before settling on her. Where there should have been whites was yellow streaked throughout with veins of pinkish red, tiny black pupils in the center. The eyes glowed with some half-dead light buried in the thing's bald, misshapen head.

Gem didn't move, even as the thing rose up on twin spindle legs. It was naked, sexless. The eyes looked away from her, scanned the street and surrounding neighborhood, then back to Gem. After a prolonged stare, the eyes and head tilted up.

It remained in that position for a few seconds without looking back. Gem risked a glance behind her. Only a quick peek to see what it was looking at, lest the monster realize she wasn't paying attention and pounce. The attic window of her house was lighted. Her father was home, then, sequestered with his radio in the attic.

The creature hissed, never taking its eyes from her father's window, and smiled. The mouth glowed like the eyes, the emergent light a physical expulsion from its lips. A white, milky gas. The lower jaw wobbled, enough to imply laughter.

Gem scrambled to her feet. If her father was home, he'd protect her. She ran across the yard, not knowing if the monster was chasing but not wanting to look. She made it to the back stairs. Her socks were soaked through. They slapped against the peeling wood of the steps, feeling heavy, slowing her progress.

Across the porch, she grabbed the kitchen door handle and caught a brief glimpse of the creature scrabbling up the side of the house, past the porch railing. It opened its ugly milk mouth and hissed, *"Daddy,"* as it climbed towards the attic window.

Daddy! Gem repeated silently, then ran inside. The house echoed with subdued *thump-bump*s of footsteps and the scraping of claws against the shingles outside. She ran into the living room, past the ticking grandfather clock, turned onto the stairs. She wasn't going to make it in time.

Top of the steps, right turn. She ran up the carpeted attic staircase two at a time.

Daddy, look out!

"Roger," Jim Davidson said into the large microphone. "Twenty-Two-nineteen here, Eastern Standard. How's the weather in your parts, over?"

He seemed oblivious to the dark, red-tinged monster which had crawled onto the back of his leather desk chair. It stroked his long gray hair, playing with the pony-tail. He did not flinch. The window behind them remained closed and latched. Didn't matter, she decided. None of this made sense anyway.

She shouted, *Leave him alone!*

"Cold," a voice broke through the static on the speaker. "Only five degrees this morning. Over." From his thick accent, the owner of the voice was in Russia, or maybe Greenland, speaking Celsius instead of Fahrenheit.

Dad?

Her father clicked the Talk button again. The monster's guttural voice whispered, *"He's mine."* It continued stroking the man's hair, leaning its repulsive, wet body against his shoulders. *"They're all mine."* It swept its free hand around the room.

Somehow, Gem understood the gesture to mean the rest of her family.

Her father straightened, turned his head to look at her. "Gem?"

Gem laughed triumphantly and ran toward him. *Yes, Daddy! It's me!*

"Gem?" he repeated, louder this time. He hadn't been looking at her, but at the top of the stairs. She hesitated beside him, wanting to reach out but not wanting to accidentally touch the thing on the back of his chair.

Come find me, Daddy! Look for me!

The demon whispered in his ear. He sighed and turned back to the microphone.

Come find me, Daddy! she repeated and closed the remaining distance between them.

The demon jumped off the chair and rose up in front of her, growing twice its original size. Then it ripped open.

White, bone-like sticks broke through the skin. Each end was tapered to needle points. The tips of its fingers split, stretched into long blades of bone. If the bottoms of her socks hadn't been so wet Gem would have slid directly into them. She stopped a couple inches away.

"Come any closer, Sweetie, and I'll rip you apart." Its voice, its *hiss*, bounced beside her ears, never quite reaching her head. Its tone and inflection were familiar. The same voice she'd heard – they'd *all* heard – in the Watts' house. In her dream. *This isn't a dream,* she thought and immediately wished she hadn't. The creature's face folded in on itself, a nightmarish expression of hate. *"And I'll do it, slowly."* As it spoke the mouth flopped open and closed, matching the words no more than might a puppet, occasionally baring broken, flat teeth.

Gem blew out her breath in a sudden surge of anger. She didn't care anymore. This wasn't real. None of this was real!

The demon stretched taller, wider, too big now for such a low-ceilinged space. Blades and bone protruded further from its skin. Gem charged forward, wanting only to toss aside the mirage and wrap herself around her father.

The pain of the claws piercing her belly, scraping along her spine and breaking out through the back didn't reach her brain immediately. First came the realization that her forward momentum was stopped. Only her blonde hair continued on, falling across her face, brushing across the skin of her assailant. She unconsciously pushed the strands aside with three fingers, then looked down at the finger-blades sticking into her. No pain, even now as she realized what happened, only the feel of them pushing into her stomach, more scraping against her spine and a metallic taste dripping down the back of her throat. Gem froze, afraid any movement would tear her in half.

Daddy, help –

The creature's arm tensed, then lifted Gem off the floor and across the room. The blades pulled free with a horrible slurp. She raised her arms a second before she hit the attic window....

...and landed hard on a polished wood pew. Gem twisted in an agony she didn't yet feel but knew would be coming, laying on her back and wrapping her arms across her belly to keep the intestines from spilling across the floor. She waited for the pain, but felt nothing but her own arms around herself. Gem stared up at a small water stain in the ceiling and waited to die.

Nothing happened. When she looked down, no blood. Gem moved one arm, then the other. Nothing but her white shirt. Slowly, carefully, she slid to a sitting position on the bench and lifted the bottom of her t-shirt a few inches. Smooth belly. No open gashes or even a scratch.

She took a breath, tried to calm her breathing, slow her out-of-control heart. This was a doozy of a nightmare, one of those vivid varieties after eating too many slices of pizza before bed.

Nevertheless, when Gem looked around an overwhelming joy washed over her. The church was lit by bright colored sunlight streaming through stained glass. This was *the* church.

Saint Gerard's next door. As it used to be.

God had come back.

Gem looked around the room slowly, worried any sudden motion would shatter the illusion or, worse, release the scream she knew lurked someplace hidden in the back of her mind. Rows of pews filled the hall. The altar stood where she remembered it. This couldn't be real. Things could not simply switch back because she wanted them to.

The place even *smelled* familiar. Vanilla. It didn't take

long to spy the candle on the altar. She used to like lighting candles here, as if the light and scent would reinvigorate the silent tomb the church had become. Not that Gem knew what it was like before it closed or during an actual service. She had begun coming here surreptitiously after everyone had gone, at first just to see. But later, because she'd felt drawn here. As if this were a secret place no one could see or find but her. Gem imagined when filled with parishioners the building would look and feel much like it did now. Maybe a little louder.

In this moment, the church was empty, as she'd always known it. After it had closed and Joyce and Becca moved into an apartment in Westminster did Gem finally take a chance and climb through the rear basement window. She'd discovered that it could be easily jarred loose from its clasp one morning after unsuccessfully trying to get in through the back door. It was a secret egress she'd made good use of. She would drop into the small alcove in the basement using an empty bookshelf beside the window for footing, then wander upstairs into the church, careful to move past the glass front doors quickly so she wouldn't be seen by neighbors. Not that there hadn't always been the possibility of someone seeing her running into the Lindu's back yard or even crawling through the window. Still, being caught *inside* felt like a far worse situation to be in.

And now, she was again alone among this musty tang of dust and lingering hint of vanilla from the candle. The Watts' version of this place smelled like Pine Sol and rosewater. But that had been nothing but a bad dream. Not this. The air here, the air *now*, lingered like the scent of an old friend.

She slapped her open right palm onto the wood. It was hard. The sound echoed. *This* place was real. But... could God have really taken back the house like this? Back from the demon....

Gem leaped up and slammed her right knee against the pew in front of her. She cursed, but her voice was still silent. For the first time she decided that was a good thing. Was it swearing in church if you made no sound?

She looked around, amazed that she'd completely forgotten about the monster that had crawled out of this building just a few minutes before and stuck her like a pig. No sign of it, now. She stepped sideways along the pew then into the aisle beside the windows, standing in a puddle of color, a wash of sunlight though the colored fragments of glass. A moment ago it had been nighttime. Now it was daylight with all its brilliance. Gem found it hard to be afraid in this light.

Had that been a dream, too, back at her house? Her throat tightened. *I hope so*, she thought. *I don't know*. The demon and her father, even the work the Watts had done in the church. More and more the scenes in that *other* version of this place felt less like an illusion, more a distant but *true* memory.

Gem turned the handle on the lower portion of the window and pushed it open. Crisp Autumn air, the chill of coming winter and smells of dead or dying leaves. She turned her head sideways for the narrow view it offered. Her house next door, bright and quiet in the afternoon light. No sign of anyone home, or at any other house along the street. The air chilled her face, a reminder that this was, indeed, real.

She straightened and looked back inside the church, waiting as her eyes adjusted to the darker interior. No, she decided, walking towards the front of the church. This wasn't real. None of it was.

"This is not real!" she said, shocked by the existence of her voice again.

What did *that* imply?

Gem sighed and sat heavily in the front pew. Then she did nothing more. Just sat, tired of so many changes. She'd just sit here and wait for something to happen.

The outside air seeped in through the open casement, chilling the room, but everything would be alright. It was how she felt the few times she came here, in the months after the church closed up, before that final ceremony last winter to deconsecrate the church so the Watts could come in and change everything. Joyce Lindu and her daughter had packed up and moved on, like Ray Lindu had done long ago.

Thinking of Mister Lindu, Gem turned her head quickly left and right. No one there. She was alone.

Was God still here? Now, or when this moment had once been, when she believed with so much passion that He lived here, when she wondered if the creator of the universe was lonely in the empty church. An embarrassing memory now, even though it had been less than a year ago. Sitting here, alone, Gem wondered again why she never walked out of her house to join the congregation when they arrived every Sunday. They would park along both sides of the street and send the neighborhood into quiet chaos for an hour or so every Sunday. Sometimes she'd lay on her bed and watch the cars arrive, people walking together towards the doors, talking with each other, sometimes laughing, doing whatever they did when they were inside, singing hymns to the accompaniment of the lone organ. In those voyeuristic mornings Gem would feel an ache in her stomach, an overwhelming desire to sneak next door. *Can I come in?* she might ask. Wondering if she'd be smothered in a dozen welcoming embraces, or simply ignored.

Always, the idea of passing her mother or brother on the way out crushed the idea before it grew into anything more than a daydream. Her father probably wouldn't mind, but her mother would, no question there.

Sitting now in the silence of this non-existent church, Gem began to understand why. She was tethered to the faith, or lack thereof, of her family. Mom and Dad never said anything overtly *bad* about church. Not really. Once maybe.

Those people aren't as holy as they'd like you to think.

Her mother said that once, or something close to that, with a quiet smirk on her face. It had been in response to Eliot's usual complaint one Sunday that "the Singing Jesus Folken" had woken him up. He always used words like "Folken." Too much into his video games and *Lord of the Rings*. Along with inheriting most of his looks from Mom (Gem looked more like her father's side of the family), the two of them shared an annoying trait of talking in riddles, spouting phrases which never *completely* made sense. Gem supposed she'd inherited more than a few oddities from Deanna Davidson herself, but she could at least claim to recognize other, more grounded attributes of Dad. At least she liked to think so.

On the morning of Eliot's "Jesus Folken" comment Gem had looked up in time to see her mother smirk, catch herself and work a frown across her pretty, indifferent face. She looked out the window to the church next door, a trace of her earlier smile working itself back, and whispered, "Those people aren't as holy as they'd like you to think." Nothing else. At least not anything Gem remembered.

Then the church closed, like a train leaving the station without her, sliding towards the horizon to someplace else.

Gem rolled her eyes and sighed. She was starting to think like a bad romance novel. She leaned back in the pew and tried to regain some semblance of cool. Too often lately she would fall into these weird fairy tale modes of thought.

Granted, she was changing - physically and emotionally. "Hormones running rampant" was a phrase her mother used whenever Gem complained about anything. Mom would sigh and whisper, *Oh, Mother*, apparently talking to Nana's ghost or maybe the "goddess" if that happened to be her deity of the month. She'd say, *Oh, Mother, get me through these next few years until Gem's hormones settle down.* It was annoying.

Gem looked around the silent church, at the myriad of colors dancing across the walls. The altar was a light, polished wood, bare except for the short white candle in the center, flame burning small and straight casting its trace of vanilla into the air. It was nice to be back, even if she was only dreaming.

"I'm sorry," she said. "I'm sorry I didn't come sooner."

The sight of the candle on the altar suddenly bothered her for some reason.

She almost laughed at the thought. She had plenty of reasons to be *bothered*. She should be on the floor drooling and screaming and pulling her hair out, or whatever a *Girl Gone Mad* did under these circumstances. Maybe she *was* doing all that and simply didn't realize it.

Maybe she was dead, dead and damned and in hell....

She growled, biting the thought away. She was in a church, *this* church, maybe for the last time. She wouldn't get this chance if she was, well, *down there*.

Would she?

She suddenly remembered why the candle bothered her. She'd brought the vanilla here only once.

A man sobbed somewhere in the house.

Gem thought, *Oh, no. No, no, no. Not this. Please.*

She stood up, ran to the candle as she had done last year, blew it out.

Not this, please, she tried to say aloud, and her stomach hurt when she couldn't hear her voice any more. She looked down at her belly, pulling her shirt up a little to make sure the stab wounds hadn't reappeared. Nothing.

Yet.

The man's quiet, sad voice reached her again. He was whispering, crying. Gem straightened her shirt and picked up the candle.

Not this time, she told herself. *Leave now!*

She *hadn't* left the last time, and apparently she couldn't do so now. She began to walk, unable to make her legs turn and run in the opposite direction, towards the far corner of the church. A narrow door opened into a hallway leading to the Lindu's miniscule living area – she'd would be hard-pressed to call it a "house," more like an annex to the church. In the Watts' version, this door was gone.

For the first time since arriving, Gem wished she was back in *that* reality.

The man's voice was louder as she opened the door and walked down the hall clutching the candle to her chest, careful not to spill the melted wax on herself. Her footsteps were too loud. The crying stopped. Halfway down the hall Gem shouted in surprise and stepped back. Some of the wax spilled, its heat burning through the shirt against her left breast. Ray Lindu stood in the doorway of his daughter's old bedroom and stared at her. He had a few wrinkles around eyes, puffy from crying. The guy was still handsome, in a *way-too-old-to-think-about* kind of way.

He'd come back after all these years. The deserter had probably come back to say goodbye to the place.

"You're little Gem Davidson from next door aren't you?" In a flash his expression changed from some deep sorrow to his usual, charming self. "Though I don't suppose *little* is the correct term anymore." A quick flashing gaze, lingering a bit too long on the spot of cooling wax, then back up again, his face neutral.

Get me out of here, God. Why is this happening again?

Mister Lindu, she said with no voice. This moment had already happened, on the last day she'd visited the church before the deconsecration ceremony (after *that* night the Watts had changed the locks on the windows).

He raised his arms a little and smiled. The guy had perfect white teeth. "In the flesh. To what do I owe the pleasure of your company?"

He stepped completely into the hallway. Gem stepped back. She didn't like how he said *pleasure,* then *or* now.

I'm.. I'm just. I don't know. Just....

What could she say?

"Just visiting?" Still, that half smile. Almost a snarl. She remembered the man being charming, always friendly, one reason why everyone had been surprised when he left his wife and daughter out of the blue that night. With a quick glance around the hallway he added, "Me, too. One last look around. The place hasn't changed at all in six years." He shrugged. "Nothing ever really changes, though, does it?"

Yea, she didn't say. *I guess. I mean no. I should go.*

She turned, but he touched her arm. Just a touch – he didn't grab her. But the touch was enough to freeze her in mid-turn.

"You know," he said, "technically this is still my house." Another step forward, fingertips still lightly touching her arm. His eyes...

She thought, *Run, just run!*

Gem looked beside her at the bathroom across the hall. She could lock herself in there.

His eyes....

Gem didn't think Mister Lindu was supposed to be

here any more than she was, so maybe he wouldn't tell.

His stare was moving more blatantly, up and down across her body, no more pretense. The fingers, long, wisps of hair just below the knuckles, moving further around her arm. Not quite a grip, but getting there.

Gem stepped back. His hand fell from her and hung dead at his side.

"Don't go," he said, stepping forward, keeping pace. "Stay. We can reminisce together." His voice sounded different, husky, more like the voice of the demon that had crawled through the window.

It was too much, all of this. Her heart tried to burst from her chest. This wasn't happening again, couldn't be. Ray stepped so close that he was pushing himself against her. Gem felt the candle press between them. Both of his arms rose up as he shouted, "Stay and play with me!" not in his own voice, but the monster's. He hadn't said that last time, not *quite*. His body pressed forward and Gem screamed soundlessly, shoved him back using the candle then ran back through the door into the church. He was only a couple of steps behind her.

Car doors slamming. Through the glass entryway Gem caught sight of Mrs. Watts walking up the path. When this had originally happened Gem didn't know who the woman was but of course now she did, and if this was a nightmare *why couldn't she wake up?* Mrs. Watts was accompanied by a short, skinny guy as they headed towards the glass front door. Gem would have to pass by it to reach the basement but she did not care. Ray Lindu was probably right behind her. If they'd been looking her way instead of up and around at the outside of the building they'd have seen her. But they never looked, never saw her. Gem flung open the basement door and risked a look back over her shoulder. Ray was not there. Probably heading back down the hallway to the back door in the kitchen. She closed the basement door as quietly as she could then ran down the stairs. Before she reached the bottom she heard keys at the front doors, voices now, louder.

She ran across the open basement hall, empty, as was the small kitchen beside the alcove. She had to do this quickly, déjà vu all over again, as they say, only this moment *had* happened before.

Ray stepped out of the shadows beneath the cellar window in the back alcove, arms reaching, fingernails stretching out for her, longer and longer. Gem dropped the candle.

It landed on the Watts' living room carpet. Some of the melted wax spilled in small drops, dotting the fibers with off-white droplets. As she stared at them they, and the candle itself, faded like a dream. Leaving only the carpet, clear of stains.

Gem blinked. Joyce Lindu was standing a few feet away, half-crouched as if preparing to sprint across the room. Her mouth was open in a silent scream. Maybe she *was* screaming, somewhere in her mind.

* * *

Seyha Watts stood in complete darkness and lifted her hands to her face, clawed at the mask that had wrapped around her eyes. She dug in, stopping only at the pain of her nails pressing into her cheeks. Something warm trickled down under a blindfold which she could not touch. Blood. She'd cut herself.

Bill

Her voice was gone. The darkness had spread around her head, masking the sound of the others. Even the throb of her own pulse, which she might hear if her ears were blocked, was missing. The fear pouring into her was palpable, like a sickness. She drowned in it, more terror than she'd ever experienced.

"*Ever?*" The laughing voice was beside her in the dark. Seyha swung her arm out but touched nothing.

"*Never, ever?*" More laughter.

Instinctively she knew what it meant, and tried to think of something else, *anything* else. She stepped forward, reaching out with her foot for the edge of the couch or the leg of a table, hoping to touch a familiar shape, even the arm of Gem Davidson would be a comfort. She did not know in which direction she was walking, certain she'd run into something or some*one* if she just kept going. She called out their names, heard none of her words. Though her legs were moving she had no sense of motion, wasn't even sure if she was walking or merely standing in place kicking her legs out like a fool. The other voice didn't return. Maybe she'd moved far enough away from it.

An angry shout, directly in her ear, "*You can't escape me, Doung Seyha!*"

Seyha screamed and ran, until her shins hit something hard and unyielding. She fell forward, tumbled awkwardly onto a bench. Hard wood.

A pew. She ran her hands over the back, grateful beyond measure for something familiar to cling to, knowing now she must be in the foyer. The pew's usual rounded edge was not there, however. The shape felt too square, crudely cut. When she ran her palm across the surface her hand twitched in pain. With the fingers of her other she found a protruding splinter and pulled it out.

This wasn't the bench in the foyer.

Even with limited contact, and after so many years, Seyha recognized its feel, the pew's unsteady footing on the floor.

Please don't, she thought. *If this is a dream don't let it be that place.*

In fact, she'd never dreamed of the orphanage, not that she could remember. She thought of it often, each time catching herself and forcing her thoughts elsewhere.

The darkness lifted, slowly, layer upon layer of a curtain silently raised. Large shapes in front of her became minute details as each lifted away. When her vision cleared, Seyha wished for the darkness to return. She tried to cry out, a long, mournful, *Nooooooo,* but made no sound.

She must have passed out. Yes, too much stress with the new house and Reverend Lindu's visit. Bill was probably trying to wake her up right now.

Not knowing what to do until she was rescued from this nightmare, Seyha sat down on the last of the three rows of pews in the small chapel. Nothing had changed since she was here as a girl. If anything, the building looked more unsteady than she remembered, two walls of corrugated and rusted metal sheets, the other two uneven planks of lumber with patches of straw poking out from where they'd been stuffed to fill gaps. Daylight shone through holes in the wood where knots had long ago rotted out. Two windows by the door filtered daylight through glass coated with dirt and sand from the yard outside. Everywhere the cloying smell of dirt and body odor, sweat and cooking spices hovered in the intense heat. Thailand, just over the border of the country where she'd been born, a country which had gone mad and devoured her family, Cambodia.

"*Welcome home, Doung Seyha,*" the voice whispered from nowhere and everywhere. "*Is it good to be here again, after all these years?*" A low snicker, tripping into a growl.

Please, she said. *I've done nothing to you. Leave me alone.*

"*Oh, of course. Leave me alone. You* are *alone. Haven't you figured that out? Hush now... hush.*"

A young girl, no more than four or five years old, ran into the room and hid at the opposite end of the pew on which Seyha sat. Either she did not notice the woman sharing the bench, or chose not to acknowledge her. Seyha tried to speak, to have a conversation with anyone other than the demon haunting her mind. She could not. This was a nightmare about a nightmare. The rules would be less than kind, she was sure, so Seyha stayed where she was and only watched.

The girl's face was wet with tears as she hid hide behind the back of the second pew. At the same time, she took quick nibbles of a Fig Newton. Not the kind of bite one would normally take to eat something as fast as possible, before someone took it away. These were the hesitant nibbles of a girl who may be hungry, but did not want to eat the cookie completely.

Seyha knew what the little girl was thinking, knew her hunger. She was not afraid, just lonely. In her strange childish way, the girl was excited at the prospect of being found by Sister Angelique. Getting her undivided attention for just a few minutes, even if it meant a spanking later, was her goal. That's why she nibbled the cookie. If she ate the whole thing, the nun could not accuse her of stealing, of taking an extra snack from another child's plate. Sister Angelique would only send her away, back into the yard with the other nineteen girls and boys.

Seyha watched herself, the young *Doung Seyha* – at least the demon had correctly spoken the family name first – five years old, this very day. It was her birthday. She'd gotten no presents, nor did she expect any. All she wanted was some attention from the beautiful, strange woman now walking into the chapel.

There *would* be a present, though, a doll made of dress fragments and stuffed with leaves, smiling face drawn with a marker and made earlier in the week by Angelique herself.

Seyha watched the young nun, with her long golden hair (she rarely wore the typical habit of her order) and round blue eyes. She was beautiful and exotic in this place of dark hair and angular features. Angelique walked to the correct pew as if reading the young girl's mind and grabbed Seyha's small arm roughly and pulled her to her feet.

"Seyha," she said sternly. As an adult, watching with mature eyes, Seyha was surprised to note some amusement in the nun's expression. Though American-born, Angelique spoke fluent *Khmer* and used that gift to teach the children the English she spoke now. "Give me that cookie."

Young Seyha did not understand every word, not this early after arriving, but nonetheless handed the Fig Newton over, eyes downcast.

Say something, Seyha thought. *Talk to her.*

Sister Angelique paced back and forth in front of the girl, softly berating her in Khmer for taking more than her share. How would she like it if Makaria took *her* treat? And on such a special day as this!

The girl looked up for the briefest of moments. Seyha remembered this moment so clearly now. That acknowledgement, indirect as it was, of her birthday. The nun no longer pretended to be angry. In fact, Sister was giving the girl exactly what she craved before sending her outside into the heat. Later that night, Angelique would tuck Seyha under the blanket on her mat and push the makeshift doll into the girl's arm. She would whisper, in English, "Happy Birthday," and move on to the next child. Seyha would not understand the words, but would stare at the doll in the dim light, stare until her eyes closed from exhaustion. Seyha wondered now whatever happened to that gift.

After little Seyha was sent outside, the nun looked

around the chapel. She froze, stared directly at the adult Seyha where she sat on the splintery pew. Sister Angelique never broke eye contact with her. Seyha stared back. After a moment, the woman's sunburned, peeling forehead wrinkled in confusion and she made the sign of the cross before disappearing into the light outside.

Seyha continued to sit, alone, feeling the humidity, hearing the drone of the insects outside, always swarming, feeling for the first time that there had been good moments, brief as they were, in her life here. Even if she had not understood them.

The drone of insects grew louder. Black spots, large flying bugs moving too fast to focus on, filled the inside of the chapel like smoke. They landed on the pew, crawled over her arms and legs, over her face. Black and yellow, a lurid red stained across swollen thoraxes. She'd never seen this kind before. Seyha stood up and slapped them away, turned towards a door that was no longer there and tripped over a log, crashed into the brush.

She looked up, scrambled backwards. Where had the chapel gone?

The demonic laughter returned, low, mocking, its source always out of sight behind her.

People everywhere were shouting. Dirty faces, tear-streaked, seven men in torn uniforms shoving each other aside, dragging some teenaged girls to the opposite side of the road. Seyha looked down and behind her, realized for the first time what it was she'd tripped over. The flies were covering her mother's body, swarming almost as soon as she'd fallen, before the blood had stopped pouring from the gunshot wound in the woman's forehead.

Seyha stared while the preternatural laughter danced behind her. It was mere background noise to the *real* sounds of children and adults along the roadside, crying in confusion and anger. She stared at her mother, tried to cry out to her but had no voice. She'd never dreamed of this moment before, this vague, jagged memory of their forced evacuation, soldiers herding her family and so many others along an unending road, marching with no destination or reason, killing time until it was their time to die. They had no choice but to follow the orders of insane men who in turn took their orders from the maddest of all, Cambodia's leader, *Pol Pot*. Whenever this time rose in her mind she would always – *always always always* – push it away. Now she was trapped, staring into her mother's eyes as she had done this same morning almost forty years ago. Seyha had been only three years old at the time. She should not have been able to remember this. But she did, always. A flash photograph of *Maeh's* face staring dead across the ground into her own. She had been killed for not giving her daughters over to the fidgety band of soldiers that had joined their captors three days into the march. The men – mostly teenaged boys but towering monsters to the small girl that had been Doung Seyha laying on the side of the road beside her mother – had been so inured to death that their eyes and hearts were long dead to the act of killing.

The murder had been an automatic response by the young *Khmer Rouge* soldier as soon as Seyha's mother refused. No real thought behind it. Her mother said no, and the boy in the too-big uniform lifted his pistol and squeezed the trigger. *Maeh* dropped as if through a trap door, pulling down the youngest of her daughters who'd been holding her hand. With the momentum Seyha had tumbled over her mother's body and landed in the brush beside the road.

Then, as now, Seyha recovered quickly but simply stared into the woman's unblinking eyes. Screams from other girls as they were taken away, except for one small child laying on the side of the road, already forgotten except by her neighbors who stepped in front of the remaining newcomers, shielding Seyha from sight, distracting the soldiers with wails and shouts of indignation until they finally left, taking more than half of the women with them.

Seyha stared, waiting for *Maeh* to blink, to smile and raise a finger to her lips, put her hand over the swollen hole in her forehead. Stop the blood from trickling into her eye.

She didn't know what to do. There was nothing left in the world, nothing.

Seyha thought briefly of her father, and what might have happened to him after he'd been taken from their village six months before this march began, then squeezed her eyes shut. *No, no, no more, no more...* When she opened them, the darkness which had lingered like mist along the edges of the road now rolled forward. The land was on fire, filled with smoke. Not smoke. Black, blessed eternal night.

Before she was again blind, the demon's voice hissed in her ear, *"So much fun we're going to have, you and I."*

Seyha raised her arms over her head and screamed. This time, she heard the sound of her voice.

First Night of Darkness

Bill Watts knelt behind the couch, both hands grabbing at his chest. He'd shouted a short bark of surprise, then realized where he was and fell into a nervous silence. Seyha, however, kept on screaming. Crouched on hands and knees, her eyes wide with some terror only she could see, she shuffled away from the sofa, occasionally speaking in words Bill couldn't understand. He took in a deep breath, lowered his hands from his chest and crawled towards his wife.

Though Gem moved onto the couch and peered over the back, she still seemed oblivious to the mayhem. Her wide, frightened eyes darted around the room, looking for something that was, apparently, no longer there.

"Sey! Sey, it's me!" Bill grabbed her shoulders. She squirmed and twisted free. Gem and Joyce finally focused on the scene, momentarily distracted from their own confusion. Bill gave up trying to grab his wife, but whispered, trying to calm Seyha with his tone.

She stopped her retreat half-way towards the front door, no longer screaming, Tears poured down her face. She blinked, trying to focus on her husband's voice. "Bill, I..."

"It's OK." When he moved closer she crawled away in the opposite direction.

"Please, stay away. Leave me alone." She looked around the room, as if only now realizing where she was.

Gem still watched them over the couch back, her expression wide with shock. Not from Seyha's behavior, but from whatever had just happened to *her*, to all of them. He started to ask, hesitated, looked over at Joyce. The priest stood unmoving beside the dining table, staring blankly back at him.

No one spoke. There was no sound in the house save an occasional gasp from Seyha as she tried to calm herself.

Finally, Gem said, "What the hell just happened?" She was blinking rapidly, as if trying to work out something caught in her eye.

Ignoring the question, Joyce whispered, "Seyha, are you all right?" To Bill, Joyce looked like a lost spirit, standing by the table, face pale and eyes seeing something other than this room. It was how everyone looked. He watched Seyha to gauge her response. His wife offered only a vague nod, but it was something.

He said, "Where are we?" The answer was obvious. In his living room. Outside, it was dark. Inside, the lights were on. No one seemed to think his question was strange, however. Seyha, Gem and Joyce looked around the room.

Something was wrong with the house. When Bill finally realized what it was he stood up, stared at the windows. They were dark, which had prompted his initial theory that night had fallen, but... something was wrong with them. He cleared his throat.

"Didn't... wasn't it afternoon? Before..." *Before we all went mad*, he thought but did not say.

The girl nodded. "Maybe we got knocked out or something. I mean...." Gem didn't finish the thought. Her lower lip quivered, stammering over whatever words might have come next. Then her face folded in on itself. She put her hands over her face and slid down onto the cushions. Joyce walked cautiously, stiff-legged, and sat beside her. Gem practically leapt into the woman's arms and wailed against her shoulder.

Seyha wiped her nose with a Kleenex found in her dress pocket and stuttered a final gasp, then was silent. Bill knew, from the rare occasions he'd seen his wife cry, that she was done.

Whatever he'd experienced a minute before, whatever he'd *dreamed*, he guessed his wife had seen something worse. She wouldn't look at him. He tried to follow her gaze, noticed the thin candle she'd been holding during the ceremony. It lay on the edge of the white carpet near the dining room table. The burnt wick lay on a small, melted indentation in the rug fibers. The flame must have gone out when she dropped it. *Thank God*, he thought. If the room had gone up in flames when they'd been blind, *or unconscious... whatever happened, Lord what happened?* they'd be in worse trouble.

Bill looked at the windows again. Pitch black outside. He checked his watch. Twelve-forty. His stomach ached. Had they been out for twelve hours?

He didn't believe that. More likely it was *still* twelve-forty in the afternoon. But, the windows....

He stepped past the couch towards the nearest casement. The glass was black. It didn't look right, looked *painted*. Not until he reached for the latch did he realize he had no reflection. If it was dark outside and the lights were on here, he should see himself in the glass. The *entire room* would be reflected. Nothing at all. Painted, then. The glass was cool and smooth to the touch. Black, opaque glass. If it was painted it had been done so from the outside.

When?

He looked at the small end table beside the couch. *The lights aren't even on.* It was all too much to accept. Bill focused again on the window, and grabbed the latch.

What was on the other side?

Nothing, came the answer in his own thoughts. His mind played with images of a nuclear holocaust, the four of them somehow surviving. Outside this house, perhaps, the world had frozen over after the sun blinked out of existence. Maybe a massive space craft hovered over them, blocking out the light. Maybe he watched too many movies. One way to know for sure.

He gripped the latch in his hand and tried to turn it. It wouldn't move. He tried the other way. Nothing. Pushing did nothing, banging on the handle did nothing, slamming his arm against the glass did nothing. Slamming it again and again and...

"Bill!" Joyce's voice. The room tipped. He grabbed the latch and looked over his shoulder at Joyce and the Gem. They stared back at him. The room tipped in a different direction. Bill's arm throbbed. He let it drop to his side, felt like throwing up.

"It's OK, Mister Watts," Gem said, pulling away from Joyce and wiping her face. "We'll be OK." She sniffed loudly, never taking her eyes from him. "We'll be OK. Really."

Bill realized he was hyperventilating and tried to catch his breath. This frightened teenaged girl was trying to calm *him*. It was embarrassing, but the thought soothed his panic. He leaned against the wall, slid down until he sat on the floor. His breathing slowed. His right arm *really* hurt just above the elbow. Bill craned his neck to look up at the window. "Did I break it?"

Gem only shook her head. "You kind of freaked."

Bill laughed, though it was short-lived and without humor. "Yea...."

Seyha sniffed from somewhere on the floor behind the couch. He couldn't see her, but needed to get up, check on her. In a few seconds. Right now he had no energy.

Joyce ran a hand along the top of Gem's head, smoothing out some tangles. When she looked back at Bill her expression had more life to it than when she'd been standing shell-shocked beside the table.

"The window wouldn't open, I assume." Not a question. Bill shook his head. Joyce sighed, then folded her hands in front of herself. "Lord, lead us from darkness, help us find our way home. Deliver us from evil, give us strength to..." She hesitated, eyes closed but darting back and forth behind her lids. Bill worried she might faint. Gem folded her own hands in front of her, perhaps unconsciously. Now she lifted one and laid it on Joyce's shoulder without looking up. At her touch, Joyce finished, "...to be strong. We don't understand what's happened, here or outside, to anyone...." She stopped again, bit her bottom lip. She opened her eyes but said no more.

"Amen," Bill whispered.

*   *   *

For the next ten minutes Bill and Joyce went to every window in the living room and tried each latch. All frozen. Even if they'd been somehow locked, the levers should have had some wiggle to them. They would not move, as if they'd been welded shut. Seyha sat in one of the stuffed chairs and watched them in silence. The Davidson girl got up and ran into the foyer. A moment later she called out, "The front door's locked. The knob won't turn."

Seyha listened to their words but could not accept them. Someone or something had locked them in and painted over every window. *Welcome to the neighborhood.* She flipped open her cell phone again. Still dark, no power in the battery. She kept the phone's charger in the drawer of a small side table beside the couch, but the drawer was locked, sealed shut like the windows. She closed the phone's cover, flipped it open again, finally let it drop to the floor. She took a deep breath to calm herself, found it hard to exhale, frozen like the doors and windows. Still, air slowly escaped through lips she didn't dare open. She closed her eyes and took in more air, willed it into her nostrils and out partly-opened lips. Again. And again. She began to feel better, physically at least. Now, however, everything *else* in this nightmare came into sharper focus.

Bill came over to the chair and knelt in front of her, one hand on her knee, taking both of her hands into his other. "You OK, Sey?"

"What," she began, found her mouth too dry. She swallowed, tried again. "Bill, what's going on?"

He shook his head. "I don't know. But we're all right. That's something. We'll start with that, work our way through the rest."

Joyce called from the kitchen, "Back door's locked. Phone's dead in here, too. And the drawers are stuck tight. Hold on." A pause, then rattling. "Refrigerator, same thing. Won't open." The rattle, Seyha realized, was the collection of glass mugs Bill kept on the fridge top, mementos of his college days. She hated those things, thought their gaudy Worcester State College logos did nothing for the ambience of the room she'd created. *They'd* created.

Gem lingered at the foyer entrance, her hand resting out of sight on the edge of the old pew. She seemed to be waiting for direction. Bill said, "We might as well check the rest of the house, see what works, what opens and what doesn't." He shook his head and added, more to himself, "This doesn't make any sense."

Seyha felt a sudden jolt of realization. They were going to search everywhere, try to open *every drawer*. She stood up too quickly. A sudden vertigo forced her back onto the chair. Bill returned, hand on her shoulder. "Stay here, Sey. We'll let you know what we find."

Embarrassed at his condescension, she gripped his

hand and pulled herself up, slower this time. "I want to see for myself." The room stayed mostly on an even keel. To justify herself, she added, "I'd rather not have anyone go through our bedroom except me."

Bill looked ready to argue the point, then apparently thought better of it and nodded. She held onto his hand. As they walked across the room Seyha noted with irritation that the girl followed them. They met Joyce at the entrance to the kitchen and hallway.

"OK," Bill said. "Seyha checks the master bedroom. Joyce, the spare room on the right. Gem the bathroom across the hall... try flushing, too. Try everything."

"Sure." The girl walked past them. Joyce followed. Gem turned left into the bathroom, Joyce opposite into the spare bedroom, hesitating for the briefest moment at the entrance before disappearing inside.

Seyha asked, and was glad to hear a steadiness to her voice, "What about you?"

Bill looked across the room with narrowed eyes, towards the foyer. "I'll go back to the front," he sighed, then, "try the basement." Three words, breathed more than spoken.

Seyha could hear Gem jiggling the handle of the toilet. There was no flush, but at least she heard the handle move. From the bathroom Gem said, "By the way," her voice had a hush to it, nervous, "am I the only one who had a real nasty nightmare before waking up?"

Seyha grabbed Bill's arm. He didn't seem to notice. He was staring back at the open bathroom door. Joyce poked her head into the hallway, her face pale. Not until Gem did likewise and added, louder, "Well?" did everyone nod. No words, just stunned looks back and forth.

Seyha felt her pulse revving up. She did *not* want to deal with this. Not now, not ever. "I'm going to check the bedroom."

Gem watched her walk past, "But did you – "

"Just drop it!" She raised her hand as if to strike her.

"Fine..." Gem mumbled. Seyha would not give her any more satisfaction. She had to check... had to check the room. Like they'd all discussed.

The bedroom was at the end of the hall. It encompassed the space once used by the former master bedroom and kitchenette. The room was much bigger, now, even with the king-sized bed taking up most of the far end. The windows were black like the rest of the house, but the room was well-lit. The light was evenly distributed, too, as in a department store. No shadows that Seyha could see. She tried to focus on the dresser drawers, but couldn't shake the thought of how bright the room was. She walked to the lamp beside the bed. This corner was no brighter than any other. She looked under the lamp shade. The bulb was not glowing. She put a hand to it, touched the glass. Cold.

Where was all the light coming from?

"Basement door's locked," Bill's voice, reentering the hallway, footsteps approaching.

She had no time. She hadn't checked! Two steps to the dresser, top right hand drawer. Bill spoke to Joyce, his arm in view outside the door. Seyha grabbed the round wooden knob for the drawer and pulled.

The drawer slid open with no resistance. She closed it quickly, trying her best to make no sound. Bill had heard *something* though. His voice was closer now, in the doorway. "Got something, babe?"

Babe? He hadn't called her that in ages. He probably used it unconsciously, but it sounded insulting. Why was she being so *angry* with everyone, especially in the middle of this insanity? Stress. Too much of it, all at once. She had no time to dwell. Her hand was still on the drawer's knob.

"No," she said, pretending to give it a yank. She let go and grabbed the next one. *Do not open*, she thought, focusing everything on the small round handle. She pulled. The dresser leaned forward from the exertion, settled back down. This drawer *was* frozen. Curiosity took hold now and Seyha forgot about Bill standing in the doorway. She tried all of the others. All of them frozen. She heard him come into the room. He tried the armoire doors. Nothing. She turned around, looked at him, and he looked at her.

"Nothing?" he asked.

"No," she said. "Nothing at all."

They moved about the rest of the room. Seyha was always one step closer to the dresser in case Bill tried to check it himself. Night table, television and stereo, all of the windows, same as everything else. The lid of the hope chest opened. Bill took two heavy comforters out, dropped them onto the floor. "Just in case it decides not to open later," he said, trying to smile again. The door to the closet was open a crack. It opened further with no resistance. At least they had an option for a change of clothes.

"There is one difference in here, though," Bill said. Seyha's heart pounded. He'd seen her open the drawer! But he was looking at the closet door. "This had already been opened a crack."

She recovered enough to say, "Yes, but so had the windows in the living room, and in here. I opened all of them before Reverend Lindu came, for fresh air." Her heart was hammering in her chest. She needed to calm down!

The others stepped into the room, staying near the door. Joyce said, "Someone must have closed them."

Gem moved closer to her and wrapped her arms around herself. "There's no one else here."

Joyce's eyes were clear, almost angry. "I think we all

know that's not true. We should head back to the living room and stay together, try to get comfortable. We've got a lot to figure out."

Bill nodded.

He took Seyha's hand. Together they followed the other two out of the bedroom. Seyha tried not to think about what they were walking away from.

*   *   *

When they'd settled back in the living room, no one spoke. Gem would have preferred being closer to Joyce, but Mister and Mrs. Watts claimed the couch. Gem and the minister took the two opposing chairs. As she had done on the couch, Gem pulled her stocking feet under her. The chair was comfortable, plush like the couch, but she felt too isolated. The dining area and kitchen loomed behind her, too large a space where something could creep towards her from behind. She curled tighter, wishing the sensation away.

Joyce took in a breath, let it out with a sigh and slapped her hands flat on her thighs. "Well," she said. "We can sit here like scared rabbits – I know I feel like one – or we can try to figure out what just happened."

Bill nodded, opened his mouth to speak but closed it without saying anything. He looked like he was trying not to cry. This made their situation worse than Gem wanted to admit. What did it matter if the *man* was upset? Joyce was the strongest of them, that much was obvious. In fact, she was the only one who hadn't freaked out yet. Gem wiped the side of her face and looked to the woman for guidance. *Please*, she thought, *say anything*.

Joyce nodded, as if in agreement, then looked at each of them in turn. "Some kind of hallucination? Mass insanity? *What?*"

An idea had taken root in Gem's head long before this palaver began, but she didn't dare speak it aloud. Even if it was a better alternative to her original idea – that they were all dead, a concept she hadn't dismissed, only ignored it, hoping it would go away – it was one she felt the least qualified of any of them to suggest.

"Gem?" *Oh, man.* The woman was creepy with that mind-reading business.

"Nothing," she muttered. "It's stupid."

"What is? Nothing's going to sound strange. I mean, look around. What's your thought?"

Fine. They were going to roll their eyes when she said it, but no one was offering anything else. Gem spoke into her raised knees, "I think God's mad at us. I think he bugged out when you did your ceremony last year and now... well...."

Joyce finished for her. "And now the devil's moved in?"

Was she being sarcastic? Gem cringed with equal amounts hope and embarrassment.

"Oh, come on!" Mrs. Watts said, flinging one arm in front of her as if to ward off such a stupid idea. "Things are bad enough, we don't need to start –"

"How do you explain what we heard, or what we saw?" Joyce's voice was tight, but she was trying to be diplomatic. "I know I'm not the only one who went... well, *blind* earlier. And before that I heard a voice. We *all* did."

Mrs. Watts looked ready for a fight. "I don't see how we can rule out this girl's brother so quickly," she nodded towards the window.

Bill's voice was stern when he said, "We're not ruling anything out, Sey. But I don't see how anyone can seal us in this house so completely. We can't even open the refrigerator!"

She turned in her seat, putting a few inches between her and her husband. "You can't open the refrigerator door, so God hates us and locked us in here with a bunch of demons?"

Joyce said, "God's not mad at us."

"Well, that's good to know!"

"Sey, please!"

They were talking over each other now. Gem wanted to add her own comments, but didn't feel she had a right. After all, she'd started the argument. Saying anything else would just make it worse.

After a few minutes, the debate hadn't progressed. It trickled to an occasional sputtered word or epithet. Mrs. Watts swore under her breath and curled up on her side of the couch, sitting not unlike Gem. Bill made no move to close the gap that had widened between them. Gem felt a twinge of satisfaction, seeing everyone take her side. She cringed, suddenly afraid the demon-laugh would return, maybe say, *Yes, yes, keep sinning, little girl. Give me your soul that I might dine on it for supper.*

Joyce looked over at her. "You all right, Gem?"

Gem sniffed and said only, "Fine."

Everyone fell quiet, lost in their own thoughts. There was always her other theory, but she held onto it, frustrated that she was the only one offering any ideas. She grunted and kicked one foot out. It wasn't aimed at anyone in particular, she just wanted to do *something*. The physical act felt good. So did the grunt.

Mrs. Watts spat, "What?"

"What?" Gem repeated. "What about the dreams? If that's what they were. If I wasn't the only one to go blind, then I probably wasn't the only one who got sent to Never-Never Land." She was about to tell them all to forget it, but saw their sudden, wary looks. Bill nodded in agreement. Seyha looked terrified. *Well, good!* If she was scared by her nightmares, may as well share the pain.

"Well?" she said, feeling bold.

Bill said, "She's right." He looked at his wife. "I dreamed – if it *was* a dream, I mean – of you and me, Sey. Our first date." He smiled a little, eyes looking sideways. "It was strange, different than I remembered in a few ways." He looked up suddenly. "And I couldn't speak." He became more animated. "I couldn't talk!"

"Neither could I," Joyce said. She spoke with a tremble in her voice which filled Gem's chest with sand. She hadn't expected the similarities to be that close. "I'd speak, but no sound came out."

Mrs. Watts nodded, if you could call the slight dip of the woman's chin a true nod.

Joyce continued, "And I saw Ray – do you remember Mister Lindu, Gem? He left when you were much younger."

The place hasn't changed at all in six years, he'd said. Gem tried to keep her voice calm. "I remember him." She wanted to say more, bit her tongue and looked down. A few seconds passed before she sensed Joyce's gaze move away. The woman cleared her throat but said nothing else.

"It was just a dream," Gem said, unnerved at the emotions playing across her old neighbor's face. She didn't believe these were just dreams, at least not the kind of dreams she was used to, but wanted – needed – her to stay sane.

Joyce shook her head. "No, it was more than that. It's as if I was dropped into the jungle to show me something that, I don't know, really didn't.... "

She didn't finish. After a few seconds Mrs. Watts whispered, "Jungle?"

Joyce nodded. In faltering words, gave a quick synopsis of the vision. *Vision* was the word she kept using. The girl in the jungle, seeing Ray. Partway through this portion of her dream Joyce stopped talking mid-sentence. No one else but Gem seemed to notice, however.

"It's not real," she finally continued. "None of this is real. I mean, yes, I've been considering missionary work now that I'm no longer pastor and, yes, perhaps in South America." She shrugged one shoulder and added, "I've even been talking to our sister parish down in Ecuador, on occasion. Just inquiries, nothing too serious."

Bill nodded. "There've been rumors," he said, "of you being groomed for a bishop's seat."

Joyce blushed. "Maybe. It's been mentioned. I just don't know if I'm interested. Not right away."

He said, "It's none of my business, Joyce, but it's been six years. Have you ever *heard* from Ray?"

She shook her head, seemed to think better of it, said, "A couple of letters. Nothing substantial." She laughed, briefly and without humor. To Gem, the woman's answer sounded like a lie. Maybe the part about *nothing substantial*, or simply that she'd heard anything at all from her ex since he bugged out. Not that it was any of her business, either. Good riddance to bad garbage, in Gem's opinion.

Bill said, quieter, "I'm sorry. Still, sounds like what you saw was just a natural concern, even after all this time. He's out there somewhere living some kind of life."

"He's somewhere, all right," Gem mumbled. She flinched at the realization she'd spoken out loud.

Bill said, "What do you mean?"

"Nothing. I don't mean anything." She looked at Mrs. Watts and sighed. *Too late now.* "It's just that the last time I was here I ran into him, that's all. He'd heard about the sale of the place, wanted to visit or something, that's all."

Joyce's face looked funny, paler than usual. Gem had assumed she'd be angry to hear the guy was skulking around, but she looked... scared? "That's not possible," Joyce muttered. *She's terrified*, Gem thought. What had that guy done to her? She wanted to ask, but at the same time didn't. She had a pretty good idea, after what almost happened....

Mrs. Watts said, as icy as Gem expected her to be, "You mean he was here at the deconsecration ceremony?"

"No," Gem said, sounding shorter than she meant to. "He was sulking around here a few weeks before that. We weren't there together, that's not what I mean." She cursed the heat that burned through her cheeks. "But I, well, I was visiting one day and he was already here. I ran into him. You must have, too. You showed up at almost the same time with some guy."

Bill raised one eyebrow, but he looked more amused than jealous. Mrs. Watts didn't look defensive. In fact, she slapped Bill on the arm and said, "Told you."

Bill said, "Was the other man about Seyha's height, balding?"

Gem shrugged noncommittally. Mrs. Watts said, "Yes, Gem, I know you were there, I saw you running across the back yard with your little candle."

Gem's worry turned to anger. This lady was such an idiot. "Then you saw Mister Lindu, he was down cellar... umm, wait no that was the dream... he probably ran out the residence entrance... or something." She looked up, tried to find the water stain from the vision. "I don't know where he went. I was too busy getting the hell out of there."

Joyce turned her head, slowly, towards Mrs. Watts. "Seyha? Did you?"

Mrs. Watts shook her head. "No, I didn't. No sign anyone else was there except this girl. If your husband, *ex-*

husband I mean, was there I'd have seen or at least heard him."

Joyce said quietly, "Technically, I guess we're still married. On paper only, but I never bothered pushing for a divorce."

Gem folded her arms across her chest and curled tighter in her seat. "Well, he *was* there and you just missed him. He didn't exactly want to be seen. At least he didn't seem to."

Joyce looked down. When standing she was one of the tallest women Gem had ever met, but at the moment, sunk into the cushions, she looked very small. Her eyes darted side-to-side as she whispered, "How could he have been there?" Gem barely heard her.

"He was a prick, if it's any consolation."

Joyce smiled, a little, as did Bill. But an uncomfortable silence fell between them. Gratefully, Bill changed the subject.

"Sey and I, in the vision, we were in a restaurant. For part of it, at least. The Cabel Grille in Hillcrest. It was the first time we'd gone out anywhere since the miscarriage." He looked at his wife. "Do you remember that?"

Seyha nodded, but not before glaring at Gem, almost daring her to make a comment. The hardness of her expression softened quickly and she looked down at her lap.

"It was me," he continued, "sitting there, and I saw through his, my... eyes. But I couldn't talk. I could hear my words, the same ones I said at the time – I'm pretty sure they were – but it was in that other voice. The one we heard before everything went dark."

Joyce nodded. Gem couldn't help but notice the woman's eyes occasionally darting across the room. "I heard the voice, too. I didn't see who was speaking. Just the voice." She tapped her head. "In here."

"I saw it," Gem said, wondering why she suddenly had such diarrhea of the mouth. *So much for blending into the background.*

Bill's eyes widened. "You saw him?"

She nodded, swallowed. "Yea, I think. But it wasn't a person. It was a monster, an ugly thing, like Gollum only uglier if you can imagine that." At everyone's blank stares, she said, "Gollum, the creepy guy from *Lord of the Rings*?"

"Oh," Bill said, his hopeful expectation fading.

Gem sat straighter, feet flat on the floor now. "I'm not saying that's who it was, it's just that he... never mind, but it was like a slimy, yellow-eyed demon creature."

Gem turned to Joyce and asked, "Is that what this thing is? Sounds like how Satan would talk, I think. And he makes up lies, like about your ex, right? And my Dad?"

"What about your Dad?"

"Nothing, it was weird."

"We have to talk about it," Joyce said. "We can't get through whatever's happening by hiding inside ourselves. If we each saw something we need to tell each other. Please, Gem. You, too," she said, looking at the Watts. "Both of you."

Bill nodded, moved closer to his wife again, arm around her. She leaned into him, but showed no sign of having heard Joyce. Gem realized that her new neighbor was suddenly looking more lost than Joyce had been earlier.

Gem told them her story.

*   *   *

Seyha truly disliked this girl, but couldn't put her finger on exactly *why*, except that she felt that way towards most teenagers. They had so little sense of others' boundaries.

Gem recounted her tale of "waking up" in her own house, of the demon slipping through the window, the girl's father in the attic. Gem was shaken up and spoke almost exclusively to Joyce. It had been a frightening dream, tailored to scare a teenaged girl. Seyha felt an urge to leave the couch and give her a hug. Reverend Lindu beat her to it, leaving her chair and kneeling beside Gem's. That was good. Seyha was comfortable where she was, safe beside Bill, trying to forget her own nightmares, both real and imagined.

Any sympathy for Gem Davidson dimmed when she mentioned finding herself in this house when it was the closed church. This part came more haltingly, which didn't surprise Seyha. After all, what she was admitting to was basically breaking and entering. This justification of Seyha's accusations didn't feel much like a victory. Especially when Gem mentioned running into the long-absent Ray Lindu, and Joyce's pale-faced reaction to the news. From the good Reverend's expression, Seyha preferred not to know the details behind their marital problems. Bad enough their new home had been Grand Central for every wandering soul last year.

Joyce looked up. "Seyha, you said you never ran into Ray yourself that day?"

She shook her head. "No, I'm sorry."

"He was there! It's not exactly something I can forget!"

Joyce turned back to Gem. Seyha noticed her hand shook a little. "Why? What happened?"

It was Gem's turn to pale. She looked away, muttered, "Nothing. Nothing, I just wasn't expecting anyone else to be there. He heard about the sale of the place, said he was just taking a look around one last time. Something like that."

Joyce shook her head, said nothing.

Gem added, "But he started to get, I don't know, creepy so I left. I promise!" She stared at Seyha and Bill with pleading eyes. To Seyha's displeasure her husband offered a nod of encouragement.

Gem closed her eyes. A couple of tears came loose and rolled down her cheek. Her face twisted in soundless crying. She was fighting something; something happened that day she wasn't telling them. Seyha pushed the thought away. It was none of her business, and besides, Joyce was an intuitive type. Unfortunately, she seemed more lost than all of them. The good reverend wasn't noticing anything. Her ex-husband had been sneaking back to her house, years after abandoning her and her daughter. Troubling enough, that thought. And... none of her business.

Gem sniffed and wiped the back of her hand across her eyes. She looked at Seyha. "I'm sorry for sneaking in here. I guess. It was just to -- " Her expression changed to its usual defiance. "But you didn't own the place any of those times I came. *She* did," a nod to Joyce. "Or her church did, or *God* did. If Joyce says what I did was wrong, then it was wrong." She looked at Joyce with a bit more humility. "I mean, was it?"

Joyce offered her a vague, distracted smile, always keeping one hand on Gem's arm. "No, I don't think it was wrong. Dangerous, though. What if you were hurt? Or – " she didn't finish the sentence.

Gem shook her head. "Nothing happened." Then, to Seyha's surprise, she turned and stared directly into Joyce's face, waited for the woman to return the stare. She said, "Nothing happened, Mrs. Lindu. I promise."

Joyce looked thoughtful, even managed a private smirk. She'd obviously understood the girl's meaning. "I'm glad, Gem. Maybe some day we could talk more about your visits. Would that be all right?"

Gem shrugged.

Joyce took in a deep breath with eyes closed, and let it out slowly. Her voice had more strength when she finally said, "What about you two? Is there more to your story, Bill? I think we got off the topic of your vision."

Seyha's stomach turned sour. What she'd seen was none of their business. If there *was* a devil, he was playing games with her. She'd deal with it, hadn't spent her life *not* talking about that part of her life to let down the wall now, especially in front of the Davidson kid.

Bill gripped her shoulder and pulled her further into his arms. "I've got to admit, my dream was nothing compared to Gem's. Except for the end, when that voice came back, loud and in my head. 'I'm going to rip your heart out,' it said. Something like that. Pretty scary."

"Before that," Joyce said, "you and Seyha were on a date, and then another night out after you were married?"

He shrugged and Seyha moved with the gesture. "Afraid so. I'm not complaining. Well, you know...."

He quietly considered something. Seyha felt his hold on her loosen. She kept her gaze shifted down, noticed a small dirt spot on the otherwise clean carpet.

"These scenes felt a bit *off*. I couldn't tell you why, specifically. Honestly, I'm not sure why these two events came to mind. Or were *put* there, whatever happened...."

When his voice trailed off again, Seyha felt his gaze turn on her. Maybe he was simply trying to reason it out. Maybe there was something else.

The drawer in the bedroom was unlocked.

"Seyha." Bill said, close to her ear, like that *other* voice had been. "What about you?"

She tensed her shoulders, wanted to break free of his grip, curse them all and run out of the room. Where would she go? They were trapped, Seyha more than the others since she was hooked in Bill's arm, cornered by his question. Not knowing what to say, she said nothing at all.

"Sey?"

She could only manage to mumble, "I don't want to talk about it," and kept her gaze on the rug.

In her peripheral vision Reverend Lindu, now sitting cross-legged on the floor beside Gem's chair, said, "Seyha, we all had a scare. None of us know what – "

"I said I don't want to talk about it!" She pulled free of Bill's arm, pushing it away like a web trapping her on the couch and stood. Looking around the room, anywhere but towards their eyes, she walked past Gem and Joyce, stopped beside the window, stared into the black glass. The window looked out into nothing. Nothing. Nothing was out there, in the neighborhood, in the world. Bill and Joyce, maybe even Gem could think there was a heaven and light and joy and life after death. They could think all they wanted. All there was, was right here. Any hurt that happened just happened and you couldn't go back. If you did, whatever caused the pain would know where you'd been hiding all these years and get you again, and again, and –

Bill's hands gently touched her shoulder. Startled, Seyha screamed and spun around with one arm raised defensively. The open palm of her right hand slapped hard against Bill's beautiful, sad face. The sound lingered, an echo in the room.

He stumbled, squinting his left eye while the other stared back in disbelief. Seyha's palm burned. She held it against herself. Bill did not raise a hand to his red cheek. She hadn't wanted to hurt him. Ever. He'd come too close, too quickly. That was all.

She clutched both hands against her chest, afraid of touching him, and whispered, "I'm so sorry. Bill, I don't know what, I don't..."

A hundred expressions twisted across his face, then he reached for her, hands on her shoulders, around her back. Her pulled her to him, wrapped her up in his arms. She shook, not in fear or rage but from a monstrous bubble of sadness tearing out of her. She made no noise other than a subdued choking. It was how she usually cried, silently, shaking but restrained so no one would know. Seyha pressed her nose into the exposed part of Bill's chest where the top two buttons of his Polo shirt were undone, breathed in the tang of his cologne. It was familiar, safe. She wanted to wipe away that red spot on his face, make everything go away. Start over with sunshine streaming through the windows, everything happy. All the while she thought – she *knew* – nothing would be as good between them again. Whatever held them prisoner in this place would never allow it.

* * *

"Shh, it's OK."

Bill wished he could hold his wife closer, hold her in this spot the entire night if that's what it took. Vague whispers behind him. The conversation didn't reach him. His cheek burned. She'd hit him *hard*. The vision in his left eye was blurry. He blinked, tried to clear it. Nothing changed.

She said something, but her words were lost against his chest. From the desperate tone, he could assume her meaning. He said into her hair, "You don't need to talk. Later, but only if you want to. None of us knows what's going on. Talking might help, but it's your call. No one else's. All right? It's your call."

She nodded, her nose wiping against him. Her silent

sobs lessened in intensity. Even so, he held on.

When it seemed like she'd finished, he asked, "Do you want to lie down?"

She nodded.

"Come on. Unless the sheets are frozen like everything else, you can lay in bed for a while." He tried to make his voice light, but it came out dull and emotionless.

Seyha moved a few inches apart from him. She'd begun to relax, but now she tensed again. She shook her head and looked up only enough to focus on his chin. "No," she said. "No. We," sniff, "we should stay together. I just don't want to talk."

"I'll stay with you in –"

"No." She laid a hand flat against his damp shirt and looked into his face. "No. I'm sorry that I hit you."

Now he *did* put his fingers on his face. It felt better, but that vague blur remained. "Me, too." He tried to smile, decided it wasn't worth the effort. They returned to the couch. Joyce was no longer kneeling beside Gem, but sat propped on the arm of the girl's chair. Her head was bent in the midst of a private discussion but she sat straighter at their approach.

"It's been crazy," he said. "Let's move on for now. If and when Sey's ready to talk, we'll come back to her."

"I'm fine with that," Joyce said. "Gem?"

The girl looked surprised to be asked her opinion. She made a face, muttered, "Umm, sure."

It felt good to sink back into the cushions, with Seyha curled against him. He noticed she was sitting half-turned away from the others. What the hell had she seen? Something from her past, like him. Maybe as far back as....

"Oh, Sey," he whispered, though she probably had no idea why he'd said it. But he knew, with a calm but horrific certainty, where she'd gone. It was the only explanation.

The details of her childhood in Cambodia he didn't know, and she never shared anything. He might *never* know, but it might be time finally to change that. Soon. If she couldn't share it with their two guests, she had to trust *him* at least.

*   *   *

Joyce led them in another prayer. Seyha found it hard to join in, to accept the blessings the priest tried to offer. Joyce was obviously desperate to try *something*. She'd retrieved her Bible from the dining room table and read a passage from Exodus, about Moses and the ten plagues God sent against Pharaoh to make him free the Israelites. The idea that what was happening was the same "plague of darkness" which cursed the Egyptians, *a darkness that could be felt*, was an insane consideration. Ironically, as horrific as their situation was, the idea that it was somehow the work of God rather than some other, darker force had a surreal, almost *uplifting* effect on the rest of group. If this was God's doing, after all, how could it be bad?

But it *was* bad. It was dark and frightening and no matter how often they debated its cause, the windows were still black, the house was still sealed like a tomb. There remained the matter of the *voice* but discussion invariably progressed away from that topic. It was the most disturbing, perhaps, but also the most important aspect, in Seyha's opinion. She sat straighter in her seat, close to Bill but meeting the others' gazes until a quiet lapse eventually fell amid the volley of ideas and theories. She took advantage of the opening.

"None of this explains the voice."

The anguished turn at the corner of Gem's eyes, the heavy sigh from Reverend Lindu, told Seyha she'd been right to bring them back to this. If nothing else, maybe it would make them all shut up for a few minutes. She was starting to get a headache from all this *talking*. "We all heard it. Even during the blackouts. And no, I still don't want to talk about mine. But it wasn't a *nice* voice. Didn't sound like God or an angel to me."

Gem nodded. "She's right. I told you I saw the thing. I don't know if I believe in demons, except maybe in movies, but if I had to choose between that or an angel, I vote demon."

Joyce had returned to the chair opposite Gem. She whispered, "There are demons. Believe in God and you have to accept the devil, too."

Gem closed her eyes, wiped her face in exasperation and said through her fingers, "What then, you're saying it *was* the devil?" She dropped her hands and pointed towards the ceiling. "I thought He was in charge!"

Joyce shook her head. "To be honest, Gem, I doubt anyone here is really sure who or *what* spoke to us."

"Whatever it was, it's pretty pissed off."

Seyha looked at each of them before nearly shouting, "Whoever spoke was laughing at us, at all the bad things in our life. Laughing when our–" She stopped, cursed under her breath and tried to reign in her emotions. Bill stared at her, waiting for more. She looked at him. "Don't."

He shook his head. "I didn't say anything." His earlier smile twitched down a notch. It looked pained, not his easy grin. The red spot was still there, lingering, taunting her. She settled against him in an unspoken apology.

Joyce waited to be sure Seyha wasn't going to speak any further, then finished the thought for her. "...it was not kind. It was trying to hurt me, all of us." Her lip trembled. She licked it and very lightly bit down.

Gem said, "I don't mean this the wrong way but... Mister Lindu wasn't a real nice guy, was he?"

Joyce nodded. "Once. All the time, really, he just had moments." She was looking back and forth across the rug, as if her gaze could wipe away the lie. She stopped, smiled a little, shook her head. "No. Not at the end. Once, like I said, he was. Mostly, in the end, well, not nice."

"I know he left you, Joyce," Bill said, "but I can't ever remember one moment when he wasn't smiling, friendly. Honestly, when we heard you guys split, I was dumbstruck. I thought things were perfect. You looked so happy."

Joyce shrugged her shoulders, tried to maintain a dismissive tone. "I know. On the outside - outside the house, I mean - we might have. But the world out there, and the world," she looked up, "in here... well, sometimes houses can have secrets." She stared sadly at Gem. Seyha assumed she was looking through the girl, seeing something none of them could see, but it didn't stop Gem from squirming under the gaze.

Joyce finally looked away and said, "Anyway, as I think I mentioned, I had been thinking of doing some overseas work, maybe with Bec after she graduates, if she wants to come along. Might be a nice change. That's all there is to my story. Kind of puts the two visions into some kind of context. In a twisted sort of way."

"Or," Gem said, "this whole thing might be Satan slapping us around because you kicked God out of the house."

Seyha sighed and looked at the ceiling. "We didn't kick God out of the house."

"Sure you did. You deconsecrated the place. God goes out, demons move in. Seems that way to me."

"Gem," Joyce said, and Seyha was glad to hear a hint of exasperation in her voice, "we may not deconsecrate churches every day, but it does happen, with all denominations. Why hasn't something like this occurred before now?"

"Maybe it has."

No one had an answer for that. Not at first. Bill offered a hesitant, "I think we'd have heard about it by now."

"Maybe, unless those people are now drooling in paper cups, or decided to pretend it never happened. I mean, who'd believe them anyway? The only papers that would report it usually have Bigfoot as their leading story."

"I think we're losing the thread of the discussion."

"Why?" Gem shifted on the cushions again to a kneeling position. Seyha wondered, without much concern, how much grass and asphalt the girl's stained socks were rubbing into them. "I mean, maybe this is just some elaborate *Lifetime Channel* movie of the week. All we have to do is sit around here and talk about our *issues*." She made quotation marks with her fingers, visibly agitated, bouncing up and down on the backs of her legs, "But it's not, is it? What I saw wasn't some nice angel trying to get his wings by showing me what life would be like without me. I saw a *monster*. The thing crawled all over my Dad and then stabbed me in the gut!" She pulled up her shirt to expose her belly. With her free hand she poked four fingers into the skin. She shouted, "It stuck these nasty, long claws into my stomach and threw me out the window!" She let the shirt drop back down. "Maybe this is some bizarre tug of war. Good and Evil fighting for our souls. That sounds more like the truth. But I'm telling you," she was almost standing on her seat, shouting louder, "I really don't want to hang around here any longer than I have to, because I have a really bad feeling that... *thing* is still here someplace, like a Bad Clown waiting to drag us all into the sewer grate!" She collapsed back into the cushions. She uttered a half curse, half hiss, "Shiss!" then rubbed her face with both hands.

Seyha had to say something, before the other two tried to change the subject. "Much as saying so leaves a bad taste in my mouth, Gem's right. I understand *none* of this, but I don't want to go through another of those blackouts. I may not have seen what *she* saw, but I sure as hell never want to hear that voice again."

A terrible certainty washed over her – she'd just given the laughter its cue to come back.

Nothing happened. They were still alone, without answers.

"Well," Joyce said, wiping her hands along the smooth length of her skirt. "I don't know what else we can do about getting out of here, but we should try *something*. No sense testing the door knobs or latches. We know they're locked."

Bill cleared his throat. "As much as I hate the idea – these windows are expensive, I mean – we might want to try and break the glass. This time with something other than my arm. One of the dining room chairs, maybe." He pointed casually with the hand resting on the back of the couch.

Everyone looked. The alternating, non-stained-glass windows were solid black, reflecting nothing. As Bill had said earlier, they looked painted. Now, Seyha had the disorienting feeling that the windows weren't blackened over, but were simply *not there*. There was *nothing* there. Nothing beyond, either. The thought caused too much vertigo, so she looked away.

Bill got up and walked with purpose to the dining room table.

Seyha scratched an itch behind one ear, noticed with some irritation Gem Davidson doing the same thing. The girl knelt higher on her seat, following Bill's progress as he walked to the nearest window with one of the chairs.

"Um," Gem said, "you know, I was thinking. Maybe this isn't such a good idea. I mean, what if you break it, but we're in outer space or something? I saw something like that on a show once. A whole town got snatched away to a weird planet and put in a zoo." Her voice got louder as Bill gripped the back of the chair with both hands and hefted it in front of him. "What if you manage to break it, and we all get sucked out?"

He gave her a little nod and wink. "I'd say, Gem, that you watch way too many movies." He stepped to one side of the window. "OK," he said, "here goes!"

Gem covered her ears and curled tightly into the cushions. Seyha leaned far back in own her seat. With a small grunt Bill raised the chair to shoulder height and, using the pivot of his body for momentum, slammed it hard against the window. Gem screamed. In the moment of impact, Seyha was certain the glass would shatter, the chair continue outside and blessed daylight would stream through.

Instead, the chair broke into a few jagged pieces. Three of the legs remained attached to each other by their connecting dowels but fell away from the seat. One leg remained, cracked. The seat itself broke loose when it hit the sill and fell to the floor The back of the chair remained in Bill's knuckle-white grip.

Aside from the sound of the wood pieces falling atop each other on the floor, the impact made absolutely no sound. *Nothing there*, Seyha thought again. The reverberation must have hurt. Bill looked towards them with a pained expression, still holding the chair back.

"I," he began. "No. Oh, no, please, God."

Seyha stared at him, then was looking only at the wall. The chair back landed on top of the other pieces. Seyha blinked, looked back and forth across the room. Bill wasn't there. She stumbled off the couch, and ran to his body on the floor.

But there *was* no body.

He was gone.

"Bill..."

Gem screamed. She had her hands against her face. Joyce got up from her chair, but after two slow steps she stopped.

Gem was gone.

Seyha prayed to herself, *Our Father, who art in heaven, hallowed be thy name....*, standing in her living room where demons did not fear to tread, where her husband and neighbor had just blinked from existence. *...on Earth as it is in Heaven...*

Seyha looked at Joyce and realized that the woman was actually speaking the same prayer, out loud, whispering and staring at the chair where Gem had been. Seyha reached out to her, not wanting to be left alone. She didn't want to be alone again. Not ever again.

Joyce Lindu was no longer there.

Seyha felt nothing then. No panic, no terror. Nothing to feel. Nothing to fight, not even as she felt a tingling sensation along her skull, an aura of nothingness gripping her head like a spongy black veil. What could she do? She was dead. All of them were dead, and this was hell. Forever and ever would the darkness return.

Second Day of Darkness

It was odd how familiar this feeling of displacement had already become, sitting in a chair that no longer felt like the one she'd just been curled up in. Once a nightmare, twice – what, routine? Far from that. Gem was terrified, but of something a *little* less unknown than last time. She would wake up – she prayed she would wake up – and the darkness would lift and she'd be *somewhere*. Maybe only to see a monster in front of her, waiting to stick her in the gut again.

She raised both hands to her face in defense of what would be standing beyond the black veil. This terrible expectation was part of the game, apparently, because it was taking an eternity to happen.

Is that all this was, a game? Joyce had seen something biblical in all this, but that was how she always thought, being a priest. The way she talked, it might be *God* playing with their heads. Gem didn't think this was his style. Not since that stint in Egypt. As much as she hated to admit it, Mrs. Watts was more on the mark. Whatever was doing this was evil. Someone or some*thing* enjoyed tormenting them.

Not for the first time, Gem began to wonder if all of them were dead. Damned to live out their worst fears again and again. Wailing and gnashing their teeth while demons laughed and poked them in the stomach with pitchforks.

She cried out, mutely, and reached into the darkness but felt nothing in front of her. Alone. This time, at least, she'd gotten a glimpse of what happened before everyone blacked out. They weren't groping around the living room lost in some hallucination. Mister Watts had disappeared. He'd been *taken*.

She ignored the urge to blindly explore her surroundings. If some bug-eyed demon wanted to play hide and seek, let him. She didn't have to cooperate.

"This is an amethyst."

Her mother's voice, to the right and very close. Any sense of control she thought she had was gone. Gem leaped forward in her blindness, shouting and grabbing for her mother. *Mom, it's me! I'm here!*

Her arms closed around nothing. She tipped forward. Legs spinning overhead, her entire body twirled and spun, falling into the nothingness. She was so stupid, should have stayed on the couch not leapt off before the demons finished building their new fake world. She was falling, dizzy and lost and –

– face down onto the floor, landing hard and sudden. She couldn't breathe, not at first, only lay there, managing to finally take in air that carried the thin mustiness of a carpet. Familiar. This was her living room. She blinked and realized she could see.

When the fear of dying was pushed far enough away, Gem thought, *Here we go again. Back at home.*

This time she was going to stay far from the Watts' house. Dream or no, something bad was going on over there. No sense instigating Gollum again.

"Am-a-tist," repeated a little girl. She'd mangled the pronunciation, but Deanna only said, "Yes, very good. You use these to channel the good aura of the world, uplift the spirit, even help with tummy aches."

The girl giggled.

Gem rolled onto her back. The room looked different. The couch was wrong, so was the coffee table on the other side of her. She slowly raised herself onto her elbows. Everything on top of the table – magazines, the coffee cup – was *off*, different. The *TV Guide* was too small. Its cover sported characters from a show long since relegated to reruns on cable. Another magazine – *National Geographic* – looked vaguely familiar.

Mom was spouting her New Age nonsense again, this time to Gem's little cousin, Amanda. At least, it sounded like her.

Gem leaned back on her elbows enough to peek around the couch to spy her mother at the round table in the corner. She looked... younger.

"What's this one?" Amanda asked. Gem sat up straighter, peered over the back of the couch.

"Fluorite."

Oh, no, Gem muttered silently, *no, no, no....*

That wasn't Amanda. Gem stood and stared at the girl. She looked a lot like her cousin, but was not her. Gem recognized the Polly Pocket t-shirt. She'd loved that shirt. Cried when she learned her mother had thrown it away. And Deanna Davidson looked younger because she *was* younger.

The table was strewn with crystals and rocks laid out haphazardly beside a long plastic container, like a pill box for ultra-hypochondriacs. Dozens of compartments, half-filled with small, shiny stones.

"Floo-rite," young Gem repeated, and when Mom nodded and said, "Hmm mm," the girl beamed and held the green stone over the plastic compartments, looking for the right one by comparing it to the others. Gem's mother absently said, "That's the only one I have, so just pick an empty one and drop it in. Your choice."

The girl took this responsibility seriously, choosing slowly.

Gem walked closer, sat on the arm of the couch. She breathed in, smelled smells from long ago. Nothing could be attributed to any one memory, lingering traces of different perfume, different toys and air fresheners. It smelled like the past. Gem could almost reach out to touch her mother. Two more steps and touch herself as a child. That last thought sent shivers of gooseflesh up her arms. She'd probably break some time-travel rule, or worse her hand might drift through the girl like a ghost's.

She stayed where she was. Gem had to admit she was pretty cute at this age. In all the pictures she'd seen of herself, when her mother didn't cut off the top of everyone's heads, her hair was in pig tails. Not now. Blonde hair loose, erratic. Short, stubby fingers, face and arms chubby like all kids that age. Gem *almost* remembered this moment, this time at least. This routine. She wasn't old enough for school. Her mom just got a new shipment of crystals from the mail-order place. Gem looked around the room, spied an open box on the floor. Shredded paper spilled out like spaghetti. The places where she bought her stuff never used those Styrofoam peanuts. Too environmentally unfriendly.

"What's this one?" Little Gem held up a new stone, the smooth black surface shining in the light. *Onyx*, Gem thought. Her mother consulted a piece of paper, maybe the packing list.

"It's onyx, I think," she said, and pointed to a section of the container where similar stones were. The girl immediately started crying.

"I'll find it myself!" she shouted.

Her mother looked up, smiled. "I'm sorry. Maybe that's not the right one. You make sure."

Placated, little Gem searched for the right compartment. She eventually dropped it into the place her mother had selected.

Why am I here? Gem wondered. She looked cautiously around the room. It had a warm feel to it, the light different, soft and homey like those days when Gem was older and stayed home from school. The house always felt different on a school day. Some secret world that most kids weren't able to experience as they labored under the classroom's florescent glare. A secret place. Solitary, like the church.

Her mother got awkwardly out of her chair and held a hand to the small of her back. She was pregnant. *Oh, wow*, Gem said silently. That was Eliot in there!

"No!" Little Gem cried. "More!"

"We'll do more," her mother promised. "I just need to pee."

"OK," Gem said, moving a finger through the dwindling pile of stones. "I'll look for a spot for... this one. " She chose another amethyst.

Her mother seemed about to object – Mom hated anyone going through her stuff when she wasn't around, especially the rocks. She must have decided that Gem couldn't hurt anything since she duck-walked into the half-bath beside the stairs.

Gem was alone, with herself.

Hey, Gem, she tried to say, but like before had no voice. *Having fun?*

"Yep," came the reply. Every hair on Gem's body rose to attention.

You can hear me?

"Yep." The little girl never looked up from her work.

This was weird. Gem worried again about messing with the past. Did she ever have an imaginary friend as a kid? She couldn't remember.

Well, she'd already blown it, too late to stop now. She

said, *Can you see me?*

The girl looked up, carefully, a child peeking fearfully over the top of a bed sheet. She saw Gem, looked quickly back to the rocks.

"Yep."

Do you know who I am?

The girl found the spot with the amethyst and let the stone drop. Her tiny fingers shook a little, and it fell into the wrong spot, tumbling between three moonstones. Her mother won't like that. The girl didn't notice. She said, still not looking up, "Yes. You're me. An *old* me."

I'm not that old.

"Yes you are. You're a grown up. And you're in hell."

Gem leaned back against the couch, almost fell over. She worked one leg over the arm until she straddled it. Things were starting to twist around again. She felt as she had when the darkness crept over her a few minutes ago. Being dragged away to a place she didn't want to be.

She whispered, *I'm not in... I'm not dead.*

The girl looked up, shiny gaze now steady. Though her voice resonated that of a three year-old's, the words belonged to someone much older. "Yes," she said. "That's where you are. That's where I'm going to be some day, I guess. Mommy's teaching me how to get there."

No. She's good! She's a little lost in her own world, but she's not bad.

"She's not *saved*," the girl said, making child-fingered quotation marks on the word. "Isn't that what the priest lady says? Or she will, they always do. Like a broken record. Ooh, ooh," she pointed to the rocks. "This rock brings you health. This rock makes your aura focus on the Here and Now. Goody goody, Mommy." Her voice dropped to a soft growl. "Teach me more!" Then she giggled.

The door to the bathroom across the room was half-open. Gem heard the toilet flush. A minute later water was running. Her mother's voice: "Gem, I can't hear you. I'll be right out."

"It's OK, Mommy," the girl said. "I'm just telling the older me how we're all damned to an eternity of torment and bad cooking because of our mother issues."

Deanna came out, walking the same half-waddle all women in their last trimester walked. "What did you say, Gem?"

The girl picked up a reddish stone. "What's this one called, Mommy?"

"It's a Peridot." She looked over the box. "Oh, no. Gem, no. You can't mix amethyst with moonstone. No… they're not compatible." She plucked the amethyst from the container, let it drop in with its sister stones. As she did, the girl turned to Gem and raised her tiny eyebrows, up and down twice.

Mom? Gem hoped her mother could hear her. She needed an ally, even if she was only *Mom From The Past.*

Her mother did not respond. Only turned sideways and sat down. She resumed sorting through the remnants. Gem didn't know what to do. What was this all about? Her mother might be a little flaky, but she was the most spiritual of them all. These rocks were only a hobby.

Little Gem looked up. *That's not me,* Gem realized. *None of this is real.* The girl said, smiling, "Playing with stones does nothing, Me," still in her toddler voice. Gem's mother didn't notice. "Only distract, divert. It's the *secrets* which rot the soul. The secrets," she lifted a moonstone from its compartment, "the secrets," dropped it back into its place, "that we hide behind sticks and stones. Some just keep more than others. Like our mommy here, like the Watts, like the Lindu's…."

Gem pointed at her. *Ah ha! So this is all fake. I'm not in the past after all.*

"Well, duh," Little Gem said, with an exaggerated roll of her pretty eyes. Her voice never lost its childlike lilt. "No matter. If I'm the devil like you and Miss Saigon seem to think, then I probably *am* lying." She began to hum, dropped another crystal into its proper place, looked at her mother. "Mommy, I need to tinkle."

"Oh, Gem. I wish you'd told me earlier."

The girl looked sad. "I'm sorry. I'll go by myself. I'm a big girl now."

"OK, but please remember to flush, and don't use too much toilet paper."

She jumped from the chair. As she passed, Gem instinctively moved further onto the couch. The girl whispered, "I'm a big girl, now, Gem, did you hear? Have a nice time in hell!" She raised on small fist in front of her, middle finger extended, then skipped to the bathroom.

The room glowed red, flickering first in a wild amber light. Heat ripped along her back. Gem turned in a half circle on the cushions. The house was on fire. Where the front had been now stretched a rocky, surreal landscape of steaming sand. The ground pulsed with flame just below its surface, then everywhere it erupted, spurting fire like jagged glass, too bright to look at. The glass fire reached into the sky, solidifying, returned as crystal shards onto the superheated sand. Glowing embers the size of mini-vans scattered in their wake. Even the clouds hovering overhead ignited, turned to ash to form fetid, black snow. The heat came next, oven-ready walls of it slapping Gem backwards off the couch-turned-boulder. Behind her, the table was gone. Far off in the new distance, mountains sagged under thick red tongues dripping from the sky. Gem could see no people but the air was filled with their screams. She covered her ears and realized her arms were burning, flailing wings of fire. Her scream joined the chorus of this false world.

She ran backwards, arms tightening to black under the flames but she dared not put them down, dared do nothing but stumble back until she collided with the swinging doors leading into the kitchen. A cool, luxurious breeze washed over her like a wave. She kept moving backwards, sighing in relief as the heat and pain disappeared. The back of her knees collided with a kitchen chair and Gem lowered her arms for balance as he sat with a painful thud into it.

It took a moment for the scene in the kitchen to register. Joyce was standing by the sink, staring back at her with a mix of surprise and terror. Then the woman was gone, faded like a camera flash's after-image. Gem dared not move, hardly breathed, because with Joyce suddenly gone the only other person in the room was a muscular man standing two chairs over from her and wearing only a pair of white underwear. Ray Lindu turned around to face her. He smiled, amused at something that Gem could care less about and said, "Hello again, Rock."

*　　*　　*

Joyce turned her head to the right, stared at the woven *Fluer de lis* pattern of a worn couch above her, tried *not* to identify what she was seeing – *where* she was – then rolled her head left. She was laying on her back atop a thin, patterned carpet, in the valley between a glass-topped coffee table and a worn, rough-textured couch. The coffee table partially obscured her vision but she could see past it to the stairs and a tall grandfather clock ticking away the silence.

Daylight spilled from the picture window by her feet. She sat slowly up and leaned against the couch – one that was older, more coarse than the Watts'. There was a vague sense of familiarity to this place. If she looked around would she see the others scattered around the room? When she did, using the coffee table for leverage, a quick scan of the room showed she was alone. Then a woman laughed behind her, distant but clear. Joyce turned around, heard the voice again. It was coming from upstairs.

At the edge of the staircase, the voice was only slightly louder. Words unclear, but happy. More laughter. A man's voice, now, the words no clearer than the woman's but their timber resonated through Joyce like a punch. It was familiar enough to redden her face, push her away from the stairs. A man and a woman, talking in hushed tones, behind what must be a closed bedroom door. That was all, nothing more.

She shouldn't be here.

Joyce turned the knob on the front door. It didn't budge. She tried the lock, nothing. Trapped, like she'd been at the Watts' house. The man's voice returned. She covered her ears and headed towards the opposite end, towards a set of swinging doors, glancing out the front picture window as she did. The street looked familiar. Of course it did. She'd known where she was as soon as she heard the voices, though she didn't remember ever having been inside this place. Even if she hadn't, obviously Ray....

No, no, no! Stop this. God, please, what are you doing to me? I'm sorry for everything. Please, don't do this.

She shoved aside the doors and stepped quickly into the kitchen towards the open back door, which slammed shut just before she reached it. The louvered blinds covering its four-pane window, and those over the sink, swayed in the sudden gust.

She stood motionless, staring at the knob, wondering what to do, knowing it would not turn if she tried it. The other woman's voice called from upstairs – clearer now, the bedroom door apparently having been opened – "Gem, you didn't go outside, did you?"

"No, Mom," said a small voice behind her. Joyce cried out and turned to face a little girl sitting at the far end of the table. Two coloring books were laid out in front of her, with a dozen scattered crayons of various colors and sizes.

Joyce recognized Gem immediately, though she was no more than three or four years old. Her small face turned towards the swinging doors leading to the living room. She said, "Mrs. Lindu is visiting!"

She turned back towards Joyce, face neutral and unsmiling. "Hi," she said, quieter now.

Joyce stared at her for a long moment, trying to understand where – no, *when* – this was. She had to say something. "Hi, Gem." At least she still had her voice. *Little victories.*

"Hi," little Gem said again. "Mommy's busy right now."

Gem was looking past her towards the kitchen window.

Joyce said, "Your Daddy's home, too?"

The girl focused on her again, saying nothing for a long time, long enough to make Joyce uncomfortable. "No," she said at last. "Just her friend."

The man's voice, his laughter, drifted down the stairs, following the soft footfalls of Deanna Davidson – Joyce had to assume it was her coming to greet her guest. As if responding to the sound of the man's voice, Gem put down her crayons and covered her ears with both hands, much like Joyce had done when she was standing by the staircase.

Moving one hand away and content with the silence, Gem dropped both and picked up a new crayon.

Deanna's thin robe was wrapped loosely around her lithe body as she breezed into the kitchen. She was almost as tall as Joyce, though with a more willowy figure to compliment her height, and disheveled black hair. She carried herself with more grace and confidence than Joyce ever could have, keeping one hand loosely on the robe's sash and lightly brushing the silk with her fingertips. With the other, as if she'd just arrived at a party, reached out to take Joyce's. "Joyce Lindu," she said affectionately, "what a nice surprise!"

What the hell is going on? she thought.

Joyce absently took her hand. The palm was warm and soft. "I –" she began, swallowed, didn't know what she should say. "I'm sorry for intruding. I don't know how to get out of here."

Deanna laughed, released Joyce's hand and gave her a playful slap on the shoulder. "Do any of us?"

"Mommy..."

"Not now, Gem." She never turned to her daughter but her tight voice was a warning. "Joyce, I'm sorry I couldn't be more presentable, but I have company, and we were so occupied with each other I never heard you..." she considered her words for a moment, "...pop in!" She laughed again. Gem covered her ears again, left them there, watching the exchange.

Joyce wanted to strangle this woman. Since it was all just a dream, maybe she *could* –

"Hey, Joyce."

Ray walked into the kitchen wearing only his white Fruit of the Looms. Gem squeaked in terror and shifted her hands to cover her eyes. Ray smiled over at her and grinned wider. "Heya, Rock!" Gem made another anguished noise and worked her fingers such that her ears could be plugged without uncovering her eyes. Even her little body curled away from him on the chair.

Joyce wanted to scream, to faint; wanted to die in that moment. She knew it had been Ray upstairs, but seeing him here, like this, was too much.

This hadn't happened. She'd never been in this house. Never.

But *he* had. If she'd suspected once upon a time, now she had her proof, belated as it was.

Ray stepped forward and kissed her lightly on the cheek. It burned.

"What are you doing here, hon? Did the toilet back up again?"

"Wha- what?"

Deanne laughed and moved beside Ray. She snaked her right arm around his muscular left.

Joyce watched them, somehow seeing Gem so terrified – or maybe the girl was simply embarrassed – as a comfort. She turned her attention to her, not knowing how to deal with the couple... *the couple, my God what is this?* – but she knew, of course. Had always known. What Joyce could not decide was the point of it all, the *intention* of these visions. Good or bad. Helping, or taunting. Somewhere unseen was some monstrous cat playing with its mouse until it grew bored of the game and devoured it.

"Joyce..." Ray, light tone, an undercurrent of impatience.

Joyce looked back, and against her will found herself looking down at his legs, up along his mostly naked body. Deanna's own thin, smoothly-shaven leg poking from the robe, close to his. Joyce blinked to erase the image, stared rabbit-like into her husband's eyes.

"This didn't happen," she said, defeated, not caring anymore. She only stared at him and said, "Why am I here, Ray?"

Deanna sighed and pulled herself away. "Ah, well, play time's over, honey." She kissed him on the cheek much like Ray had just done to Joyce. One hand still rested across the robe, fingers splayed over her belly. She now tightened the sash and slapped Ray on the butt. "You can let yourself out. Come on, Gem, naptime for you!"

Gem slid off the chair, keeping her small hands positioned in front of her face to avoid seeing the man in his underwear. When they were gone, and the swinging doors had settled, Ray wandered to the nearest chair and sat, draping an arm over the back of the seat.

"Is that some deep, philosophical question, Joyce? *Why are we here?*"

"No. It's not. I'm actually in the Watts' home, or floating in some cloud above it. I don't know. I *do* know that, at this moment, I'm not standing in our old neighbors' kitchen with you. I *can't* be and you damn well know it." She waved an arm around the room. "This is an illusion, a mirage. I think it's time to stop letting it control me. Now, I ask again, why am I here?"

"No," he said, leaning further back – showing off his body. Joyce turned away, looked at the refrigerator. He continued, "This isn't real. You're not exactly floating above the house, but *that*, I assure you, is the real world. For what it's worth." He sat straighter, realizing perhaps his preening was not having the desired effect. "Feel better getting that off your chest?"

She didn't like the condescension in his voice, or the way he looked at her in his usual, infuriating slow scan up and down her body. It was only for show, of course, because compared to Deanna, Joyce felt ugly. She turned her back to him, stared out the small window over the sink.

And saw herself, stepping from her car in the driveway next door, looking at Ray's car, then back to the house. A quick glance over here, almost *directly* towards the window through which Joyce was watching *her*, then quickly turned away. Joyce almost remembered this moment, now. A familiar, deep pain blossomed everywhere inside of her. She pictured her daughter Rebecca, not the child she would have been in this moment of time, but the *real* now, the pierced and punked-out college student, her daughter *and* best friend. Somehow, that helped, even if she might never see Bec again.

Without turning away, she whispered, "Who are you?"

The scrape of a chair on linoleum, barest thud of his weight as he stepped forward. "Oh, I'm Ray. I guess." His voice was too close. She tightened her shoulders a second before his ugly, perfect hands settled on top of them. Not violent, ironically gentle.

"And you're Reverend Joyce Lindu, former pastor of a small Episcopal parish who now finds herself lost and wandering amid lost dreams and shattered hopes." He squeezed her shoulders. Nausea tightened her throat. She would not get sick. She was about to shrug him away when he let go and stepped away, muttering, "Lost dreams and shattered hopes... I should write that one down." Scrape of the chair again followed by the sound of his sitting once more.

The *other* Joyce, the one outside, stepped in through the church's front door. She remembered always coming in through the main entrance to reach the residential section at the other end of the house. Rarely did she use the small door at the end of the driveway. The home seemed so much bigger that way. If fact, everything that was truly *theirs* was meager, humble. Once she thought it was a good thing, a way to keep priorities straight. *The last will be first*, and all that. Now, it only fed the disease running through her gut. She'd never felt more *last* than now.

"Poor Joyce," Ray said, with no trace of sympathy. "Lost her man and lost her church. At least now you're free to run away and hide from your sins in some filthy jungle thousands of miles away. Take our daughter and heed the words of James, put your faith into action. Bury your head in dirt and poverty so no one – " he sighed, not completing the thought. "Ah, whatever. Have fun, I say."

Joyce turned around. After the sun glare outside the room was dark, Ray's body was a blur of shadow. She must not let this thing, whatever it was, destroy her. *Ray* hadn't, even after that horrible final night with him, when every illusion she'd built around herself fell apart so violently. She had to take control, had to show some damned *nerve*. She cleared her throat, managed to whisper, "If you're an angel, or created by one, you'd agree with that sentiment. If you're something else – "

"A demon, perhaps?"

She fought a jolt of fear. "Perhaps," she said. "But if that was true, you'd want me to do anything *but* help the needy." Her mouth was dry. She hated herself for it.

"The *needy*," he groaned, and stared up at the ceiling. With an exaggerated sigh, he said, "There will always be poor. Didn't The Man say that once? You and I both know the only reason for any of this is to get as far away from that house next door as possible. Am I right? Hmm?" He smiled, without any trace of humor.

"What do you want from me?"

Ray smiled wider, and stood up again, stepped forward and brushed two fingers across the front of her blouse. "Oh, I don't know." Another slow look along her body. Joyce tightened every muscle in order not to react, positively or negatively, give him, or *it*, any satisfaction. "How about a little fun, for old times' sake?"

Joyce leaned back against the kitchen counter. Before she could stop herself she said, "Don't touch me." Her voice was a miserable, weak squawk.

Ray laughed, raised both arms in a gesture of mock

acquiescence. He leaned against the kitchen table, waggling his legs side to side in a childish, unspoken invitation. That was when Joyce noticed the red, plum-sized mark in the center of his bare chest, just below the rib cage. It looked like a birthmark, though she knew full well he had no such blemish on his skin. She focused on this, willed it to grow larger, more painful – Ray interrupted the thought with, "Ah, the Holy Mother. So chaste, so pure." He straightened, crossed his arms over his chest as if unconsciously covering up the stain. "Well, if it's any consolation, Joyce, my little jaunts next door – or *Ray's* jaunts, since we've worked out that minor detail – didn't last too long. The ravishing and quirky Mrs. Davidson would soon be much too busy having little Eliot to worry about any flings with her brackish rogue of a neighbor." He slowly ran an admiring hand along the stubble of his chin. Then he sighed and brushed off his chest as if having just eaten. The birthmark was gone. "You know," he said, focusing on the imaginary crumbs, "I always wondered why you didn't offer to baptize the boy. Pour water over his head..."

Too much, all of it, too much....

"...bless him in the name of the Father, and the Son, all that –"

Joyce screamed and threw her body forward, fists in front of her. She slammed them against his chest. He hardly flinched, and did not try to stop her.

The swinging doors to the kitchen slammed open. Gem – the teenaged version Joyce had left behind in the Watts' house – stumbled backwards, arms against the sides of her head not unlike the toddler version of herself had been doing. Her legs hit the kitchen chair and she sat down hard. Their eyes met for only a moment before the kitchen disappeared and Joyce found herself falling forward until both hands scraped across the hard-packed ground.

Long strands of dried grass tickled her face. She raised herself to a kneeling position. All around rose the screaming, humid jungle.

*   *   *

Seyha Watts stood, rigid, in a foul-smelling hallway, waiting as the blackness thinned then blew away in an unfelt breeze. She did not know this place. Bare walls around her, lime green paint stained with grime. She tried not to focus on one spot too long. Unavoidable, however, was the smell. Garbage, rot, and death. She wanted to go home. Wanted to be back in her carpeted, white-walled home with Bill and the sun streaming through the windows with the late-summer breeze blowing in. Wanted to be thousands and thousands of miles from this broken, dirty hallway and its smells and the echoes of shouting, cries of unrestrained sadness and fear. A memory came rolling into her consciousness of a school library in America, pictures in a book, of this place and others like it, the scream that had suddenly escaped from her teenaged self, one that seemed like it never stopped. One which never came again. She refused to let it, or think about that moment. Now, she raised her hands to her ears against the memory of that scream and the sounds of so many others down the hall where she now stood. Like the good nightmare this was, the sounds were no quieter, the odor no less nauseating.

Why was she here? This was not a physical memory, she had never before stood in this place. The voices in their misery spoke a language she did not understand, but she knew they were speaking *Khmer*. The language of a place and a country long dead to her, from a time she had hoped had also died.

Seyha looked behind her. Aside from the voices, the hallway was deserted. She needed to move, but whatever she was meant to see, whatever sorrow forced itself upon her, it would come of its own accord. Then she could wake up, find Bill, hide in his arms until the next wave of blackness swallowed them up. How many times would she have to come here?

"Not much longer," said a voice beside her. Seyha shouted in surprise and backed against the wall to her left. The young man standing casually a couple of feet away was barely out of his teens. As far as she could discern he was also Cambodian. A uniform shirt hung loosely over his chest. A damp, nondescript stain blemished the shirt's left shoulder. Apparently the boy hadn't felt a need to clean it. Like the rest of his body, his face was thin, teeth protruding at odd angles, nicotine-yellowed and black in spots. Despite this, his smile was warm, nothing like the grimaces and leers of the boys who'd killed her mother.

"Sorry for startling you, Doung Seyha. But we have much to do and not a lot of time." He spoke fluent English, no hint of an accent. He reached out, gently touched her elbow with his fingertips. She did not flinch away though her entire body was shaking in a continuous, thin tremor. With this gesture, he led her down the corridor. She didn't talk, assumed it would be useless but realized with only mild surprise that she'd heard herself shout a moment earlier. She did not want to follow this soldier, but resisting would only prolong the nightmare.

He did not seem to want to hurt her. Seyha was not fooled. He was Death, choosing this form for this moment only. He took many others. Mostly like this, however, a skinny boy in an oversized uniform carrying a gun that could destroy worlds with an uncaring twitch. She searched his presence with her eyes, craning her neck to see around him. He seemed not to notice, or care.

No rifle, no weapon at all that she could see.

"Almost there," he whispered, allowing her to think her thoughts and study him. He was her guide through Hell, and played the part seriously.

They passed room after room, some of the doors open. From these came the smell, some worse than others. She dared not look into them, having seen too much only from the corner of her eye. Huddled shapes on the floor, skittering away from their passage. If she looked, she would see misery too massive to take in.

On the other side of one closed door, a man screamed in that strange, familiar language of her birth. She did not understand the words, but their meaning was apparent. A cry for mercy. Angry voices followed, more pleas from the first.

The boy slowed noticeably as they neared the next door. It was open. Again, the odor intensified at their approach. No voices inside.

Please don't put me in there, she thought. *I'm not supposed to be here.*

"No," her host agreed. "You are not. A visitor only. You should be honored." They stopped shy of the door. Seyha glimpsed two bare feet, dirty and curled as if in pain. The boy said, "Not many outsiders have seen this place, at least not in its..." he waved an arm absently up and down. "What's the word? In its heyday? Yes," he said, nodding. "Heyday. Come."

Slight pressure from his fingertips on her elbow. She held back. His hand moved up her arm and closed tighter. He pulled her forward into the room. One final shove pushed Seyha past him. The soldier remained outside in the hall. "You have a visitor, Mister Doung."

Seyha closed her eyes. Hard spots danced behind her

lids. She'd seen too much. What they were trying to show her was a lie. It was wrong!

The man on the floor whispered, "*Sumto, kum wai kinyum. Kinyum utwer awai kep kaus tha.*"

Until this terrible chapter in the history of mankind, the man's language had been her own. Over time she had forgotten it. The Sisters of Compassion weaned her on English, French and Latin. Never again in all the years since then did she try to relearn her native *Khmer*. There was no need. Seyha should not have understood the words the man spoke, but in this dream of dark magic everything was possible, as long as it caused pain.

The man laying on the floor beyond her closed lids had said, *Please, don't hurt me. I've done nothing wrong.*

Even if the soldier hadn't spoken his name, Seyha knew who this man was. It was why she had closed her eyes. What made them open, however, was the sound of his voice. A voice she never expected to hear again.

Seyha looked down at her father. He lay on his right side, curled in a fetal position on a torn straw mat. His gray pajama shirt and pants were stained in dark, heavy patches. Between the swollen mounds of bruises on his face, his eyes were open. Two thin, glistening slits.

"Father?"

He blinked, pressing the flesh of his eyes together, then apart. He winced in pain but shifted his body to angle his head towards her. The chain leading from his manacled wrists to an iron spike in the floor draped across him like the last vestiges of a blanket. His mouth opened... so many missing teeth!

"Father!" Seyha said again. She fell to a crouch and cradled his face in her hands.

Because of the extent of his injuries, her father looked old and withered. His body was thinner than the boy in the hall. His lips moved again. A tear escaped the slit of one eye. Barely audible, he hissed, "Seyha..." He moaned, more tears. His face turned down, pressed into her lap. "*Tha, tha, munmein, ne ein, tha,*" he said. "*Hadawai ban chei gai jup na ein? Pru ne ein utwer wei kei...*"

No, no, not you, the translator in her head whispered. *Why have they taken you? You've done nothing wrong....*

Why was her father in this place? Where were they? She looked around the room. It was partitioned by warped sheets of plywood. Through a break between them a second figure moved in a slow, back and forth motion. To her right was a chalk-stained blackboard. This had once been a classroom. The hallway outside, so many unmarked doors. A school.

She tried to lift her father to a sitting position. The chains rattled off him and piled on the floor. His wrists were cuffed in thick iron bracelets, the chain an umbilical chord connecting him forever to this room. The linoleum was cracked where the spike had been hammered through. She wondered if its point protruded into the room below.

"Seyha," he whispered again and swallowed, face twisting in pain as he did so. He continued speaking, at least his lips moved, but Seyha could not understand what he was saying. Now and then, a word would be clear, "confession" or "they", translated by, or perhaps *for* her, only to be lost in the context of his whispered mutterings. One was clear, *Angkar*, a word she recognized without needing translation, one of many used as unofficial title of the communist government run by the monster Pol Pot. And *Khmer Rouge*, the army soldiered by children in a world gone insane.

She bent down and kissed his forehead. Her lips pressed through layers of sweat. A sour, pungent taste spread through her mouth and she swallowed back nausea.

Memory flashes like a slide show, moving too fast, details blurred, men coming to the village and taking her father away. Not arrested, only "Summoned for consultation." She thought that was the reason. Her mother had been worried but proud: it was good. If he could be useful to the government, serve some value.... but young Seyha had clung to her father's leg in protest. He lifted her, kissed her forehead much like she had just done to him in this place, and handed her to back her mother. Seyha remembered crying because other fathers had gone away and never came home. The last memory of that moment was the pattern of her mother's skirt. Maybe because she was crying against it, she didn't remember, was never sure how true the memory had been – until now, in this place where bad memories were served with macabre delight.

Not knowing what else to say, Seyha whispered, "I'll talk to them. Explain."

At some point the man's swollen eyes had closed but when she spoke they stuttered open. He stared at her, no sign of recognition. He mumbled words she couldn't hear. Seyha tried to pull his thin wrists free of the shackles.

All this time, her host remained in the doorway, hands folded limply before him. No change in his quiet expression, no compassion in those large, sunken eyes.

Seyha screamed, *Why did you bring me here!?!*

Her voice was gone, again. Even so, she raised her head higher and craned her neck to stare at the boy. *Why am I here? What did you do to my father?*

Her tears found release, blurring the image of the soldier in the door, twisting his outline into something hunched and grotesque. Perhaps this had always been his true form. Seyha cursed it, her soundless words collapsing into chest-heaving sobs. She held her father closer, pressed his cheek against her chest. She closed her own eyes, held him close, never to let him go. Never again. This was a lie. All of it. He was not brought here. After the Vietnamese army rescued the remnant of her village as they marched endlessly across the countryside, through her life in the orphanage and beyond, Seyha imagined her father searching for his lost family. Calling their names. When she came to America, she stopped imagining. He may yet be alive, very old now and missing his family. He would never find her. She would never return, so there was no sense in hoping. But this... this was not true, such a good man would *never* have been brought to this damned place. *Never.*

The boy in the doorway cleared his throat. "Yes, Doung Seyha, he was. S-21 is what they call our little world here. Such a warm and welcoming name, don't you think?"

Shut up!

"Thousands of other men, other fathers like the one you now hold were swept away by the wave of paranoia dripping from the broken mind of the one you know as Pol Pot but whom we called *Bong Timuoy*. Brother Number One."

I said shut up!

"So many little details you conveniently decided not to learn over the years since you were snatched away from us." He sighed. "So many things we can teach and show you now!" He almost sounded giddy. Seyha gently rocked her father. He was so cold. She cradled his head and shoulders against her, but his unmoving body grew colder, heavier.

She raised her head to the ceiling and cried. The sound – and, again, there *was* a sound – was joined by a dozen others. Crying and screaming all around her. Not from the prisoners trapped in this man-made hell. These new voices belonged to children.

*   *   *

When his own darkness lifted, Bill Watts stood not far from where he'd been a moment ago, except everything around him had changed. His home had reverted to its former self, Saint Gerard's Church. He stood among a hundred-plus parishioners, fingertips of one hand resting on the back of the pew in front of him. The other held open a hard-bound hymnal. The congregation sang *Oh, Who Can Know The Mind of God?* The closing hymn, apparently, since Reverend Lindu – a little younger than a few moments earlier but retaining the same, haunted look in her eyes – bowed before the altar and led the procession down the center aisle with the Bible held reverently before her.

Bill's jaw moved in song. He tried to stop it, to look away, see who was around him. His brain didn't have control over the rest of his body. *Oh, Who Can Know The Mind of God?* was number 469 in the book, one of the more obscure hymns Valerie de Daulles occasionally chose for services. Their music director liked to call it "adding mysterious ingredients to the pot."

Bill sang against his will. As before, he was doomed to be a passive observer of some moment in his past. The absurdity should have sent his mind reeling and his heart racing, but then his body was not his to control. Seyha was not beside him. In the past few years she rarely accompanied him. When was *this* service supposed to take place?

The people in front of him moved into the aisle. Bill's body followed and held small snippets of conversation with his neighbors. He found it hard to concentrate on what anyone said. Their voices were like a radio with the treble too low, bass too high. The speech of grown-ups in old

Charlie Brown cartoons. "Woo Waa Waa," Albert Fitts said. Bill felt his mouth turn up in a smile. "Wa, Woo Woo," came his response. This got a laugh out of Al and a slap on the shoulder.

Lord, he thought, *what's happening? Save me from this.*

In a small way he felt guilty for the prayer. The visions described by Gem and Joyce were very unpleasant. He had merely re-lived his first date with Seyha, and though their dinner date after the miscarriage had undertones of sadness, it had been a moment which brought them closer together, determined to try again. Not that they were ever successful. She never got pregnant again. Even so, why would he be allowed such tender memories?

A dark, amused voice behind him said, *"Maybe you're just one heck of a nice guy, Billy."*

If he had control of himself, Bill would have leapt forward. He could not. The mocking tone behind the voice reminded him of his previous vision-dream, how it had ended with its promised threat, the monster grabbing at his heart.

Laughter, low like the rumbling of a passing motorcycle, so close Bill wanted, *needed*, to turn and swat it away. But he could not turn, could only walk with the crowd down the aisle, occasionally "Waa-Waa"ing with his neighbors.

"Where's the wife, Billy?"

Leave me alone. Leave her alone.

Laughter again. Slightest touch of breath on his neck, hot and moist. *"Too late for that, my friend."*

They were almost to the door. Reverend Joyce Lindu stood outside, shaking hands, speaking briefly with each parishioner. A few would go so far as to swallow her in a quick hug before moving on. In the corner of his vision Bill thought he noticed *Ray* Lindu, but he could not look to see for sure. Nevertheless, Joyce seemed younger here, the paint inside the church was not what it had been last year when it closed, though still a faded yellow that must have been in style decades ago but in this time already looked old and dated. This moment must have been closer to the time he and Seyha had moved to town. Beyond Joyce, the small green lawn shone bright in a morning sun that hung above them in the blue, clear sky.

None of it was real.

"Green grass, blue skies," the dark voice sighed, almost wistfully. In front of Bill, Albert Fitts reached out a hand to Joyce. Everyone moved in slow motion. Time stretched out, slowed further, then stopped altogether.

The voice continued, *"Breathe in that blue sky, Billy, pull the clean air into your lungs, praise your God for the day He gives."*

Odd words for a demon, he tried to say, then mentally winced, afraid of admitting what he increasingly believed this creature to be. No one moved around him. Albert's hand locked together with the pastor's, his other frozen in the motion of his signature shoulder rap. Beyond, cars stalled as they pulled into the street, on their way home. No, Bill realized, *not* stalled. Still moving, but so, so slowly.

Behind him the voice continued its rumination, the tone contemplative, *"Your life was always blue skies and green grass. What is your life now, hmm? Who is your life?"*

In the name of our Lord I demand you –

"Look to your right, Billy."

Bill turned his head. For the moment, it seemed, he had control of his body again. Nothing in these nightmares could surprise him any longer. He dreaded the possibility that the owner of the voice would be standing beside him, leering with a grotesqueness which Gem Davidson had so awkwardly described. On his right, a few frozen parishioners, and Seyha. She'd been standing in the back vestibule, waiting for him to arrive. Had she been... yes, she'd been downstairs, with –

"*With the children*," the voice finished. Bill didn't think he/it could have sounded any closer. It perched weightlessly on his shoulder, almost pressing its lips to his ear. Bill shuddered, felt the response in the body he occupied, his own body, phantom that it was.

"*And...*," the voice continued. It paused for effect, then, "*action!*"

The people came alive. His view of Seyha was blocked by the threshold of the doorway. Joyce smiled, took his hand. "Bill, Waaa Woo Waa Waa, Wooo."

Bill said something equally nonsensical and moved on. He stepped to the side and waited for Seyha to merge into the crowd. She appeared after a few seconds jostling her way past the slow-moving Hank and Phyllis Cowles. The elderly couple had to lean away from her frenzied exit. She did not greet Joyce, only shuffled free of the mass of people, past Bill then onto the sidewalk.

He half-ran to keep up, tried to slow himself down but he was again riding along as an unwitting passenger. When the *Bill* of this time spoke, his words were understandable, though they sounded wrong, spoken underwater.

"You OK?"

Seyha tried to smile but the expression dropped to the usual, neutral gaze she often wore in public. "I'm fine. Sorry I didn't come back up with the children after the sermon. So much to pick up and pack away."

Bill watched and felt his arm hook into hers.

"What's the rush?"

"Nothing. I just... I just want to get home, settle down. Not feeling well." She laid a hand flat on her belly which had not yet begun to show any bulge. *She's pregnant, here*, Bill realized. She hadn't lost the baby yet, not for a few more days. He remembered this morning, this *when*.

When they reached the car parked along he roadside two houses down, he opened her door. She looked tense, moved with jerky motions.

"Were the kids out of control this morning?"

His words, spoken in this *Once Upon a Time* world, struck him with an odd mix of confusion and excitement, until he remembered she'd been downstairs, having volunteered (reluctantly and only at Bill's suggestion) for a shift with the Children's Liturgy – a toned-down version of the Scriptures being shared upstairs and broken into simpler constructs for the kids to understand. Arts and crafts were popular tools. Talk a little, get them building, see the concepts as a creation of their own hands. Bill loved the mornings when he worked downstairs. Sometimes he led the group, other times just helped out. Seyha had agreed to give it a try, but only as helper, always uncomfortable talking to kids of any age. Bill always assumed that this would change once she became a mother, herself.

He got behind the wheel, started the car, waited for a red station wagon to pass behind them, then pulled into the flow of cars.

"How many times, Billy, did she go into that pit of despair you call the Children's Lit-ur-gy?" The voice dragged out the word, as if pained to speak it. *"Hmm?"*

Before he could tell the demon to shut up, the question clung to his mind. How many times, indeed? At least a couple more after this morning, he was sure.

"It's your first time," he heard himself say. His jaw muscles moved with the words, up and down, up and down.

"Amazing, the stupid details you conveniently decide to forget."

Shut up!

"Make me!"

Seyha shook her head. Now that they were heading home, her demeanor relaxed. She was calm, but still said nothing, hand still resting on her flat belly.

How many other times, Bill now wondered, had she worked downstairs after this particular day? Only *one* he could actually remember. One other time after the miscarriage. He understood, or thought he did. When they had their own, she'd go back, volunteer again.

"Of course, she eventually stopped coming to church altogether, didn't she?"

What do you care?

"Who is your life now?"

It had asked this question, or one similar, as he was leaving the church. It made no sense.

"Doesn't it?" The laugh again, an I-Know-Something-You-Don't-Know chuckle that tickled the inside of his ear.

"You know very well, William Watts." It's voice dripped with loathing, impatient with the game. *"Pain can be so easily masked when we want it to go away."*

Bill looked at Seyha again, or was *allowed* to see her by the act of his other self. She was older than him by nearly a decade, but still so beautiful, more even than their first date on that hillside. More lovely and perfect in this light of late morning than by candlelight in that same restaurant where he pledged his love and asked her to marry him. Pledged his life.

*"Who *is your life?"* It whispered.

He understood. Or thought he did. *She* was his life. Seyha was his life and his love and she was beautiful and loving and she wanted to have a family with him and grow old together and it could still happen, or she would change her mind someday about adopting and he had not made a mistake he had not misread her he had not he had not...

The voice was laughing now, unfettered and raucous.

Bill could not stop it nor block out the terrible truths... the terrible *lies*... it was stuffing into his mind. No more than he could stop his dream-self from parking in the driveway of the house they'd rented before buying the church, turning off the engine and walking quickly around the back of the car to open his wife's door. She smiled, amused at his insistence on chivalry. He was always adoring her, worshipping the ground she...

The car was gone. Bill was standing in the living room, back in the church but now, again, it was their new home. He looked around. No one else had returned yet.

Sey! he called, stunned when still no voice came from him.

Something crashed to the floor in another part of the house, down the hall, near the master bedroom.

*   *   *

She knelt as if penitent on the ground, long strands of burnt grass pressed under her knees. Occasionally, Joyce stole a glance up at the new world around her. She was back in the unnamed, unreal jungle. Then she quickly looked down again, examining lint on her skirt, turning her hands to examine the dirt now caked into her palms after she'd fallen when Ray, and the Davidsons' kitchen, disappeared. She would not think about that, or him. She'd spent these past years *not* thinking about Ray. Even if what she had been shown was true, and it probably was, what did it matter? He'd done far worse.

She raised her head again and evaluated the clearing, the same she'd been sent to an eternity ago in the first vision. This might be South America, reminiscent of the images she'd surreptitiously found on the web over the years. Those moments had been a quiet balm as she absently browsed the Diocese's *Mission Works* page, scanning images and stories of people serving in worlds much like this one.

Planning your final escape from this cold, cruel world.

Her own thought. Self-recriminations came easily, lately. If it was the truth, so be it. If the Lord didn't mind her taking a detour, why should *she*?

Flies and gnats weaved a twisting cloud around her, an undulating, constant motion. Something bit her arm. She slapped it, felt another prick on her neck. Mosquitoes didn't usually bite in dreams, did they? But this wasn't necessarily a dream. What *was* dreamlike were the fingers of acceptance worming their way into her perception, a validation of this moment. *Mental Novocain.* Accept, or go mad. Neither felt like an acceptable option.

She looked down again, bored of the unchanging landscape. The air smelled thick and humid, and it was *loud*. Screeching monkeys, chattering birds like a hundred rusty swings in some unseen playground. Their cries competed and blended until Joyce couldn't tell where one voice ended and another began. There was a constant rustling behind the oversized fronds and hanging vines. Everything about her new surroundings – and they would *remain* surroundings since she did not plan to move from this spot – felt real. Something about it didn't *look* real. Maybe this was too much a stereotypical jungle, built from her imagination rather than any true locale. Tarzan might swing by on a kudzu vine, slam a fist on his bare chest. *Me Tarzan*, he would say. *You Joyce.*

Someone said, "Are you here to help me?"

Joyce looked up, startled by the small voice. The girl was dressed as before, in a frayed skirt and nothing else. She smiled tentatively, revealing teeth stained brown with decay. *So much help these people need*, Joyce thought, more from reflex than any real concern for her. Whoever, whatever she might be, she wasn't who she seemed. Like

Ray.

She slapped at another bite on her arm and stared at the girl.

Hello, she finally said, tired of the prolonged silence. Like before, her voice was soundless, a ghost whisper. She pressed on nonetheless. *My name's Joyce, if you don't already know that. What's yours?*

"Sally." The girl lifted the edges of her skirt and curtsied.

Joyce raised her eyebrows in surprise. *That's your real name?*

Sally shrugged. "I guess so. Mom and Pop gave it to me."

Mom and Pop, she thought. Missionaries. They might not have known her real name when they took her in. *No, stop this*, she thought. *You're just making stuff up now*, even if this girl might be an actual person somewhere. Not here.

Mom and Pop, Joyce said, playing along for the moment, *they run an orphanage?* The question felt condescending. The girl's birth name could very well *be* Sally and she may have a regular family like anyone else. Joyce doubted it. This was her illusion, her preconceived Western notions played out in three dimensions.

Sally wiped her nose with her palm and sniffed. At the same time she wrinkled her face in an expression which, on a child, spoke volumes: she hadn't understood the question.

Where do you live? Joyce asked.

Sally looked around. At the edge of the clearing the trees were immensely tall. Joyce felt small beneath them.

"I live here."

In the woods?

She nodded. "Yep. I play sometimes. Sometimes my brother comes back, and he plays with me. Sometimes Mom plays. But lots of times she has to go away and Mrs.

Guedes watches us."

Guedes. Now there's a name Joyce could relate to their surroundings. Brazilian, perhaps, though Geography had never been her strength. Even so, names of actual people were an anchor in this make-believe world.

Enough, she decided. Ray had answered her questions with riddles and sarcasm. Maybe this one - if she wasn't the same creature behind a different mask - might be more cooperative.

What is going to happen, now? Joyce asked. *Why are you...*

The question which came to her, even without a voice, drew up all of the anger and fear she'd tried so hard to keep down. Joyce said nothing more, looked down again and waited for the emotion to pass.

Slowly, Sally knelt on the ground in front of her and reached out. Soft, gentle touch of her fingers on the woman's skirt. Then she removed her arm, sniffed, and settled back on her heels.

"You are so sad," she said.

Joyce only shrugged.

"Look around you for a moment, Joyce," still spoken with that young cadence but the change, the maturity, in her words was unmistakable.

The mask was slipping.

Joyce *did* look around, first at Sally, then at the wall of vegetation twenty yards away on all sides. Sally said softly, "Where are we?"

In the jungle.

"No, *that's* the jungle over there. We're in the center."

Of what?

"You have questions."

Joyce laughed, but knew the statement was just that, not a question. She waited.

After a few seconds, Sally wiped her nose again and

sniffed loudly. "You come from there," she said, gesturing behind Joyce with the snot-covered hand. Joyce didn't look back. "Now you are in the middle and need to travel forward, come to the end."

The end of what? Pardon my language, but what the hell are we going through? What the hell is going on?

Sally's smile was wide, amused. "You're so nice, Joyce. 'Pardon my language' and the worst thing you say is 'hell.'" She giggled, then her smile dropped. "I'm sorry. I wasn't making fun, honest."

They stared at each other for a few more seconds, until Joyce raised both arms away from her sides and waved her hands as if to say, *Well, go on!*

Sally smiled again. "Why are you so attached to Gem?" she asked. "You hover over her like a protective mother-bird."

That was an odd question. *She's just a girl,* Joyce said, hoping it wouldn't sound too defensive even in silence. *She shouldn't have to be going through any of this, let alone the rest of us. She's scared.*

Sally looked down, nodded slightly as if considering the answer. Without looking up, she said, "You've been considering leaving the priesthood, devoting your life to missionary wor-"

Stop! She tried to shout. *Stop now! What do you care, who the hell are you? Are you an angel or a demon? What are you?*

"Well, there you go," Sally said, unfazed by the outburst. "Some assertiveness in your questions." She sighed. "I think you can guess I'm not going to answer that. Especially when you won't answer me." She niffed again. "Who are you trying to save, Joyce - Gem? Maybe some nameless little girl five thousand miles away? Your daughter?"

Cold crept up Joyce's arms. In contrast, her face began

to burn. Fear and anger fighting for control. Sally continued, knowing she'd hit a nerve.

"What happened wasn't your fault. You did what you had to do, the only thing you were capable of at the time."

She was talking about that final night, the last time she'd seen Ray until these nightmares began.

"Of course I am," Sally said. "Whoops." She tapped her head with one finger. "Yea, I'm in your head. Sorry."

She hoped this creature *was* an angel. Joyce could throw herself into this small girl's arms and confess her sins, never let go, demand to be forgiven and blessed. Like Jacob in the Bible, wrestling with God.

Sally reflexively waved away a sudden cloud of gnats. "Hiding in someone's arms is simply another way of hiding from Truth. Bill Watts is finally learning this. Or will, soon enough."

Bill?

"We all have truths. Some are good, some are bad. The bad we hide from, bury in darkness so no one can see. But Truth...." she laid the index finger of her left hand perpendicular atop of her right. "I'm capitalizing the T in Truth, by the way... Truth has to be embraced. All else is a lie. Secrets are lies. You would know Bill Watt's Truth if you hadn't been so lost in your own all these years."

Joyce began to protest, but the girl's words laid over her. She was right. Joyce knew the dwindling attendance at Saint Gerard's was the act of a flock wandering away towards safer ground, a better shepherd. The closing was inevitable. She'd been distracted, unable to keep watch.

"You think often in biblical metaphors, you know."

Joyce actually laughed, briefly.

"That's ok," Sally added. "A lot of pastors do, and most don't realize."

What is Bill's Truth?

"Did you capitalize the T?"

She *so much* did not want to smile. *Yes, what is Bill's Truth?*

"Too late for that, Joyce. Truth will be known. It always will. He's been hiding from it in the arms of his wife, like an ostrich burying its head in the sand. Secrets are never kept at bay, as much as we want to believe they are. But they're cancerous, poisoning everything around us." She wiped both palms across her dirty skirt. "Even so, Truth will be known. Bill's will be known, and Seyha's. Deal with it then."

Had she just been reprimanded?

"Yup."

What about *Seyha?*

"She's a bitch."

Joyce had no response to that. Sally raised a thin corner of her mouth, almost a knowing smirk, and said, "Aren't we all at times, though? No, Seyha simply has no Truth. She used to, but long-ago denied it, buried it, built her house on top of it. She's built her own truth, now, and you went through each of its rooms and blessed it, remember?"

Her house?

"Her fortress, with Bill playing the part of sentry, standing guard, protecting her."

From what?

Sally almost half spit out a contemptuous laugh. "Her fear. Hubby guards her lies because they keep her safe, and because if he faced them himself, after so long, they could just as easily destroy him. Bill knows this, deep down. We all know this."

Somehow, she was sure this person would never tell her outright what was happening. But there was an honesty in the words, even if what Joyce was hearing still didn't make sense. Clues and riddles, but better than what she had before. She pressed, *What about Gem?*

"Just in the wrong place at the wrong time."

Joyce blinked. After a moment, she said, *You don't mean that.*

"No, sorry. Just thought it was a stupid question."

...Why?

Sally sniffed and wiped her palms on her skirt again. "Why?" Her face wrinkled, as if she'd smelled something vile. "Joyce, what the hell do you think you saw back there?" She gestured towards the jungle behind her, this time with less gentleness. "Your life and the Davidsons' have become very entwined over the years. More than just that vile tryst between Ray and Deanna. You've quietly obsessed over her family, long after Ray had gone. Long after *you* had gone. Gem has been doing the same thing in the closed church this past year, though for different reasons."

Don't I have the right?

Sally shrugged her bare shoulders. "Easier than taking any real responsibility, I guess."

That was when the sound came. Distant at first, like a storm far off quietly announcing its approach. It was a rumbling, the groaning of the world somewhere behind them.

The girl looked up, startled and a little frightened. Odd. Joyce had assumed she was the one in control.

Sally looked back to Joyce. That *was* fear in her eyes. She spoke with a sudden urgency. "Everyone has secrets, Joyce. Some small, insignificant in the scope of one's life. Gem's are like those; personal, little half-truths."

Something large and heavy fell to the earth, a tree perhaps, closer but still what Joyce would consider 'in the distance.'

"But those of the family are our own. They shape us,

even when we do not unders...."

She trailed off, scampering to her feet. Joyce almost did the same but remembered her plans to stay where she was.

"Joyce, no more time. We have to go." Sally was bouncing on her toes, looking alternately at her then at the woods behind. She was terrified.

What's coming? she asked.

Sally held out her hand. "Please, we have to go."

The world behind Joyce tore apart. Crashing and rending of the tress, no longer distant but filling the clearing with their presence. She turned, still kneeling but beginning to rise. Behind her, trees toppled like toys, giving way to something wide and tall and sickly-pale pushing through, into the clearing. There was still enough growth to partially block her view, but the size and shape reminded her of a charging elephant, only three times taller and wider as it closed in on them. They didn't have elephants in South America, did they?

Sally took her hand and yelled, "Run!"

Joyce stumbled to her feet and didn't question the command. She held the hand tightly and ran in the direction Sally was already moving, across the clearing. Whatever was coming now emerged from the forest behind them. No more sounds of trees being crushed underfoot like sticks. Only the heavy *thud-thud* of feet shaking the ground in small earthquakes. When they reached the far tree-line and stepped over drawbridge fronds that bowed under their weight, Joyce looked back with a quick toss of her head. What she saw made no sense. Not an elephant – it was monstrous, toad-shaped but nothing she could immediately register as familiar. The wide, flat face was in motion, twisting with an almost-human expression. It charged towards them, half-crossing the clearing during that one brief glimpse.

Sally was a step ahead. Joyce gripped her hand tighter and they ran along a narrow game trail, the forest's green walls a blur beside them much like in her first vision. The sound of crushing life from behind. No animal roar, only a deep panting, the air wet with the breath of –

Joyce tripped and let go of Sally's hand, rolled across milky leaves which offered no hope of concealment. She continued to roll for cover, when a shadow passed overhead and a foot pressed onto her back, long and fleshy like a human's but a hundred times larger. Short, chipped claws poked from toes which arched overhead and beyond her vision.

The creature's weight pressed the air from her lungs, kept pushing, straining her ribs. Just as Joyce expected all of her bones to shatter, the weight stopped, lifted slightly but still pinning her, forcing her breaths into strained wheezes.

When Sally screamed, Joyce twisted her neck enough to see the girl's legs stagger a half-step further along the path, uncertain whether to continue running. The monster's weight shifted and Sally froze, something cracked like a wet snap, then the little legs rose out of view. A bloody mucus dripped in splashes over the grass in time with the sounds of crunching and chewing too loud to block out even if Joyce's scream was not silent.

The creature's face lowered enough to reveal an inflated bottom lip. Like its feet, the face was almost but not quite human, too wide and fleshy, elongated and twisted like a cancerous balloon. She could not see its eyes. The jaw opened again. Something hung between its broken teeth. Joyce closed her eyes and tried not to hear its breath and swallowing --

Then the monster leaned forward, more and more and crushed her into the hard-packed earth. Her breath sprayed out in a red fountain.

She lay in silence. Deaf and blind. Dead, crushed deep into the soil of the jungle. Nothing around her. She'd been wrong, all her life. No white light, no loving embrace of the Lord at the end of the tunnel. Nothing but emptiness, the void of the universe before God made the world with all its welts and sores. She would spend eternity here, cursing the nothingness, cursing herself.

She reached up and touched her face.

How had she done that?

Above and around her, the emptiness of death thinned. Something glowed far away. Not death, only the Darkness, washing away from her like a wave spent and now receding, leaving its oily residue behind. The amorphous veil around Joyce's head was soon gone, no mask of black around her. She stared up at a familiar ceiling, freshly-painted. She was back in the Watts' house. A deep, painful sorrow filled her chest, threatening to choke her like the foot of the imaginary beast. Of course, she hadn't died, only suffered through the sick, cursed games they'd all been forced to play. This time she had thought it would be different.

And it was.

This time, she'd lost the game. Tricked into complacency, to deny a faith which had carried her through so much, cursing God as nothing more than a pipe dream. The vision in the jungle or the one which would probably begin again after another short reprieve were nothing to the horror of those few, short moments, her denials like Peter's during Christ's trial. She lay on the new carpet, stared up at the ceiling, and cried silently. That was all she could do. She had no strength for anything more.

*   *   *

Gem dared not move. One arm remained against her head, pressing out the screams that were no longer filling the hell she'd left behind in the living room. The other had fallen to the top of the table to keep herself from falling past the other side of the kitchen chair. As soon as she landed, she'd noticed Joyce standing across the kitchen – only to *poof* out of existence few seconds later. Ray Lindu turned casually around in his own chair, thankfully not the one beside her own, and nodded. The fact that he was sitting there almost naked didn't seem to bother him. Not that it would, she supposed. *Don't think that way*, she thought. *He'll pick up on it. Don't think, don't move...*

"Hello again, Rock," he said, any look of amusement he might have had dropping away from his face after Joyce disappeared. No trace of the lurid, gross older guy she'd come across in the past, either. Except, of course, that he was sitting in her kitchen without any clothes on. When he got to his feet, Gem forced herself to look down at the floor, towards the refrigerator then out through the window as he walked in his Fruit of the Looms towards the swinging doors, no longer paying her any attention. When he spoke again it was a shout, almost bored, "Deanna, your girl's here...." He reached for the doors but stopped when Deana called back, "Little Gem or Big Gem?"

Gem looked up at the sound of her mother's voice. Ray turned his head to look at her, slowly, his lips bending into a tight sneer. "All grown up," he shouted back.

Find something, she thought. *You have two seconds to grab some kind of a weapon.* She tried like hell to maintain eye contact while taking mental inventory of what might be within reach on the table.

Ray pushed himself out through the leftmost door as her mother bounded into the kitchen through the right. He muttered, "Headin' home," and though they did not touch, the flashing look they exchanged before being cut off by the swinging doors was enough to make Gem squint in confusion.

She blinked away the haze in her brain and watched her mother, saying nothing as Deanna pulled the sash of her robe tighter around herself and walked across the room towards the sink.

The initial fear of seeing Ray in her kitchen, in his skivvies, began to fade. What the hell was Mister Lindu doing here? It didn't make any sense.

"Want something, Gem?" Her mother faced the overhead cabinet next to the sink, raised on her tiptoes with the robe lifting slightly as her hand reached for a glass.

"Wha...?"

Not changing position and in the same tone as before, "Want something?"

Gem waited. So did Deanna. Or *whoever* she was. Flashes of the previous vision, a toddler version of herself walking by and giving her the finger. These weren't real. These people weren't *them*.

What the hell was Ray Lindu doing in her kitchen in his underwear with her mother in a bathrobe?

Anger, a black tide of it, rose up and Gem rose with it. She stood, pressed the chair away from her with the backs of her knees.

"This did not happen," she said.

Deanne didn't turn around, didn't react at all except to repeat, "Want something?" A slight waggle of her right hand before the glasses. Gem crossed the room in three long, thunderous steps and screamed, "I don't want any fuc –" but she got no further. A wall slammed into her, or *she* slammed into *it*. Her face and chest and arms collided with an invisible barrier a second before her brain could comprehend anything was there.

She didn't stumble backwards, only slid down the unseen wall, crumpling in a heap in the middle of the kitchen. The room tilted, not because she was hurt, Gem didn't think she was, just dazed, but it was all so wrong. Invisible walls, living rooms turning into hell, Ray Lindu in his underwear and screwing her mother.... *No, no, no, no, no, no....*

"Gem," Deanna's fingers in her hair, a rare, gentle caress. "It's OK. Come on up." She allowed herself to be lifted off the floor, stood unsteadily on her feet. Mom would help. Mom would take care of her. That's what she was supposed to do, wasn't it?

Nevertheless, the black tide rolled back in. Gem wanted to ignore it and give in, let everything be, lean into her mother's arms and go to sleep. Instead, she lashed out, knocking Deanna's arms away as she stumbled back against the kitchen table.

Her mother's arms coiled themselves against her chest. She gave no sign of surprise or irritation in her calm, pretty face. "What is it, Gem?" As if she'd just been interrupted reading a good book.

What the hell *was* it? Was she supposed to have seen this, or did she accidentally stumble into Joyce's dream and saw something she wasn't supposed to?

She wanted to go up to her room and hide, but didn't want to run into *him* again. She wasn't supposed to have seen this.

Deanna's tight smile said otherwise. It was her *Oh really, is that what you think?* look.

Strangely enough, that expression calmed her a little. Gem leaned her left hand on the table and raised herself back up to a standing position, pointed with the right towards the swinging doors, the window over the sink, then out the back window - the appendage was taking on a life of its own. She pulled it in and pinned it with her left arm.

She didn't want to ask her mother the only question she

could possibly ask in this situation, so she turned around and sat back in the chair at the end of the table, as far from the woman as she could manage.

Deanna stood in the middle of the room, arms still folded, the short robe shiny in the afternoon sunlight, and also said nothing. The universe would not move forward, Gem thought, until she said her lines again.

She would not. *Screw 'em.* She was just a kid, didn't matter what the adults did. What they did was... what they did was what they did.

Her father, in the attic, talking to people on his radio, hardly ever coming down these past few years. Didn't he used to play with her a lot, and play with Eliot? *Eliot.* Did he know?

Her mother's posture unfroze enough to slide one hand down and press against her belly. Gem saw this, guessed it was in response to her thoughts of Eliot and in that moment knew what the act implied. No, Eliot did *not* know. This was a time before the episode with the rocks in the other room. She couldn't know that, either. But she did. That's how this all worked. Whatever you thought was the truth.

More time passed, Gem's thoughts slowed, and her mother was perfectly content to stand there like a mannequin for a lingerie company.

She wouldn't be allowed to leave this kitchen until she said something.

Gem sighed, looked at the tabletop when she spoke. "Whatever. You had an affair with Mister Lindu, right? Is that what I'm supposed to believe? Well...." She traced the *boomerang* patterns on the table's Formica surface with her finger. "Well, ok, whatever. This could all be fake. I mean, not like there's a floppy hell-monster climbing up the side of the house, either. It's all fake."

Deanna's voice came soft and full of an emotion Gem didn't recognize at first. Love, maybe? Or shame.

"I'm sorry," Deanna said.

The black tide returned, a little, enough to force her gaze to meet her Mom's. "*Are* you? Did you and... *did* you? Really?"

"Not for long. But yes. It happened. It ended."

Gem found herself staring at her mother's belly. "You're pregnant with Eliot aren't you? You did this while you were pregnant?"

Deanna stepped forward. Gem wanted to push her away, but stayed where she was. A part of her, the sad, whiny little girl part which should have burned away by now but which was making a comeback in the last few minutes, *wanted* her mother to approach, make it all better. Deanna did the fingers-in-the-hair thing again, saying, "Oh, Gem. No. No. Not while I was pregnant."

Gem leaned forward, waiting for the other shoe to drop. Deanna stepped back across the room. "You're a smart girl, Gem. You figure it out." Gone was the weird tenderness in her voice. Deanna emanated bored indifference again. "You staying for dinner?" She bent down and reached for a frying pan under the counter.

Gem put her fists against her cheeks and pressed, not knowing what else to do with them. She looked outside. Their short backyard ended with trees. It was summer, leaves in full bloom blocking most of the view of the houses on the other street. She considering running outside and heading that way, escaping this nightmare. It wouldn't work. She wasn't really here.

Ray wasn't really here.

"Easier that way," her mother said from the stove. Something sizzled into the pan. Gem didn't remember seeing her get anything out of the fridge. Maybe she was frying the toaster. "Everything's fine, Gem. Don't worry. Just a bad dream. Get washed up for dinner."

"I'm not having dinner, Mom," she said, surprised at the calm in her own voice.

"Oh," came the reply, uninterested. "That's too bad." Then Deanna turned around and smiled, the expression wrong, too pointy. Heavy footsteps approached the swinging doors. The mother-thing said, "You'll be back. I'll keep the food warm."

Gem was in the Watts' living room, sitting on one of the plush chairs. Joyce lay on the rug near the other chair, a dazed look on her face, tears running down into her ears. Between them, Bill Watts knelt. Long streaks of tears lined his own cheeks. When he realized where he was he gasped like a drowning man coming up for air. He said nothing, not at first, only stared down in horror at his clenched fists. He opened them slowly. Empty, save a row of red impressions burned into both palms by his fingernails.

He looked across the living room and whispered, "...true."

*   *   *

Seyha no longer held her father. He was gone. She instead held a dirty white doll in the crook of one elbow. Half of its hair was missing, unconsciously pulled out by her teeth as she slept with it each night. Not that she could see the doll in detail. The room was illuminated only by two votive candles glowing across a sea of bodies huddled around her on the floor. She remembered the doll. Not the same given to her by Angelique on that first birthday after she'd arrived, but another, given a couple of years later from a crate sent by faceless people living in another world.

Slowly, carefully Seyha sat up on the mat, twisting her

legs to keep from touching the cool wood floor. The mat was woven bamboo, big enough for a child but not a full grown woman. Her back twisted from in pain from sleeping on such a hard surface. She was still crying, her father's terror a weight crushing her down. She lay down again and cried out the sorrow and anger all the louder, into the crook of her arm and the doll's head.

Seyha knew where she was now, the recreated world of her childhood. The shelter she'd been offered from the monsters which had eaten her family. She curled on the mat and played the part of her younger self trapped in the body of a grown-up.

Another child in the room began to cry, a boy indistinguishable amid the dozen or so children sleeping or shaking under the light of the candles. His cries joined her own, then overpowered it. Another joined in, then another. Soon most of the children were awake and crying, calling names Seyha did not know in words she no longer understood.

No one came to comfort them. Seyha heard her own voice calling for her mother, then for Sister Angelique who was undoubtedly awake on the other side of the heavy wool blanket which partitioned the adults from the children. Two other women lived and worked alongside her. They could not possibly sleep with such a racket, such a cloud of despair pouring into every corner.

Seyha cried louder, competing with the children for the attention which would not come. Every night this happened, as far as she could remember. A peaceful night's rest, if it came, was lost in the crowd of memories of nights like this. One child would have a dream, a memory she should never have to remember, then wake up sobbing. Startled from their thin sleep, others would join her, crying out of reflex or confusion, awaking into a strange dark. The music of their injured lives rose from the mats until every child wailed in a communal hymn of misery.

Every night....

She thought, *I'm not here! I'm not* here!

Seyha tossed the doll aside. It landed against a little boy who cried all the louder for the contact. She stood, towering over the children like a farmer amid a garden of reaching and thrashing limbs. No one ever came, because the song always ended with the deeper, more peaceful sleep of exhaustion. Sister Angelique knew this. She stayed on the other side of her blanket, waiting them out.

Seyha stepped carefully between mats, even as fingers touched her legs or closed around an ankle. She told herself, *Just keep moving.* One hand released her ankle, but another took its place. She was an adult in a sea of babies, someone who could stop the fear, who could turn and kneel beside at least *one* of them, hold and *shoosh* them until they felt safe again.

There was nothing inside her which could be given or shared. She couldn't make these little ones safe, since she, herself, was not. The temptation to at least try *did* blossom, briefly, the final flare of a match before snuffing into a sulfuric whiff. She cleared the last child's reach and stood before the door. She could still turn around and dive into that sea. Not to comfort or caress, but curl onto her mat and sing their song. If she did, she would never stop. They would climb over her, begging for a touch, or a kiss, stain her with their dirt and snots and tears and the crying was becoming louder now and nothing else existed but the sound and the misery and she had to get out and run away and never stop.

Seyha stumbled forward, cursing her legs for being so weak. Her ears buzzed with the volume of the voices, no longer a natural sound. The roaring of waves crashing below a thousand jet engines. At the door, she fumbled with the rope and plank latch. Louder, louder, blinding in its fury. She began to cry again, fought it. Too loud. Too much.

Every night. Every night.

When the door opened the sound of misery magnified a thousand-fold, slamming into her, ripping out her soul. The cool night offered no relief. The sound was everywhere. She couldn't move. Two large hands grabbed her and squeezed. Seyha thrashed, tried to jerk herself free. In the sudden brightness of the living room, Bill's face was pale.

"Seyha! Calm down."

She was home. She was lost.

Bill did not let her go. God bless him he did not let her go. He pulled her forward. Too close. She couldn't breathe. She struggled to regain the open air she knew she'd never feel again. Bill's voice faded to a pinpoint of sound. She fell into a new, deeper blackness, and never landed.

*   *   *

Moments earlier, Bill stood in the deserted house and heard a crashing noise from down the hall. Something had fallen to the floor, the sound distant enough he guessed it originated from the master bedroom. He tried calling Seyha again. No response. Given his lack of voice he understood that he was not, in fact, *back*. Still dreaming, trapped in another illusion.

He stepped into the hallway, kept on walking. Nothing which had happened to him thus far had been in his control, so there was nothing he could do to change anything.

He stopped outside the master bedroom door.

What or who was waiting inside? These visions of his

seemed so mundane, except that whatever was behind them was trying to turn some of the happiest moments of his life inside out, make them darker than they'd really been. Overall, though, his life had been good. He walked it every day, with Seyha and the Lord and the people of the church and his employees. If there was some dark truth which these visions were trying to show him, they could never change the reality of that.

How much had he prayed since the chaos began? With Joyce, yes, but alone, in his own head and heart?

Bill hesitated outside the door, not wanting to look inside, and whispered a prayer in a voice that did not exist. He wasn't certain even if he *could* hear himself, if the words would make any sense.

He would make it through whatever was waiting in there. They both would.

When he glanced behind him, his heart beat faster. A moment ago, there had been nothing behind him but the empty hallway and kitchen. Now there was *literally* nothing, only black. Darkness had swallowed the kitchen and obliterated the entrance to the living room. In this dream world, only the hallway and the few rooms branching off it remained.

The darkness crept forward, swallowing a picture of his parents on the wall. The house slid soundlessly under its black tide. He stayed where he was, watching its approach.

As it passed the bathroom and spare bedroom, the doors slammed closed and a hundred fists banged against them, shaking the hinges. *Bang! Bang! Bang!* The violence was muffled behind the encroaching black wall. Still, he remained still, not wanting to move into his bedroom.

He closed his eyes, took a breath, considered letting the darkness and whatever monsters had been loosed inside devour him. That would be preferable to whatever waited in the bedroom, he was sure of that now.

Lord, help me, he thought. *Save me. I don't know what they're going to show me, but it's bad. It's a lie! Please....*

When he opened his eyes there was only the black wall. It pushed softly but insistently against his face and chest. Bill fell back against the door frame. He spun, fell into the bedroom.

"No," he whispered.

His voice had returned but he didn't notice, too terrified at the expectation that something out of his worst nightmare would be standing in front of him. He stared at the carpet between his hands. Nothing happened. No sound

Slowly, he looked up.

The room was empty. Nothing between him and the far windows except the four-post bed and hope chest.

One of the small drawers from Seyha's dresser lay on the floor in front of him, its contents spilled in a scattered pile. Underwear, rolled socks....

Bill crawled forward, knelt over the drawer. "Please help me," he whispered. "I don't know what to do." It looked like someone had pulled the drawer too hard, spilling everything onto the rug in a long, scattered line then simply let it fall on top of the mess.

Seyha had checked these drawers, hadn't she? Of course she did, but that was in the "real" world. This was only a dream.

It's not real.

It's not.

He turned the drawer upright and picked up some socks, dropped them back in. A couple of envelopes with old credit card bills. Some old pictures of him, others of the two of them.

Something else.

This object was round, plastic. One side was a powder blue, the opposite white. On the blue side he saw a white sticker, words typed. A prescription. His vision blurred.

"Please, God, this is not true... it's all a dream. It's not real."

He picked the object up, gripped it under the fingers of his right hand. It was no bigger than his palm.

He knew what it was, even before reading the words on the label. Bill could barely summon the strength to whisper, but he had to say *something*, exorcise the demons around him, those pressing this blasphemy onto his heart.

Pictures in his mind, past scenes: *Seyha never returning to help with the children's service, turning around in the supermarket if going forward meant passing a leg-kicking kid screaming from the back of a shopping cart. Her blank expression and stuttered protests every time he talked of adoption, since having children of their own seemed less and less likely.*

He squeezed the plastic case. A crack shot from the tip of his middle finger, under the label. The label - with her gynecologist's name printed at the bottom - the doctor who obviously had no qualms prescribing birth control bills to a woman whose husband wanted as many kids as God would bless them with.

"These are lies!"

No demon laughter in response. All was silence except from his own voice.

Bill squeezed as hard as he could manage. Cracks in the plastic burst upward, sending some of the small white pills popping into the air. They bounced off his face like tiny slaps.

He closed his eyes, shouted, "It's not true!"

Why would she take these? She couldn't -

His throat tightened, closed up. Pieces of plastic ripped into his palm along with his own nails. He squeezed harder, needing to feel the pain. He was crying, eyes closed, mouth open to tears falling over his lips, crying for himself and Seyha, for the children they could have had... anytime they wanted.

But she did *not* want to. She did *not* want to....

"It's not..." He opened his eyes as the bed shrunk and faded to some impossibly far distance.

He was back in the living room. His mouth frozen as it formed the final word. Joyce was lying on the floor, eyes unfocused, staring at the ceiling. Gem stared at him with an equally blank expression from one of the chairs.

Bill looked down, expecting to see shattered pieces of blue and white plastic mixed with his blood. His hand was cramped but otherwise intact. It held nothing. Four distinct indentations in his palm where his fingernails had pressed.

Nothing else.

"...true," he finally finished.

He let the word drift upward, followed it with his eyes towards the stricken expressions of Joyce and Gem. He was about to turn around to find Seyha when she appeared only a few feet away. Her eyes were closed tight as she thrashed the air in front of her. He almost ran to her, reflexively pull her close, then caught himself. He looked down at his clenched hand, forced it to relax. The palm was dotted with crescent shaped marks from his nails, but no pills, no cracked plastic case.

Seyha did not seem to be coming out of her vision. Her arms were now bent and raised to her face, a long sound like a cry but muffled forcing its way out of her. She was shaking. *To hell with her*, he thought, hating himself for thinking it. He didn't even know if the vision was real. He got to his feet and stepped forward. Her pain was his pain and he could not leave her like this. He would check the drawer later, if it even opened. Until then, he reached up and took his wife's wrists.

She screamed and lunged forward, but he held on, perhaps too tightly but he allowed himself that single concession to his slowly ebbing anger. "Seyha! Calm down!"

Her eyes shot open, scanning the room. He loved her and hated her in that moment and could not decide how that was possible, only that it was probably true. She'd lied, she'd lied for all these years.

You let yourself be lied to, Billy.

Not the demons voice, but his own. He would not accept blame for this.

Seyha's eyes turned upward in their sockets and she fell limp in his arms. He held on, letting go of one wrist and moving his arm around her waist. Joyce was beside him. Together they carried her to the couch.

He looked away, towards the hallway and unseen bedroom beyond.

Second Night of Darkness

Bill cradled his wife in his lap as she lay curled on the couch beside him. She was asleep, snoring softly, her system having shut down from whatever stress had come with her vision. He envied her that.

Her respite was brief. Seyha moaned. He gently slid his hand over her hair, now and then pulling a stray strand from her face, now and then tempted to pull a few others out by the roots. Joyce and Gem were sitting in silence, apparently waiting for Seyha to wake up. Looking at the windows, in the silence, Bill tried to process what he'd seen. No, he hadn't *seen* anything. Only a vision, a dream. A lie of the devil, perhaps, to put a wedge between them. He waited for the mocking laughter to return at the thought, but the room remained silent. He would check the *actual* drawer for himself. Seyha told him they'd all been stuck, just like everything else. He'd seen her try one himself. Not that one, however. Not the top, right-hand one.

Stop it! Stop thinking! Take care of her now. Later, first chance, he would check.

It couldn't be true. They'd been trying to get pregnant for years since the miscarriage. Never, not once, did she ever imply she thought otherwise.

Before he could play out every conversation, every sideways glance, Seyha opened her eyes and looked up at him. His heart leapt. She was so beautiful, and was looking only at him.

Who is your life, the voice had asked.

*   *   *

Even after Seyha woke up, no one spoke, each too exhausted from their respective jaunts through the Darkness – that was how Joyce had decided to think of it, Darkness with a capital D. She tried to catch Bill's gaze. He looked less calm, eyes occasionally darting to his wife, never lingering on one place too long, scanning the few corners of the house visible from his vantage on the couch. Whenever he noticed Joyce staring, he would look away.

Ironically, it was his wife who first spoke. Whatever was happening to her was probably worse than anything Joyce had experienced. At the very least, it was worse in its *effect*. They needed a glimpse of what was going on with her, if for no other reason maybe learning a little of what was happening in her head might help to lift the carnival tent and reveal some reason for all of this.

The scolding she'd gotten from the girl in the jungle kept playing in her mind. She might have a better idea what was happening between these two if she'd paid more attention over the years. Saint Gerard's wasn't such a big parish people would get lost in the crowd. And Bill was always there, always active. She should have done more, talked more, *been* more. But she wasn't, too lost in her own misery, too busy keeping it safely tucked away. Now the church was gone, and she was trapped in its echo with a congregation of three people. The remnant flock.

Seyha caught her staring and said, "Please don't start another of your therapy sessions, Reverend." Her voice was thick, almost dreamy.

Sitting cross-legged on the floor, Gem visibly stiffened. Their positions had reversed since coming out of the Darkness. Joyce now sat in the chair, Gem on the floor beside her. Before the girl could say anything, Joyce replied, "On the contrary, Seyha. I think you, more than anyone, need to tell us what you've been going through."

Seyha wrapped both arms around one of Bill's and shook her head. "I don't want to talk about it."

Joyce turned sideways in her seat and absently rested her hand on Gem's head, gently stroking as one might pet a dog. Gem didn't stop her. On the contrary, she scooted the few remaining inches between them and leaned against the corner of the chair.

"It's past time. You need to talk... now." Her sudden assertiveness felt foreign, almost false. She knew, of course, that she did not want to discuss her *own* episode with Ray and Deanna Davidson, either. She was being a hypocrite, but that was too close, here in this house. Gem must have some memory of that time. But she was so small then. *Doesn't matter*, she thought. *Broken marriage, bad man. Nothing else.*

It was a familiar mantra, convincing herself so she could convince others. She imagined Jungle Sally kneeling before her, shaking her head in disgust. Joyce raised her hand from Gem's head, fine blonde hair at her fingertips. The girl needed her to be strong, like her daughter had needed her. *Nothing else....*

Seyha hissed, "You stay out of my life." She stood up from the couch, fists clenched at her side. Poised for a fight.

Bill looked up but surprisingly made no move to calm or comfort her. *He wants to know, too*, Joyce thought. She cleared her throat, but otherwise struggled to keep her voice neutral. "No, Seyha. I will not. Whatever you're experiencing is tearing you apart. Not to mention the effect on everyone else."

Seyha's arms shook at her sides as if struggling to free themselves from restraints. Joyce pressed, "We seem to be reliving moments - from our pasts, mostly. I don't claim to know much about you, and that's my fault entirely, but the little I do – correct me if I'm wrong – you survived that nightmare in Cambodia. Pol Pot's regime and... the *Khmer Rouge*, I think his army was called?"

"Shut up, you bitch! None of this – "

"We've covered that," Gem said in a half groan. Joyce cringed. *No, girl, be quiet. Of all people, don't you speak.* But it was too late. Seyha had a target, a diversion.

"You get out of my house, now!"

"You open the door, lady, and I'll gladly –"

"Gem..."

Gem looked up. As sternly as possible while trying to keep her voice level, never looking away from Seyha Watts, Joyce said, "Be quiet, please." The girl obeyed without argument, aside from a frustrated sigh.

Seyha's upper lip briefly rose in a snarl. Whether this was directed at Joyce or Gem, she couldn't tell. It didn't matter. "Leave me alone," she said, then walked around the couch, heading for the hallway.

"Seyha, I don't understand what is happening but if we're going to deal with this we have to talk!" She had to raise her voice as the woman moved beyond the dining area. "There's a reason this is happening!"

The bathroom door slammed shut.

Bill moved to the far end of the couch, but did not rise to follow. Reluctantly, he turned to face Joyce. As before, when they made eye contact he looked away, down to his lap, fascinated by the palms of his interlocked hands.

Joyce leaned back in her chair and took a breath. She was shaking. A vibration under her skin, the first tremors of what could be a major quake if she wasn't careful. She said to Bill, "She was raised in an orphanage, right?"

Bill shrugged. "I guess so."

"You guess so?"

He bit his lower lip, let it flip free. When he replied it was a whisper, perhaps afraid his wife would hear. "Yea, sorry. She *was* an orphan. That's the best I can do. Anytime I ask, she changes the subject, or says she doesn't want to talk about it. It was a Catholic orphanage, that much I'm pretty sure of. Run by some nuns. Sister Angelique was one. The name stuck in my head because it was so unique. She'd mention the woman in passing, in a conversation when her guard was down." He unlocked his hands and wiped the right knuckle under his eye, then did the same to the other. He sniffed. "Whenever this occurred I'd try to open the door a little more. But, she'd slam it shut pretty quickly."

Gem wrapped both arms around Joyce's left leg, like a frightened child to her mother. Joyce rested her hand on her head again. All she could offer the girl was her presence.

Gem said, "What if we're, I mean, I was thinking that, if we...." She sighed, rested her head against Joyce's leg. "What if we're in hell?" She curled her arms tighter.

Bill started to say something, closed his lips and looked around the room, focused finally on the hallway. "No, that's not true."

Gem straightened, still leaving one arm around Joyce. "No? Can you explain this any other way? We're forced to relive bad things, watch demons chase our family and attack us. That voice, that stupid *psycho* voice everywhere! That's no angel!"

Bill nodded. There was no arguing her point. He finally said, "One flaw in that theory, Gem." He put his hands flat against his chest. "I don't remember dying."

Gem's building energy kept her from staying in one position for too long. She shifted first on all fours as if preparing to pounce, then kneeled with her back straight.

"Neither do I," she said, "but what about a nuclear bomb? If someone nuked Ledgewood or Worcester we wouldn't have time to notice. Just *whammo*! I sure wasn't ready for heaven. I never even got through the Old Testament. Go directly to hell, do not pass *Go*, don't...." She looked at Joyce. "But you're a minister, Joyce. Doesn't that mean anything? How come you're down here and not up there? At least *you* deserve to be."

A flattering if not entirely logical question. Joyce held onto it, a brief lifeline to pull her out of the sudden despair Gem's words planted inside her.

"No," she said in reply. "I can't accept that."

Bill leaned forward and planted his feet on the floor. "So, wherever you happen to die, that's where you stay? Some make-believe version of our house in this case? Seems a bit New Age, if you ask me."

Joyce found herself unable to keep the thread of his argument. She thought instead of Ray. He was back, perhaps not real but no longer relegated to random snippets of memory. Playing the part of her host in these nightmares. Enjoying his role of *tormentor* all over again. She'd spent years finally accepting he was gone, that she would never lay her head on his chest at night, never speak to him again. Gem claimed to have seen him, *here*, before all this happened. But he wasn't back. He couldn't be.

"Joyce?" Bill's voice was quiet. Her expression must have conveyed something welling up inside her, an overflowing horror no different than what everyone else had bottled up. Everything was upside down, everything was wrong. Bill slid off the couch and crouched beside her chair, opposite Gem. Now there were two of them kneeling before her, penitent worshipers, *no, don't think that. Don't think. Just don't think.*

It was dark again, hands on her. Not dark, her eyes

were closed. The room was tilting. A chasm opening behind her. Her chair felt like it was sliding along an angled floor, backwards into the abyss. She'd made Ray go away, that wasn't wrong. She'd saved her daughter, saved herself. He was the evil one. *He* was in hell.

She cried out, briefly, eyelids tightening. *I need to stop this. I need to stop.* Bill whispered that she was alright, stroked her arm, said her name, said "Here." Why did he say that? Something wiped her face, drying tears she didn't know were there. It helped. "I'm sorry," she whispered, mostly to Gem because she wanted to be strong for her. Too late for that.

If this was hell, then they were damned to take turns blubbering like fools for eternity.

That thought struck her as absurdly funny.

She smirked, felt the room straighten a little. Even so, she couldn't stop crying. She *wouldn't* stop. What else was there to do? It was her turn. Another laugh, which she doubted the others heard. Hands on her, no more talking, just the touch of another, living human, giving love the only way they each could. Being present.

Dead people didn't do that.

Gem muttered, "Excuse me for a sec." There was a pressure on Joyce's leg as the girl used it for leverage and stood, then walked across the room towards the hallway. Joyce kept her eyes closed, preferring to maintain her own darkness a while longer.

*   *   *

Through the closed bathroom door, Seyha could hear the priest crying. *You selfish bitch*, she thought, directing the chide to herself. *Oh, poor Seyha, no one understands me!* Meanwhile Joyce Lindu, a woman who had never done anything to her, offered nothing but love to the both of them was crying in the living room while her hostess hid on the toilet.

Seyha curled her hands into fists and pressed them against the side of her head. This was *not* her home. They were trapped in a carnival fun house, falling and tripping into God's open mouth as he stuck out his tongue and laughed. She could not do anything for Joyce, for Bill or anyone else. *Stupid Gem thinks she's so smart and grown up. To hell with her. With everyone.*

Seyha gasped and raised her head. What was she thinking? She closed her eyes, tried to pray, to ask Bill's God for support. There were no words. The space above and around her was empty. Once, she thought maybe there was a God. Sitting in the chapel with Sister Angelique and Mrs. Tan. They would teach prayers, train them in the Sacraments, give the children bread and even wine when they were old enough to receive. In those moment, sometimes, Seyha thought that maybe God was real, and he was good. He'd saved her from the soldiers, hadn't he?

The next logical question, as always, never failed to close her mind and heart. She didn't have to think it anymore, so reflexive it had become. For every one child rescued a dozen mothers and fathers, sisters and brothers were killed, whole families destroyed. If God was real, if he was bigger than the evil in the word, something so horrific would not have happened, nor the thousands of other tragedies before or since. Bill would argue that point, of course, but he wasn't here. Only room for one on the toilet.

Seyha sat straighter atop the closed toilet seat, leaned back, stretched her legs. After all that had happened in her life, she now found herself trapped inside her house with the world outside black and dead. Or simply *gone*. Her past, the unreal nightmare existing only in flashes of memory and brief revelation each night before falling asleep, had finally caught up to her. No one understood what was going on, but Seyha thought she might. *Khmer Rouge*, death and torture and needless pain. It had not been left behind in some forgotten backward country. It was hunting her. Death, riding across the globe, looking for survivors. She was prey that had escaped. But the hunter kept hunting, never tiring, always searching her out. Now, a net had been thrown over her and anyone unfortunate enough to be nearby. A net of darkness. Doung Seyha should not have survived, but she'd slipped the net, met a man, found happiness. All, apparently, an illusion. A way to let her guard slip lower, as Death crept closer.

This world, right now, was the real one. All else had been a gilded mirage.

She looked around the bathroom, built in part with her own hands, designed by her, tiled and painted by her. She'd been proud of this small place. This cell. If she stayed in here, far from Bill and the others, maybe they'd be set free when Death's arm reached into the net to take her away. Her world was not theirs.

Take me, she thought. *It's me you've wanted. Let them go.*

Joyce had stopped crying a few minutes ago, her sobbing replaced by quiet conversation. Eventually, even that came to an end. Everything outside the room was silent.

Except for the footsteps thumping along the hallway and the knock on the bathroom door.

She didn't say anything, not until the knock came a second time. Seyha stared at the door, expecting a long bony hand to reach under and click across the tile floor towards her leg.

She swallowed, managed to say, "Who is it?" As much as she'd prayed for the others to be released, she wanted Bill here. Never again, though. She needed to be alone, so the darkness would release him. Maybe then... but she did not finish the thought. The knob turned and the bathroom door opened. Seyha had tried to lock it when she first entered the room, but like everything else it didn't work.

Part of her was relieved that Bill, or Death, had finally come for her.

When she saw who it was, Seyha strained to keep the sudden cramp of anger at bay.

Gem Davidson stood on the threshold, holding the knob. "You going to be here all night? We need to stay together, if you hadn't figured that out."

Seyha swiveled on the toilet seat and faced her. "Get out of here. You've caused enough trouble tonight."

Gem laughed, actually *laughed!* It was mocking, though without the powerful, cruel tone of that *other* voice from the darkness. Even so, not what Seyha expected.

Gem looked around. "Nice place. I suppose there wasn't room under the bed to hide?"

Seyha stood up and stepped forward, placed her hand flat against Gem's chest. Before she could push the girl into the hall, Gem also stepped forward. Seyha had to either step back or stand nose to nose with her. She stepped backwards. Her foot hit the tub. Gem knocked her hand away. "Don't touch me again, lady, unless I say you can." To Seyha's dismay, Gem reached back with one foot and slammed the bathroom door closed.

* * *

Bill looked up at the sound of the bathroom door slamming closed. "That can't be good."

Joyce leaned forward and looked towards the hall. "We should probably go get them." Her tone implied how Bill felt – *why bother?* No one was going anywhere. He shook his head, leaned back into the cushions.

"No, leave them. Maybe that's what she needs. A good argument. If anyone can get her going, it's Gem."

He smiled, but the expression faded quickly. He struggled to look calm, because inside his heart was racing. *This is your chance. Go to the bedroom, see for yourself one way or the other.*

"What happened with you?"

He looked up at Joyce's voice, startled. She wanted to talk. He wanted to scream.

"Nothing. I mean, not *nothing*, just more cryptic scenes with me and Seyha, our past. Nothing tangible. You?"

Joyce sat on the edge of her own seat, and didn't appear to want to get too comfortable. She leaned forward on her elbows, gave the hallway a quick glance, and said, "It was pretty bad." In wavering, sometimes indecipherable mutterings, Joyce outlined what had happened in the Davidson's kitchen. Bill managed to follow her story enough to understand that she had gone through hell when she was pastor, and no one in the parish, he included, had any clue.

He wished he cared more than he did in that moment. Every word, every detail of Ray the cheating pig or their neighbor in her robe narrowed his chance to run into the bedroom, see if the drawer would open and prove that the vision was true. He didn't think he'd have the nerve to check once Seyha came out of the bathroom.

Silence had been filling the living room for a while before he realized, Joyce was no longer speaking. She didn't look annoyed at his lack of response. In fact, her face had color, more than earlier. Talking seemed to have helped, even if it was mostly to herself. All Bill could focus on was his narrowing window of opportunity. A big part of him didn't want to know, but he didn't think he had any real choice in the matter. Not anymore.

"What's wrong," she asked.

As soon as Bill stood up the shouting began from the bathroom. *Out of time.* "Nothing." He walked towards the voices. "Maybe nothing," he added, more to himself. He walked quickly, not slowing when something crashed from the other side of the closed bathroom door. Seyha was screaming - might, in fact, be killing the girl, but he didn't care for these few seconds, walking into the bedroom, never slowing, reaching out for the top right hand drawer of Seyha's dresser.

Do not open, he commanded it, then pulled it free. It slid soundlessly out of its slot and came loose. He'd pulled it all the way out, held aloft only by the small wooden knob. So much junk crammed into one tiny space. Gravity pulled the opposite end down and Bill let it go. It crashed to the floor.

Behind him it sounded as if Seyha was taking a sledge hammer to the Davidson girl's head and demolishing the bathroom at the same time.

He kicked the drawer away.

The blue and white pill case was on top of the stack, having been under everything when the drawer was closed. He reached down, ignoring the sudden creaking and buckling of the house around him, and lifted the case, let it lay in his open palm. Seyha's name and their address on the label, her gynecologist's name printed at the bottom. He'd met the guy once, at the supermarket with Seyha. Did he know that his prescription had been kept secret?

He stood at the threshold to the hallway, not remembering walking there. Joyce had just pulled Gem out of the bathroom when its door slammed shut and cracked down the middle. The scene was reminiscent of his last vision, but Seyha must be inside, going berserk ... no, there she was, just beyond Joyce at the entrance to the kitchen, looking around in a panic.

Looking for him.

He tightened his grip on the pill case and began to walk.

* * *

A few minutes earlier, Gem leaned against the closed bathroom door and crossed her arms defiantly in front of her. Less than four feet away Mrs. Watts faced her, her olive complexion tinged with red as she flushed with a simmering fury. Gem spoke with as much venom as she could muster, "What is wrong with you?"

Seyha took a step forward. Gem tensed but forced her body not to react. She would *not* let this woman intimidate her. Seyha shouted, not caring how loud her voice carried in the small room, "How dare you come in here! Get out now!"

Gem was pleased with herself that she was able to take a half-step forward, narrowing the distance between them. *Two can play at your game, Mrs. Watts.* "No." Gem lowered her arms, not wanting to look defensive. "I just left the nicest lady I've ever met crying like a baby, and here you are hiding in the bathroom."

Now Seyha took a step forward. She began say again, "How dare you –"

"How dare *you?*" Gem interrupted and matched her volume, took another step so only a few inches remained between them. "Have you any clue what we're going through? Oh, poor pitiful Seyha," she knew using her first name was baiting her but she really didn't care. "Having bad dreams? Wake up, lady. We're *all* having them. You're nothing special."

Seyha's face got so red Gem could almost feel the heat. The color brought out minute blemishes in her skin, concentrated in dark spots around her otherwise perky little cheeks. Mrs. Watts shouted, "You come into my house uninvited and start traipsing around like—"

"Oh give me a break!" Gem almost raised her hand, thought better of it and settled for stuffing her hands into her jeans pockets. "You still on that spiel? How long are you going to play the mean neighbor? As much as I hate to admit it, lady, we need you with us. We need to stay together!" Gem couldn't remember calling anyone "lady" this much in her life. It was better than some of the other words that occurred to her.

Seyha stepped back a little, but her face retained all its fire and rage. "You don't need me and I don't need you. You'd be better off out there with the others. Leave me alone. It's safer that way."

Safer that way? That was bizarre. Gem wasn't sure what she would accomplish in here, except maybe to vent at the Wicked Witch. Now she had something concrete to latch onto. "What do you mean *safer*? You think you're causing this?"

Seyha's eyes briefly broke contact with Gem. When they came back, they were still angry, but there was something different in them. Gem didn't think she'd make much of a psychologist but if this was what they termed a "breakthrough" on talk shows, she had no clue what to do about it.

Seyha, at least, gave her an out. "Just leave me alone."

Gem didn't take it. Too late to back down, now. "We've left you alone. It hasn't helped. Not to mention every time you come out of your dreams you spazz out."

"Don't lecture to me, Gem. Just mind your – "

Gem couldn't give her any advantage, not if the woman was going to start up with *that* line again. "We're all freaking out, but you take the cake. What have you seen, Mrs. Watts?"

"Leave me – "

"What have you seen? Haven't you considered that maybe they're all connected? Don't you even have a trace of worry for Joyce? For Bill?"

"That's Mister Wa–"

"Bill, Bill, Bill," Gem said, wishing she'd been able to make the statement sound less juvenile. She felt a twinge of guilt for enjoying how the taunt hurt her. For a brief moment she came to her senses and realized she was standing in a bathroom scolding a grown woman! The sensation was scary, that Gem might be losing control herself. It felt good, too. Hopefully she'd be able to stop when the time came. Nothing to do now but press on. "Personally, I don't think there's anything we can do. I think we're in hell and it's too late for any of us."

Seyha didn't counter that, not right away. Gem found herself out of breath. She was so wound up, so ready for the inevitable fistfight.

The woman's eyes narrowed, her face twisting into a grimace that Gem did not like. All at once her own sense of power began to melt into fear of this crazy woman, of the scary new mask falling over Mrs. Watts.

"You don't know what hell is, you little shit. I've been there!" Seyha stepped forward until there was no distance left between them. Her words were physical across Gem's face. Gem clenched her hands behind herself, refused to back away. Seyha continued, "I've been there and I can tell you all about it, but I won't. Do you know why?"

Two really good comebacks occurred to her, but Gem filed them away under *Don't Even Think Of It*. All she said was, "Why?"

Mrs. Watts pressed her body against Gem's. "Because all you know are fat pillows with Barbie prints, thick blankets and a nice, safe world." Her face changed again. For a moment, brief but clear in the flash of its existence, twisted into a rendition of the demon crawling out the window in Gem's nightmare. Then she was human again. Sort of. "Some of us were *raised* in hell, Miss Davidson. So just leave me alone and go back to your friend, the priest."

Seyha turned away and glided back towards the toilet. Gem was certain if she'd looked at the woman's feet they would have been an inch off the ground.

She *did* want to leave. Badly. But she'd come in here, and she wasn't leaving until this lady either came out or beat the snot out of her with the toilet plunger. Granted, the latter looked like the higher possibility, but she stayed her ground. Where else was she going to go?

Seyha's back was still to her, shoulders hunched.

Gem knew her next words would guarantee a ticket to the aforementioned plunger-beating. "Is that what you saw, then? Cambodi-"

Seyha turned. "Get out of my bathroom! Get out of my house! Get out of my life!" Her screams crashed off the walls. Looking around for something to kill Gem with, she lifted the porcelain lid of the toilet and slammed it down. It hit the base and shattered into a half-dozen jagged pieces, some falling to the floor, others into the bowl. A large chunk held on by one twisted plastic hinge. Seyha screamed, kicked at this piece, sent it flying into the tub.

Gem opened her mouth, couldn't speak, couldn't take her eyes off the plunger which now toppled over and rolled to Seyha's feet. The woman didn't notice it. *OK*, Gem decided, *time to go.*

The door opened behind her, knocking Gem a few unwanted paces further into the room.

Joyce stepped past her and shouted, "Sey, what's going on?"

Gem let her pass, having to press her butt against the sink to make room. When she moved towards the door another loud crack echoed behind her.

Now what? She turned around, expecting to see Mrs. Watts breaking something else. In truth, the woman was stepping backwards, past Joyce then Gem and into the hall, all the while staring at the far tile wall. A long, deep fissure worked up from the tub's edge to the small, blackened window.

Gem was glad not to hear any hiss of escaping air. Before she could wonder how the woman had managed to do *that*, another crack appeared – both audibly and visually. It began where the first ended, traveled diagonally downward, stopping only when it reached to lip of the tub a few feet from the first. There was now a jagged triangle in the wall.

The vanity mirror beside her shattered. Pieces of glass fell into the sink, bounced out and spilled onto the floor. Gem took a step backwards further into the hallway. Joyce did, too, turned and put an arm around her shoulder to lead her out.

The mirror's frame bent and twisted as if an unseen hands were crushing it like an aluminum can.

Another crack from the tub. Then another. Seyha shrieked behind them, or maybe it was Bill, walking towards them from the bedroom. He looked into the room. A face seemed to have formed in the wall over the tub, an angry, angular face. Pieces of tile fell, adding to the grotesqueness of the image. Joyce pulled Gem along the hall past Seyha, towards the living room. The last Gem saw of the bathroom was a black hole in the wall where the vanity used to be, then her view was blocked by Bill's advancing form.

The bathroom door slammed shut. Seyha and Gem both screamed. Something pounded against the door from inside. It struck again, and again, more sounds of smashing and breaking glass and cracking porcelain and splintering wood.

One long crack appeared in the bathroom door, stretching its full length.

Gem imagined all the anger and spite from their argument taking on a life of its own, slamming into the walls, bouncing back stronger each time.

The hallway fell quiet. No more breaking. No more pounding. Seyha moved beside her husband and the couple stood motionless, staring at the cracked door like headlight-stricken deer.

No one moved.

Directly behind Bill the door to the spare bedroom slammed shut. The Watts twisted around and shouted. *Everyone* was shouting now, matching in volume the new sound of giant fists pounding from inside the spare room. Monsters, coming to life. *Feeding time*, Gem thought, then wished she hadn't.

Bill stuffed something into his pants pocket and said, "Get into the living room, now!" Gem grabbed Joyce's hand and tried to run, but Joyce wasn't moving. She stared at the spare bedroom's door, blinking in time with every angry slam of whatever was inside.

Gem pulled. "Joyce," she whispered, "please!!" The woman blinked faster, turned her head, and must have seen something on Gem's face because she first started walking then ran out of the hallway. She was pale. *Oh, God*, Gem thought, *let her hold it together, for a little longer, please....*

As they entered the dining area, the kitchen in front of them filled with smoke. Gem slowed. Someone collided with her from behind. She ignored it. The kitchen was nearly filled with....

No, Gem realized, *it isn't smoke. It's darkness. The* darkness, coming after them. Joyce had regained herself and now it was *she* pulling *Gem* past the dining table into the living room, not stopping until the couch and chairs were between them and the large opening into the kitchen. Bill and Seyha were right behind them. The foursome stood together behind the last chair, facing back from where they'd come. Waiting for the flood of black to spill into the room and drown them.

It did not come. The kitchen was gone, the half-wall opening now a black window. Featureless, no swirling curls of smoke. It looked solid, like the windows outside. For the moment the darkness was contained to that one room. The hallway was still open, still accessible.

Not that anyone would suggest going back *that* way.

Everyone waited. Nothing more happened. No echoing anger, no giant's fist slamming into doors.

Joyce muttered, "Dear God in heaven, what was that? What was that?"

Gem spoke before she thought to keep the comment to herself. "I think the house is mad at us."

*   *   *

How long had it been? Bill guessed maybe thirty minutes, but time was elusive. His watch was frozen in the eternal moment when all of this began. The episode in the bathroom could have just as easily been only ten minutes ago.

Since they'd returned to the living room, the house had groaned and creaked like a ship drifting out to sea, ready to come apart any moment.

Everyone sat, looking around, *waiting for the next piece of shit to hit the fan*, he assumed. Waiting for the darkness to come back. As it was, it had not spread any further than the kitchen, but that sound... as if the walls were filled with it, straining to break loose.

Seyha stood behind Bill's chair, the same position she'd taken when they'd come back from the hallway. He'd given up trying to get her to sit. Her hand rested lightly on his shoulder. Bill felt the round plastic case in his front pocket, pressing its existence, its *reality*, into his leg. *Not yet*, he'd decided earlier. *Wait. Don't think about it.* Every time he considered the meaning behind the pills, the lies he'd been fed and gladly swallowed for... how long? Eight years, almost nine... he would visibly shake the anger away. No one noticed. It didn't matter if they did, anyhow. He took in a breath, let it out slowly and forced himself to reach up and hold Seyha's hand. Her fingers closed over his. Bill did not squeeze back, not trusting himself.

Joyce looked up and stared at them for a long time.

"Seyha," she said finally, her voice soft, "I'm sorry if I'm pushing you, but I'd like to hear anything – anything at all." As she spoke, the priest looked left then right, as if wondering if her voice would be the straw that finally tore down the house.

Seyha's fingers tightened around Bill's. Joyce must have noticed because she held up a hand. "It's OK. It doesn't have to be detailed, not if it upsets you. But it's *already* upset you."

Surprisingly, Seyha replied, "Yes." Her voice was thick, the hand holding his shaking a little. "Yes, it is. I've spent all my –" she stopped, took in a deep breath, let it out. Bill felt his own body tighten. *Stay quiet*, he told himself, hoping Joyce would not push. If Seyha was going to tell them anything, it would be now or never. Part of him, a darker part which found root inside his mind in the past hour, wondered if it would matter at this point. He thought again what Gem had said, about all of them being dead. In torment. Everything they've seen, lies. He closed his eyes, knowing the irony of *that* idea being wishful thinking, and waited for his wife to say more.

* * *

It would be easy to lash out again. Run into the bedroom if she dared go back in that direction, hide behind the same walls she'd become so adept at raising. The walls kept her safe, even happy if she didn't think too much. Everything was unraveling, peeled away by this prison. The house was closing in around them. There was no place to go. How much longer before the only thing left was this small square of carpet?

And even now, Joyce kept pushing. Seyha couldn't find any meaning behind anyone else's visions, except perhaps Bill's. Those had loosed a fear in her, as if something was trying to lift a curtain, force her hand by showing her secrets a little at a time. She wondered what he'd seen this last time. It might have something to do with his sudden coldness. Had he come out of the bedroom when all hell broke loose with her and Gem? She thought again of the unfrozen dresser drawer. Some secrets needed to stay hidden, would cause more pain than any possible redemption from some vague concept of truth.

Everyone was waiting. If she was careful, she could toss them a bone. Let them in a little. The pain of seeing her father in such a state was too fresh, to horrifying to acknowledge to these people. But maybe something earlier. Whatever was controlling their world might end up showing it to them, anyway.

"I was on the side of a road," she began, then stopped. Her throat was dry. She licked her lips. The simple act of speaking made her feel exposed. Standing behind Bill's chair, keeping him between herself and the others, she rested her free hand gently against the back of his head. He did not move, had hardly returned her grip of his fingers. *What did he see?* She had sinned against him – was *still* sinning. *Push it away*, she thought, wanting to let go of his hand, yet not daring to.

"I was at the side of a dirt road," she said again, "in Cambodia. The day my mother was killed by *Khmer Rouge* soldiers, for no other reason than she refused to allow my sisters to be taken." Her voice sounded surprisingly strong. She'd never in her life uttered these words to another person, not even Bill. Instead of pain or a loss of control, Seyha felt stronger for them – a small bit of strength, mixed with anger. She took hold of that anger and continued. "I had three sisters, all older. I don't remember much about two of them, but I remember the oldest, a little." She looked away. What she was saying didn't sound right. Having always held so many minute details to herself, speaking them aloud they sounded... *wrong*.

"What's the matter?" Joyce asked.

"Nothing. I just..." something hurt in her chest. *No*, she thought, *be strong*. Panic blossomed into a fire, spread to her stomach. She'd looked away, but turned back to Joyce, eyes wider. "I.... I'm not sure... she was my sister, or my cousin." A laugh, then. Short-lived, the first sign of madness. Her voice sounded too high, almost a squeal. "All of a sudden, I don't know if she was my sister, cousin or just a girl from my village. Any of them, actually. This one, the oldest, was very close. I remember her playing with me once. But...." Darkness crept along the edges of her vision. Not the darkness which had swallowed them twice already. This had no substance, no texture. Still her vision continued to dim. *Going to faint again*, she thought. *You are so weak.*

Bill got up and walked around the chair. He held her in both arms, saying nothing as he led her back onto the warmed cushion, guiding her as he would a helpless old woman.

Seyha stared at her hands resting on her lap. She wanted to die. "How can I not know if she was my sister? All of a sudden, how can I not know something as simple as that? I can't even remember her name." Another humorless laugh. "Can you believe that?"

"You were just a baby, Sey." Bill's voice.

She leaned into the chair, closed her eyes, wished for sleep, if she couldn't have death. Talking about this had been a mistake. She felt worse.

"Sey," his voice had a hard edge to it. Was he angry?

She opened her eyes, looked up at him. He sat on the arm of the chair, one foot resting on the edge of the cushion beside her. When their eyes met, he smiled. Not a happy smile. In fact, she couldn't remember him ever looking more miserable.

"That's better," he said, still in that cold voice. "You need to stay with us. Focus. Please. You may not think this is helping, but it is. For now, let's say she was your cousin. She was close, no different than a sister." His hand on her shoulder, squeezing a little too hard. "It doesn't matter. Later, maybe. But don't let it trip you up."

He wasn't mad. He was being strong. It felt good to let him be like this, for the moment at least.

She looked only at Bill, and said, "They wanted to take her and the other girls away. I guess everyone knew why. I didn't. At least, I don't think I did. She, my... cousin, was very pretty. I remember that. Everything is in spots, the memories. I think my mother said *No.* Then someone shot her. Just... shot her.

"I was holding her hand. When she fell she pulled me down with her. I remember wanting to yell at her to get off me, she was too heavy. I wanted to, but knew enough not to say anything. Everyone crowded around us, yelling, shouting. I climbed out from under my mother. She was dead."

The burning pain in her chest and stomach faded. Not gone completely, but *bearable*. She didn't cry, felt no sadness. In this moment, Seyha never felt more *empty*. And, oddly, it felt good.

She risked a glance around. Gem looked about to cry. Her face was red, bunched up like she was fighting the emotion. A crying face. As much as she didn't want to like this girl, Seyha decided she probably wasn't all that bad.

"Anyway," she looked back to Bill, then quickly away from the pity in his face, down to her lap, "they took the other girls away. I don't remember where. After that, nothing but walking, all day. Holding someone's hand. Different people, I think. Whether they were my aunts or just other villagers I don't know. I don't even know how many days it was."

Joyce asked, "Where were they taking you?"

Seyha lied, "I don't know." From the sudden tenseness of his hand on her shoulder, she assumed Bill knew. He'd done a lot of research on her homeland over the years, until she insisted he stop. Bill probably knew more than *she* did at this point. Seyha had done some research of her own, years ago when she could read English and was safely ensconced at the Saint Margaret's school just outside of Boston, no more than sixty miles from where they lived now. She'd been thirteen, or fourteen, a ward of the Commonwealth, brought to America through some program between the Church and the Sisters of Compassion. The smell of mildewed pages, echoing silence of the small library, so strong even now in her memory. Sitting at a long table, alone, Seyha had scanned a new arrival, fresh plastic dust jacket. A book about home. Until that terrible day in the library, "home" had meant

Cambodia. She read about the death marches, saw the photographs. She remembered being fascinated by it all, even recognizing some of the events and locations. Whether these came from her own limited memory or through tales told by the other children she didn't know. Near the back of the book, she found a page with photographs of bodies, black and white images of gray corpses piled like lumber. She had slammed the book closed. Covered her face and screamed into her palm, reaching up and pulling a fist of hair from her head. Seyha had come to her senses in the nurse's office, staring at the ceiling. Today that book was likely on a forgotten shelf in the same library, old and musty, its plastic covering cracked and yellow-taped.

Seyha said none of this to the others. She could have, but Gem didn't need to hear about that kind of grief. If they ever got out of here, the girl would probably end up running to her own library to see what all the fuss was about. For now, she needed to give some sort of "happy" ending.

"I don't remember what came next, probably because I was so dehydrated I was almost dead myself. When the Vietnamese army invaded, they intercepted our little caravan. They killed our captors, brought us to a refugee camp. I don't remember when I arrived at the orphanage. Like you said, I was very young."

Again she realized how dry her mouth was. She was thirsty. Probably an unconscious reaction to the memory of that walk, scanning the road for anything to grab and eat. The kitchen across the room was black as a starless midnight. The bathroom was currently occupied by monsters. She almost asked if anyone else was thirsty, decided against it.

No one said anything for a few minutes. Seyha leaned

sideways against her husband. She *did* feel better. Nothing had changed in their situation. They remained trapped in this house-cum-prison. Inside herself, she felt a little cleaner.

That was, until Bill spoke up. Until he asked the next question which filled the chasm which had cleared itself inside her with fresh new pain. Renewed her guilt.

I have sinned against you, my wonderful, loving husband. I have spit in your face and you will never forgive me. Never. And I'm so, so sorry for what I have done to you.

*   *   *

As Bill listened from his perch on the arm of Seyha's chair, his emotions oscillated between empathy and anger - the latter at himself for forgetting even momentarily what she'd done to him, but also that this moment of openness to finally happen now, of all times.... She was sharing a terrible moment in her life to near-strangers after years of Bill trying to coax the words from her, pry open the door she'd closed so completely. Now it had opened, not by his doing, not *for* him. All because of this twisted version of reality God or Satan or big-headed aliens had dropped them into. He hooked his thumb into his jeans' pocket, ran fingertips over the outline of the plastic case, physical proof that their relationship had blossomed this last decade over a lie. A quiet part of him hoped it *was* God dragging them through this. Otherwise, like Gem said, they might be at the mercy of something which actually *relished* the misery of others.

More and more, this latter possibility was feeling like truth.

Seyha was done talking. The lingering silence was an opportunity, one Bill might never get back. As much as he did not want to speak to her right now unless it was a scream, her past was open to him, a little. He would push, use this newly-found confidence fueled by hurt.

They'd been trying to have children for years. Both of them. *Only* him. He forced his hand away from his pocket. She hadn't been trying, never intended to get pregnant. This brought him to another thought, but that way led to places too dark to consider. If he followed the thread too far, they may never find their way back.

"Sey," he said, hesitantly. He gently laid one hand onto her shoulder. "Why...." How could he say it? The idea that once he exposed her secret it would be the irreparable destruction of their marriage was too much to risk.

It already happened, though. Hadn't it?

"Sey... I need to ask you something. It might not make any sense, but I want to ask."

Seyha glanced up at him, then quickly down to her lap. In that flash Bill recognized her old reluctance returning like a cold mist between them. Mouth shut, lips pressed together. The door was closing. Years of habit almost ended his question before it was asked. Joyce nodded from the couch. *Go on*, the gesture said.

He cleared his throat, wanted to squeeze her shoulder harder. "Maybe it has to do with your time at the orphanage, I don't know. Are you," he laughed, hearing the rest of the question in his head and knowing it was too stupid to ask out loud.

Ask it. Start.

His words were forced, spoken robotically. "Are you afraid of having children?"

He sensed this was the wrong - or the *right* - thing to say, by the subtle pulling away of his wife from his hand. Not enough to make him let go, but the warning was implicit.

He would not stop, not this time. He pulled his hand

away. "Sey, I'm just - "

She whispered, "Stop…. Not here. Please, Bill, don't."

He slid off the arm of the chair and knelt in front of her. Gently, he took hold of her wrists. "Talk to me. You don't get it, do you? This place isn't going to let you hide anymore." The more words he spoke, the less any fear of what might happen could keep him from putting everything on the table.

Is *it everything?*

He blinked away the thought and slid his grip, from her wrists to her hands. Seyha turned her head away, as far over her shoulder as was physically possible, closed her dry eyes, and said, "Leave me alone. Please, Bill. Not now. I don't… I just don't…"

"Tell me!" He squeezed her hands. He didn't want to hurt his wife but, oh, he was going to make her answer, shake her, scream into that beautiful face that was turned away like a dog who'd done her master wrong, if that was what it took. His hands were shaking. Louder, still feeling he had control over himself, he said, "Tell me. I'm your husband. The lying ends now."

He was light-headed and his ears were ringing from some bizarre reason. Fear, most likely, but he could not give into it, not now nor ever again. No turning back. Everything or nothing left. He let go of her hands and stood up. Only then did he hear the sounds of the house around him, groaning and straining like a ship in a storm.

Seyha was looking at him now, a mixture of fear and defiance. *Don't you dare*, the look said.

Bill reached in his pants pocket and pulled out the case of pills. "What the hell are these?" he hissed, wishing he could run away and never hear the answer.

The house groaned again, only this time, it didn't stop

*　*　*

It sounded like a train crashing through the house. The noise was so loud Gem stopped listening to the Watts' conversation and curled on the couch beside Joyce. Before she could raise her hands against the side of her head, the sound suddenly stopped. A moment of silence, then –

CRACK.

Something snapping, a monster's footstep. She didn't dare look around, afraid of what might have made that noise. Beside her, Joyce turned, looked beyond the couch towards the other side of room.

There was no more sound. A silence that echoed worse than any crashing or groaning, quiet enough to hear Joyce whisper, "God, please, no..." as she raised her hands to her face. Then she was gone.

Bill and Seyha turned their heads. He was holding some plastic thing in his outstretched hand. Seyha mouthed, *Bill,* then something thick and unreal crawled across the back of Gem's skull.

She closed her eyes and thought, *Not again. Please God don't send us back into –*

That was as far as she got.

Third Day of Darkness

The snow between the church and the Davidson house was a kaleidoscope of colors and shapes. Above her the night sky was starless and black. Joyce was floating, hovering twenty feet above the ground. A choir of voices drifted through the glowing stained glass and filled the neighborhood with music and light.

Of all the dreams she'd been thrown into, this felt most *like* a dream, moving through this nighttime winter landscape which tipped and swayed below her.

From the front yard came the familiar creak of the *Saint Gerard's Episcopal Church* sign hanging from a roadside tree. Otherwise, the neighborhood was quiet except for the drifting hymn.

Joyce was weightless, adrift in the night. Even as she began to fall, slowly, like the blow of snow from the roof, she had no sensation of herself, of *being* anything at all. She hovered over a figure as it stepped tentatively from next door. Fur-lined boots silent in the snow, long blonde hair poking from odd angles under her cap, Gem stopped, hesitant, letting a gust of wind swirl the snow around her.

The double front doors opened and four men emerged outside, each holding a corner of the altar. This was the night of the deconsecration ceremony, last December, when Saint Gerard's would be no more. Joyce settled lower and was seized by a fear that she would continue down, into the snow and earth to be forever buried and forgotten.

She bent her legs defensively, stopped a few inches above the top of the snow.

Gem, she said.

Of course, her voice was no more tangible than the rest of her.

Gem Davidson blurred, stretched forward, then was standing by the front doors, walking alongside and talking to Paul Giroux as the high school student helped three others carry the top portion of the altar to Maurice Baer's waiting panel van. Gem questioned him, gesturing to the wooden altar, but their words oscillated between audible and indistinct like snippets caught on a distant radio station. Paul invited Gem to Saint Cecelia's to see the new church. From a sudden reddening of Gem's cheeks he *might* have said more but Joyce couldn't be sure. Too much confusion in the sounds and scene around her.

Joyce drifted backwards, turned towards the church again.

The double front doors closed slowly, now only a thin line revealing the final ceremony of Saint Gerard's church inside. She stretched forward as Gem had done, sucked through that narrow gap before it closed completely. No sense of warmth inside. She was not real enough to feel temperature. The church was crowded, alive with bodies sitting in the pews. Joyce traveled above them, the *Ghost of Christmas Past* come to haunt, but to haunt whom? She looked up, saw *herself* rising from the pastor's chair at the side of the sanctuary. Her too long neck bowed slightly under the weight of this moment – the closing of a parish. She was such a somber figure from this perspective. That wasn't how she remembered feeling. *Relieved,* in a way, seeing the building, the eyesore which had marred the landscape of her life, finally cast aside. Not the church itself, but the home. No longer a constant reminder of bad memories for her and Bec....

She closed her eyes and chided herself for being so selfish, then and now. The church was too much of a burden to carry when she had so much baggage of her own, all of it weighing her down. It had slipped through her grasp and she'd let it go. The sheep had lost their shepherd and were moving to a better, safer pasture. And all she could think as she stood there this night was the vast relief of its weight no longer on her shoulders.

Joyce suddenly flew forward towards her other self. She stood in the center of the sanctuary, whole again.

We who are gathered here, she felt more than heard herself read from the thin black volume in her hands, *know that this building, which has been consecrated and set apart for the ministry of God's holy Word and Sacraments, will no longer be used in this way.*

She drifted away, let the Joyce of this time continue reciting as her spectral-self looked out over the congregation, found her daughter sitting with her trademark half-smile in the third row. Bec had driven up from school for the ceremony, forsaking her usual black wardrobe for one of Joyce's more conservative dresses. A rare sight, and one which she remembered being grateful for. Even so, the shiny stud in the side of her nose, another through her left eyebrow, reflected the light when she turned. The adornments somehow added a touch of style to the otherwise plain, earthy dress – a dress like her mother. Plain, used up.

She fell into herself again, felt her mouth say, *Let the bishop's Declaration of Secularization now be read.* Her head turned toward the young bishop, Mark Camez, who rose with his trademark ease and casualness. She held out the book, thumb holding the page open, then again drifted out and above the body, out of the memory, to be set adrift over the heads of the a parish.

She wavered over the altar like Christ on the crucifix, staring at Rebecca, and the man covered in blood now sitting beside her, one stained arm draped over Bec's shoulder. Ray had somehow squeezed himself next to an oblivious Leo Wiegers. He laughed soundlessly. When he saw Joyce floating above the sanctuary he waved her towards him with his free hand.

She tried to shout *No!* but of course she had no control. At the edge of her locked vision she noticed Gem skulking in the back of the church watching the proceedings with an unmistakable look of sorrow, then Joyce was stretching out, sitting in the pew beside Ray. There shouldn't have been room for her – or Ray for that matter – but she could not turn away from him to see if Mister Wiegers had been relegated to the aisle by her intrusion. She couldn't look away from her husband. His face and shirt were covered in blood. Mostly his shirt, askew with buttons in the wrong holes as if hastily donned. It was white, once, but the center was a bright splash of red. At one point the blood had washed upward across his neck and chin. He pulled Rebecca closer, though their daughter didn't seem to notice. Without looking away from the proceedings on the altar Rebecca whispered, "This is wild, like one of those fever dreams." Joyce didn't know if she'd said this in December or, more likely, it was in response to this new, carnival-ride version of events.

Ray nodded. Two dried lines of blood ran over both lips and the stubble of his chin. He turned towards Joyce. "Is this what you want to see, my love? See me dead in all my bloody glory?" When he laughed the twin streams flowed in spurts from his nostrils. "I should say all my *gory*. Excuse me a second." He pursed his lips and spit a wad into her face.

Too late Joyce raised her hands. Her palms smeared the

congealed blood across her cheeks and nose, inadvertently pressing it past her own lips. She spat and lowered her hands, stared at Ray, eyes and tongue stinging. She was not frightened by the sight of him. In fact, she liked what she saw. *God forgive me, but this is how he should be.*

Ray raised his free hand again. His bloodshot eyes wrinkled with a dark amusement. He said, "The woman wants forgiveness. Coming right up," and tried to snap his fingers. They were too wet to make a sound. Still he waited, head cocked. Nothing happened. He pulled his arm away from Rebecca and turned towards Joyce. "It's been so easy to see me as a monster, Joyce."

You're not Ray, she tried to say.

He nodded, "Yes, yes, we covered that already. Fine." The blood was gone, shirt properly buttoned. This clean-shaven rendition of the man now stared into her eyes. "Ray was pretty monstrous in what he had done. But no monster is an island." He paused, looked away for a moment, then resumed his stare. "Not the best metaphor, sorry." She could not stop him taking both her hands in his. "When someone is guilty of so much, it's easy to blame him for everything. But you need to ask yourself, Joyce, what was your part in all of this? Not just this." He freed one hand and slapped it against his chest. Blood sprayed out from between the shirt's buttons and up through the loosened collar. He raised the stained hand above himself.

"But here." He smiled. "Did I do all of this?" He suddenly pushed her off the bench and stood. Being in the front row she fell backwards onto the floor in front of the sanctuary. He stared down at her with an expression of unmasked contempt. "Such a powerful man, he was, to have destroyed something so holy of God's." He looked around at the congregation which was again on its feet and singing.

"Such a busy man Ray was. So good that you were rid of him at last."

He walked down the aisle until lost from sight behind the crowds standing in their pews. The last thing Joyce saw was her daughter looking down at her, confused. "Did *you* cause this, Mommy?"

She closed her eyes and leaned back, unable to accept what they were saying - even though his words carried the same accusation as those of the girl in the jungle, as her own self-recriminations. Joyce's head never connected with the edge of the raised sanctuary floor. Instead, it fell softly to a pillow. Her body stretched out under sheets and bedspread. The feel of the bed was familiar, but not recent. Not her bed. Not anymore. She opened her eyes to broken darkness. The ceiling, illuminated by slats of light sneaking through the blinds from the streetlamps outside, was one she'd lain awake many nights staring at. The *old house*, as she referred to the residential side of the church. She never wanted to come back here.

"Leave me alone," she whispered. "Just let me die." Whether this was said to her captors, God or herself, it didn't matter. Like an incantation, hearing her own voice broke the despair somewhat.

Slowly, reluctantly, she sat up and swung her legs over the side of the bed. The lines of light shining in from outside allowed her to see enough of the old room to find her white terrycloth robe atop the hope chest. Her back was to the closed bedroom door. Through this, or perhaps the too-thin wall between this and Bec's room, drifted her daughter's crying. Then a brief grunt of words, indecipherable except for Ray's heavy tone.

Joyce's skin tightened, began to tingle with the stress of those two sounds.

Please, God, no. I'm sorry. It was all my fault and I'm sorry but please don't do this to me again. Please don't do this to us *again.* She kept the thought rolling through her mind as she wrapped the robe around herself. *Please no, please no,* as she unsuccessfully tried to stop herself from tying the sash, hesitating by the door, hearing the heavy thud of Ray's steps moving away down the hallway. *Kill me now, send me to hell, but please don't,* as she opened the door, quiet as a mouse. The old kitchenette and the pathetic square table where they ate their meals was on her right. Gone now, in the Watts' world, the entire room absorbed by the master bedroom. The light over the stove had been left on, spilling into the hall, casting her robed shadow vaguely across the runner carpet. Joyce was not in control of her own movements, so she padded to Bec's bedroom as she had done that final night years before. The door was open. Her daughter, thirteen in this moment, almost fourteen, stared from the gloom, face wet with tears reflecting the distant light. Joyce blinked, the Joyce of *this* moment, trying to decipher the mystery of why her daughter, a young woman in her own right even then, sat awkwardly on top of the bed, fumbling to put her pajama top back on, settling instead on holding it against herself. She looked away from her mother, who could – then and now – only stand in the doorway, confused and lost and seeing the last shreds of her life drift away.

*   *   *

Gem Davidson opened her eyes and saw the red, slightly chipped dinner plates on which so many meals had been eaten in her family's house. They had nicer ones, tucked away in the living room, but according to her mother those were for "special occasions." Gem couldn't remember any occasion special enough to take them out of the dust-covered china cabinet. Always these older, dishwasher-safe plates were the tableware *du jour.*

The Davidson's dining room was small, an extension of the living room not unlike the Watts'. The table was big enough to hold the four of them on the rare occasions they decided to sit and eat together. This was apparently one of those times. Her mother sat opposite, spearing a piece of steaming broccoli with her fork and talking to her father, who hunkered over his own red plate. Though her mother was speaking, Gem couldn't understand what she said. Her ears were plugged up, making everything sound underwater. To Gem's left, Eliot was oblivious to the world around him. Her brother clinked his fork down onto his plate and grabbed a glass of milk. The sound of the fork on the plate was loud, clear. Only her mother's voice, then her father's distracted grunt of a reply, were vague and obscure. Eliot drank half of his milk in one prolonged gulp, slammed the glass down with an audible thud, and resumed his eating. Chicken breast, mashed potatoes, and bright green broccoli. Nice meal. She looked over at the kitchen door. From this angle she could just see the calendar hanging on the wall by the phone. *November.* Aside from the fact that the same page could potentially hang for months before someone remembered to flip it, Gem figured this time it was accurate. Her mother had cooked a big meal so, although the entrée was chicken instead of turkey, this was probably Thanksgiving. Two days of the year warranted a formal sit-down, at least in Mom's mind - Thanksgiving and March nineteenth, Dad's birthday. The oven was fired up and the family ate whatever came out of it, at the table, together. The routine of eating *at the table* was key - there were numerous other evenings when everyone sat together to eat, but in front of the television with plates on their laps.

"Eliot," she whispered, "can you hear me?"

He looked up, a small blob of mashed potatoes perched on his bottom lip. "Sorry, what?" he said.

"I said, can you hear me?"

He smirked. The potato lump dropped free. It didn't land on the plate. More than likely it was hanging from his pant leg. She wasn't going to tell him. "No," he said, snorted, and poked a broccoli tree.

"I'm serious." She was still whispering, but her parents stopped their indecipherable chatter and focused on them. Eliot absently wiped his mouth with the back of his hand.

Gem said, "What's going on?"

Her mother's voice was clear now, "I'm afraid I don't follow, Gem. What do you mean?"

Gem considered everyone's questioning expression, then sighed. "Nothing. I'm just trapped in the neighbor's house with a bunch of demons, or maybe they're just mean angels. We can't decide. Nothing to worry about."

"OK," Eliot said, and cut a piece of chicken.

Deanna Davidson's smile hung limp on her long, pretty face. "Gem," she said, "you're so funny."

"Yea, whatever." She wanted to add some remark about their neighbor standing naked in the kitchen a little while ago, but held herself, not sure if all these moments could be brought together, anyway.

"This chicken is good, Mom," Eliot said before he'd finished chewing. "How come we never have stuffing for Thanksgiving?" With so much food behind his teeth, the holiday came out as "Thaffesifiing." He swallowed the lump, picked at something stuck between his front teeth with the fork.

Deanna clucked her tongue. "Stuffing is too hard to make."

Gem felt one of her *daughter-buttons* pushed. She slapped her right hand flat on the table. "Stuffing's so easy, Mom.

How do you – " She stopped. The broccoli speared onto her mother's fork was spotted with black. Gem squinted. Maybe it was spinach. She looked down at her plate. Nope, no spinach on her plate. Now, *that* would have been harder. More than *stuffing*.

The chicken breast, half-eaten on her mother's plate, had three – *two and a half*, Gem realized – fuzzy green spots of mold. Gem understood then that the dark spots on the broccoli were decay. *Bad veggies.* Old and moldy. Her stomach flipped. She looked at her own plate. Everything looked fine.

Eliot had managed to free whatever had been trapped between his teeth. He flicked the half-eaten maggot onto the table. There were more, whole ones on his plate, squirming in and out of his potatoes, circling the broccoli like animals in a miniature zoo.

Gem's nausea grew almost too fast to control. She covered her mouth, aware of breakfast eaten ages ago but still sitting in her stomach. She looked again at her plate. She hadn't eaten anything *here*, not yet at least. Even so, her food looked decent enough. She carefully used her fork to lift the edge of the chicken. If there was anything under there she'd lose a week's worth of lunches all over the table.

Nothing.

"Is there something wrong with your food, Gem?" Deanna asked the question with such clipped frustration that Gem knew the answer had better be "no".

Gem poked through the mashed potatoes. Nothing impaled itself on the tines. "No," she said, and managed to swallow to convince herself she wasn't going to barf. "*My* food's fine," she said, "but..."

What could she say? Her father's plate had a long crack running through the center. Something white and fuzzy with dark tinges dripped off the edge of the meat.

Something moved in his potatoes but Gem looked up to his face before she could learn what it was.

"Dad, you OK?"

Her father was looking down at his plate. She was pretty sure he wasn't seeing whatever *she* saw. He probably didn't see the plate at all. Usually at these events, with everyone together, he was in a great mood, wide open and talkative. Something fell from his down-turned face onto his plate. It wasn't a bug, or mold.

He was crying. When Gem reached out, her hand came in contact with some invisible barrier between them. She pushed a little, felt it give at first, then resist. It strengthened the harder she pressed against it. It felt like someone's arm or shoulder. She pulled her hand back with a squeak.

"Now what?" her mother sighed.

What was wrong with her family? Were they always this... disinterested? She supposed they were. Her father sniffed, releasing another tear onto his spoiled food.

"Dad," she said again, "what's wrong?"

He just shook his head, slowly, and said nothing. No, this wasn't her father. Not this pathetic, sad man beside her. She reached out, fingers stretched, and again touched the invisible shoulder. She pulled her arm back.

"What are you doing, weirdo?" Eliot was looking at her while he slurped a wriggling...*no, no, no*. Gem looked away, but said, almost as a reflex, "Nice of you to notice me, dork," then regretted it. Why couldn't she just be nice to him? He was only a jerk to her because that's how she usually treated *him*.

"You've gotten so wise, Gem," the man now crouching between her and Eliot said. He hunkered so low that his eyes barely rose above the table.

Beautiful was the only word Gem could think to describe

him. Long blonde hair danced over his shoulders, thick with a slight wave to it. He didn't look much older than her, face smooth with a chiseled sort of health that said, *I Work Out But Don't Flaunt It.* His blue eyes gazed at her with – *wait a minute,* she thought. Things had become so bizarre she hadn't been the least bit surprised that this Adonis just blinked into existence beside her.

At least he didn't have claws.

"And *you* are?" she asked, trying to be casual.

"Eliot," Eliot said, and laughed.

"A friend," the newcomer replied. He nodded across her lap. "Your Dad looks upset."

Gem looked back at her father, then waved a hand towards him. The invisible shoulder no longer barred her way. More than likely the body it was attached to was kneeling on the other side of her chair. A very muscular one under a white polo shirt. "That's not my Dad. You guys have been trying to make me think he's this lost puppy, hiding away from the world. He's not like this in real life. When he comes down, he's happy. He even acknowledges that I exist, at least more than the Ice Queen over there does."

Her mother slammed down her fork. The plate broke in half, sending something with way too many legs scurrying for cover under a large bowl of infested potatoes at the center of the table. "Excuse me, young lady! How dare you speak to me that way?"

"I'm talking to Handsome, over here," Gem said with a growing sense of liberation. If they – whoever *they* were – wanted to play games, she didn't have to follow the rules anymore.

The handsome boy furrowed his brow. "You should not speak to your mother that way. Honor your Mother and Father."

Gem smiled, reached out and gently laid a hand on the young man's cheek. "Yes, I know. I actually read that part." By now Eliot was resting his chin on one fist, watching her while he chewed. The top of his head moved up and down with the motion. "You're nuts," he said, "you know that? You have an imaginary friend now?"

Gem's defiance melted when she remembered what her brother was chewing. Didn't they see how rotten everything was?

"No, Gem," the boy beside her said. He rested a hand on the back of her chair. "They don't. And you can't just point to them and say their food is spoiled. They won't listen. They don't want to understand the reasoning behind it. You have to approach this carefully. *Show* them how bad the food is."

She looked at her mother, who in turn shot venom from her eyes. Deanna put the fork into her mouth, lips tight. She pulled it free, never taking her eyes off her daughter. Gem's father sobbed again. That was enough. She was frustrated at the total cartoon-ishness of how her family was being portrayed.

"This isn't your family, Gem. Not the way you usually see them. Outwardly, they're as normal as you remember, though a bit aloof and eccentric sometimes. This," he craned his neck and scanned the people seated at the table, "is how one might physically represent how they are... inside."

She thought about that for a minute. "You mean, like their souls or something?"

Eliot was looking nervous. "Gem, OK, that's enough. Will you please stop?" She felt a pang of guilt at how much she was scaring him, but if this wasn't real....

"Eliot looks normal," she said.

Her brother gritted his teeth, puffed through his lips,

"Gem...."

The Adonis nodded. "True, but he's just a little jerk." She stiffened. He quickly added, "Your words, not mine."

"But," he clapped his hands together, "to the food! The best way to show them that what they're eating is rotten is to take a bite or two from their plates. Show them how bad it is."

Gem looked plate to plate. Moldy, crawling with insects. She winced. The old nausea kicked back in. "No thanks."

"This isn't real, Gem. None of this is. You won't get sick. You'll be protected."

She looked at him, her sour stomach forgotten. "You mean like, you're my guardian angel or something?"

"Let's just leave it at that," he interrupted. "But do it now, we're running out of time." He reached for the fork, handed it to Gem. She accepted it, but her hand was shaking. She didn't want to do this.

"Taste their food, and show them. Let them see its corruption. Hurry."

"Is this some kind of lame metaphor or something?"

Her father sniffed deeply, but looked up as Gem reached for his plate with her fork. No way she would take that big chunk of meat. She might be able to keep down some potatoes. *This isn't real*, she reminded herself. *None of this is real. It can't hurt me. Show them.*

"Open their eyes," the young man said, standing behind her now. Gem reached forward and scooped up a wad of her confused father's potatoes.

"What are you doing?" her mother asked, eyes narrowed and suspicious.

Eliot's plea sounded like air escaping from the stretched neck of a balloon. He was almost crying. "Gem, *pleeeease*, stop it."

The mashed potatoes served as the grazing land for five small maggoty things. And that was only what Gem could see. She managed to bring the fork halfway from her father's plate to her own when she stopped. She couldn't do this. Looking down at her own plate, at the clean, steaming food, it occurred to her that maybe there was another option.

When she looked up at the boy, he was glaring down at her. Still, absolutely gorgeous, but his face now tightened with anger. "No," he said. "There is no other way. Didn't Jesus spend time with sinners to show them the Light?"

Gem tried unsuccessfully to return his stare. "What are you talking about? These are mashed potatoes." When he rolled his eyes, Gem felt a twang of embarrassment. "What, is there some big – what's the word – symbolism in all this that my tiny brain is missing?"

"Look – "

"No, *you* look," she said, waving the fork between them. "Wouldn't it make more sense for me to eat my own food and show them how much better it is than that junk they're dropping down their throats?"

His face twisted into a pout which, she had to admit, made him look really cute. "No," he said. "It wouldn't."

She waved the fork, sending mashed potatoes and a couple of wormy things to the floor. One landed on her jeans leg. She swiped it away. "Well, I'm not eating this! There's no way this can be good for –"

"Eat it!!!" he screamed, rising up as if on his tiptoes, so much higher he loomed over her now. He was no longer beautiful. His blonde hair was still wavy and conditioned, but his eyes were wild, darkened from their former sky blue to the yellow and red of the demon which had crawled from the church window. "What," he hissed, "makes you think," he grabbed her wrist, forcing the fork towards her mouth, "you're any better," her lips almost brushed the food, "than the rest of your family?"

"Gem?" Eliot said. For a moment the demon's grip loosened. Both turned to face her brother. Eliot was staring at his plate, then hers, confused. "What's wrong with my food?" The room tilted, then twisted in on itself, like a television with its horizontal hold askew. When the world righted itself a second later, Gem stood on her back porch, alone.

*   *   *

Bill Watts watched his younger self sitting in the backyard. The G.I. Joe action figure in one hand battled an almost-identical soldier (whom the boy had named G.I. Jimmy) in the other. Young Billy supplied the requisite fighting noises, his mouth twisting in a "crash!" and "hay-yah!" Bill smiled in spite of the horror he'd been facing with Seyha's lies only a few minutes earlier, the mockery that his marriage had become.

Now he was here, in yet another moment from his past. Long ago, this time. He walked closer. The occasional section of undisturbed grass was a cushion under his loafers. His mother's yard looked different than the last time he'd come. Less grass, more toys. His younger self didn't appear to see him, but that didn't prove Bill was invisible. He didn't want to risk having the boy turn around, see a man who probably looked like his father standing behind him. Wasn't there some time travel rule around that? *No, that's ridiculous.* He wasn't traveling in time. His emotions had become hardened to the shock of these visions. This time he was more frustrated than frightened, being tossed around in memories that would twist in on themselves, become darker than they should have been. He did not want this memory to twist.

He stopped a few yards away from himself. His parents could never afford to buy an 8mm movie camera like his friend Andrew's family, such a luxury didn't fit into the budget of a Worcester cab driver and a part-time supermarket clerk. Bill never saw images of himself as a child except in still photographs, yellowed and buried among his mother's possessions now tucked away under his own bed. He saw himself clearly now, sitting on the grass amid a plethora of bare spots worn from so many hours of playing with action figures and Hot Wheels. Monkey didn't help matters. The Labrador Retriever's bathroom habits wreaked havoc with the lawn. Bill looked around. Had Monkey been around at this point of his life?

Yes!

His heart soared with delight. The lab lounged just around the corner of the house, never far from her "brother," as little Billy liked to refer to himself when talking about the dog. Billy, of course, had come up with the name *Monkey* when he'd been five. *You name her*, his father had told him. She was his birthday present. A rainy September twenty-second, the small puppy licking his face and peeing on the rug.

Monkey! he had shouted, and the name was so wonderfully unexpected it stuck. Monkey. The details of that day were relayed to him often by his parents, usually at his urging. He loved to hear the story, wanted to remember the moment. Dad's cab parked in the driveway - he had taken a break from his shift to celebrate - the man stood in the middle of the room and laughed. *Monkey it is, then.*

I miss you, girl, Bill said, not surprised that his voice was silent. The dog did not look up. He crossed the yard and knelt down beside her, scratched behind her ears. The dog, dreaming, thumped her tail on the grass. Bill's heart opened so wide in that moment he wanted to cry and lay down and hold his old Monkey Dog.

Eventually, he stood and walked back to the spot where he'd been standing earlier. Little Billy stopped playing with his figures, looked around, then groaned in frustration.

"I'm so bored," he growled to no one.

Bill laughed noiselessly. *Yea*, he thought, *I'll bet*. The neighborhood was situated at the outskirts of an industrial complex in the northern section of the city. Half of the buildings were long vacant. There were other houses on their road, most with older kids or retired couples. No children Billy's age. One neighborhood boy came close, Walter. The kid mostly kept to himself, or was driven for play-dates across town. But something about Walter always gave him the willies. Now, watching himself reluctantly pick up G.I. Joe again, because there wasn't anything else to do, Bill knew that he would gladly have had Walter over on this day, if only for a change of routine.

Bill looked around, felt the warm sun on his face. Summer vacation. He'd hated summer vacation. No school, all his friends – Andrew especially – too far to reach by bike, at least at this age. It took a long time for Billy to convince his Mom to let him make some trips in subsequent summers. Even so, most of his friends were off to one fabulous outdoor camp or another. Too expensive for the Watts' budget, nothing they could justify since his Mom usually stayed home during the day and only worked weekends. Most of these long, hot summers were spent with her and Monkey, watching television, waiting for his father to come home at supper for an hour or so before heading out to scoop up the evening commuters.

Maybe, God willing, he'd be allowed to stay here, in this time. Maybe he could see Dad again. At this thought he did cry, a hitching sob which caught in his throat and went no further.

Why am I here, Lord?

"Billy!"

Through the screen door his mother looked so young. Bill walked quickly to stand beside himself, no longer caring if he was seen. He shouted, *Mom! It's me! Can...* no, of course she couldn't hear him. He looked down, fought the urge to kick one of the discarded Hot Wheels with his toe. He was pouting.

Why am I here? he said.

Billy continued the battle, ignoring his mother.

Mom came out, wiping her hands on her skirt. She did that gesture a lot, usually after making lunch or dinner. There was rarely anything on her hands. The woman could pound bread dough and not make a mess.

"What's the matter, Billy," she said, kneeling beside him. "You don't feel good?" The adult Bill sat on the grass beside them. It was surreal and beautiful, seeing his mother and himself like this. A home movie to watch at last, in three dimensions.

"No, I'm OK. Just *bored!*" He said this last word with exaggerated emphasis. Mom ran her hand over his messy hair.

"I know. I talked to Andrew's mother a little while ago. She said he can come over all day tomorrow. He's still signed up for camp, but she said now and then he can come by anyway."

Billy didn't look convinced. "I don't know. That's all he talks about at school. Going to camp, going to camp. He wants to be a junior counselor in a few years. He's not going to miss one single day."

A smile, so beautiful on this otherwise tired woman's face. "Well, she said he's – what was the word – 'psyched' to be coming over tomorrow."

"Really?" His face lit up.

Bill remembered this, in pieces, like those old pictures in an album. He must be about nine or ten here. Andrew Brenner did come over, and often that summer. Billy would have gone mad with boredom otherwise.

The boy seemed happier, but his eyes remained downcast. Bill thought he knew what was coming next. It was a conversation he'd had with his mother, and sometimes his father. Too often. As if asking, again and again, would reveal some secret loophole he could take advantage of. When he heard himself say the next statement, Bill understood how painful it must have been for his mother to hear.

"I wish I had a brother or a sister. I don't mean like Monkey. I mean a real one."

Bill stared at his mother's face, watched a hundred emotions battle each other for control. She took in a breath, let it out slowly, rested her hand on the boy's head.

"I know. But you know that's not possible."

He knew it, both then and now. His mother almost died when he was born. So had he, in fact. Something wrong with the placenta during labor, undetected fibroid tumors in her uterus. Undetected, at least, until half-way through her pregnancy. For a while the doctors thought she was having twins. No twins. No brothers at all, then or ever. After delivery, when she'd stabilized enough, they performed an emergency hysterectomy. Little Billy was looked upon as a "blessing," a word he heard too often in childhood.

Billy wasn't done reaching for the ever-evasive exception to this rule of nature. Mom pursed her lips, preparing herself.

"Why can't we adopt?"

He knew the question was coming, but hearing it now, in light of all that had happened in this current nightmare, was a shock. *No*, he moaned in his private silence. *Stop. Stop, stop, stop.*

"Billy," she said, "please. Your Dad and I are talking about it, but do you know how expensive it is? We're saving up, I promise. Soon. But I can't guarantee it."

"But..."

"No, buts. Andrew's coming over tomorrow. You'll have all day to play. He can even stay for supper."

He nodded, knowing he was defeated. "OK."

She stood up. "Come in and wash your hands for lunch."

Bill stood, too, trying to focus on the scene before it was lost to him forever, but thinking about the conversations - the borderline arguments (though they never argued, only 'discussed,' a fact he was once proud of but now knew was their biggest downfall) he and Seyha would have around adoption. He'd been dumbfounded how she could be so against it, being an orphan herself. She'd tighten her lips and pull away, ending the conversations.

He took a step back, opened and closed his fists. Of course, now he knew. If she didn't want children of her own why would she consider adopting?

His younger self took longer to move into the house, never in much of a rush. His mother waited patiently, holding the screen door open. Such sadness on her face. The older Bill continued to clench his fists, open them, clench them again.

"When I'm grown," the boy said, picking up his soldiers, "I'm going to have lots of kids. Ten, maybe twenty."

Bill looked down at himself. He'd never said this aloud, did he? He thought it, often, imagining visiting this very house in an oversized van, a dozen laughing and screaming children piling out like clowns in a circus...

"...surrounding their Nana," the boy was saying, in parallel with Bill's thoughts. This part of the conversation never happened, but Bill no longer cared. He remembered. He remembered this once-private vow made to his mother. Repeating it often, until it was too late.

His mother scooping up her grandchildren, all of them, into her arms, smothering each one...

"...with kisses," the boy said, walking past his mother, the door closing behind them. Bill's feet were locked in place on the lawn.

"...having a big dinner with all of us, everyone..."

...shouting and telling jokes, even Monkey, too old to possibly still be alive by then, wagging her tail...

"...under the table." The boy's voice faded as he and his mother moved further into the small house. "I promise, Mom."

I promise.

His mother's voice, light, pretending not to be as moved as she obviously was, "That's nice, Billy. That..."

...would be so wonderful.

He was alone in the backyard. Monkey ran around the corner, realizing too late she was left behind. Bill forced himself to step forward, ripping free the imaginary roots binding him to the earth. He opened the screen door for the dog. Monkey started in, stopped then looked up at the man beside her. Her tail wagged and she leaped up, paws on Bill's chest, and gave her old "brother" a dripping lick across his face.

I love you, girl, he said. Then Monkey got down, bounded through the open door.

"*There* you are, Monkey Dog, girl!" came his own small voice inside the kitchen.

Bill let the door hiss shut. They never adopted. His

father died only a few years after this moment. Heart attack. His death laid down more of a burden on them. He had life insurance, so the mortgage was paid off. But a single parent family, with an income consisting only of what his mother could take home from her expanded hours at the *Haven Market*, wasn't the best candidate for adoption. Not that she would have had the time to raise another child.

Someday, he had promised secretly in his heart. He'd mentioned his plans, only once, to Seyha, before they were married. If she had shaken her head, said *no, bad idea, Billy boy*, would he have married her? Maybe not. Probably. It didn't matter. He had loved Seyha Watts with all of his heart. And she loved him. They would have kids. Almost succeeded, that first time early in their marriage before Seyha miscarried. Nothing after that. They tried… so many tender moments of love-making flashed through his mind, each punctuated with his wife, every day, secretly opening the dresser drawer, taking a pill, never giving their family a chance.

She did not want children.

Maybe it was something else. A possibility that she was simply reluctant to risk getting pregnant and losing another child…. She wasn't *avoiding* children, not really, only the chance of going through that same loss. Bill turned the idea over, waiting to see if it had merit. She'd been distraught when it had happened, as much as anyone would be so soon after discovering she was pregnant. Of the two of them, Bill had been more open with his disappointment. Seyha was not one to wear her hurt, or any negative emotion, long in front of anyone. Bill included.

It was possible, and hopeful. Lies born from fear, not malice. He could grab onto this like a lifeline and curb the deep ache of her deception. Either way, however, it was still that: deception.

It was too late to ever fulfill his dream for his mother, anyway. She was gone with the Lord, a year and a half now.

Bill sighed, turned and walked along the backyard, not knowing where he was going, nor caring. As he neared the edge of the property he turned back to face the house. There were no children scrambling out of any van or swarming around their Nana.

Nana was gone.

He wiped his face and sniffed.

Oh, Sey, he said. *What's wrong with us? How could you have done this without me ever knowing, whatever the reason? How could you lie to my face, every single time?*

"Hi." A girl's voice, behind him. Bill turned to see a young dark-skinned girl with tangled hair standing on a grassy stretch at the edge of the property. She wore only a wrinkled, brown skirt, looking so out of place in this middle-class neighborhood. Bill could only stare.

"Hi," he finally managed, noticing but not caring in the slightest that his voice was back. "And you are?"

"Sally." She curtsied, lifting the edge of her skirt but never taking her eyes from him. "Please to meet you!"

*   *   *

It was night. The air was warm, *summer* air with a cool breeze played across Gem's face as she stood on the back porch. She looked through the screen door back into the house. The only light came from the blue numbers of the microwave clock spilling across the darkened kitchen. Twelve forty-nine. Late. Silence. No voices, no clinking of forks on plates. Was this the same night? No. Thanksgiving would have been colder out here. She sighed, relieved to still be able to hear herself. She didn't know *when* she was. Standing on her own back porch, she still felt lost.

A new voice reached out faintly in the night air. Crying.

Gem thought of Ray Lindu in the closed church. The muscles along her back tightened. She turned slowly, even as she realized it was a girl's voice, not a man's. Gem moved to the railing and squinted - as if squinting could help in the dark – and looked for the source. Something in the backyard next door. *Of course*, she thought, *where else?*

A figure sat slumped forward in a lawn chair in the middle of the yard. The square of light cast from the basement window did not quite reach the person sitting alone in the dark. Gem started towards the back steps then caught herself and stopped. If these moments, these *scenes* were supposed to be connected in any way, they were being threaded together by a madman. Nothing good would come of any participation on her part. She would stand right here all night if she had to, on her porch, and keep her distance from the haunted house next door. She laid her hands on the peeling stairway railing.

Her hands fell to her sides. The railing was gone. The crying girl hunched forward in the lawn chair directly in front of her, between Gem and the house. Gem looked back, saw herself still standing by the railing, looking back down at her. A bizarre *déjà vu* came with the sight. Seeing herself seeing herself, seeing herself.... When Gem turned back to Rebecca Lindu, the sensation of vertigo faded - best to keep her eyes away from the porch.

This *was* Rebecca, younger than the last time Gem had seen her in the neighborhood. Not much older than her own age, now. It was odd, realizing that the six years between them no longer mattered.

Rebecca didn't notice she had company. Gem never called her Bec, like her mother always did. The name never seemed to fit, even punked-out as she usually was these days. She wasn't, right now. As best Gem could tell in the dark, the girl was wearing plain blue pajamas. Feet bare on the grass, wet with dew which had soaked through her own, hapless socks.

"Hey," Gem whispered. She risked a glance back, saw herself still standing on the porch. *That* Gem looked different suddenly, younger. Had this actually happened? Had she come outside one night and seen someone sitting here? Maybe. It rang familiar, but Gem didn't trust the feeling. She turned back. Rebecca lifted her face from her hands and stared silently, her expression unreadable, vague in the dark shadow of the house and strings of black hair drifting over her eyes. The single light from the lone cellar window gave the girl a halo around her edges.

She continued staring, not speaking. Gem cleared her throat, whispered, "You OK?"

Rebecca shook her head, lowered her face once more into her hands. From somewhere in the house, a woman screamed.

Gem looked up, expecting Seyha Watts to charge around the corner in a rage. That's what the scream was, one of *anger*, not fear. More shouting, a man's voice, barely audible under the furious volume of the woman's scream.

"What's going on?"

"Nothing," Rebecca said through her fingers. "Everything. The end. I've ruined everything. I just want to die."

More shouts, the woman still screaming, still a rage but something else added, something bothersome to hear, though Gem couldn't exactly decide what it was. The man's voice returned, louder. Gem didn't have to wonder whom the voices belonged to. She gave Rebecca a final cursory glance then stepped across the wet grass towards the basement window. This had been her entrance and exit from the empty house every time she'd visited, once upon a time. The window never locked right, allowing Gem to raise it up with only a jiggle of the frame. Now, in this dream or vision, she was here again. She knelt down in the damp grass and looked into the basement, then quickly turned away, focusing on the ground directly below the window, not wanting to process what she'd just seen inside. The last time she came here, the night of the deconsecration, she'd knelt in this same spot, in the snow, staring longingly into the empty church hall with its long tables covered with snacks and coffee urns, waiting for the crowd upstairs to file down for a goodbye bash. No snow this time. Nor was the room beyond the glass empty.

The figures moving inside demanded her reluctant attention again. It was Joyce and Ray Lindu. Gem stared, struggling to find a place in her brain for what she was seeing. At first her face flushed and she cringed in embarrassment, but she was frozen, staring, then slowly understood the truth of what was happening.

"Oh, my God," she whispered. "Joyce?"

She narrowed her eyes, felt her heart already racing in a chaotic jumble of fear and anger, forcing herself to wait a few more seconds to be sure she was seeing what she thought she was seeing. Finally, she grabbed the window sash, jiggled it loose and raised it up. Sticking her head inside, she screamed, "Joyce!"

*　　*　　*

Seyha stood in the aisle, beside the first of only three short pews. Sister Angelique knelt in whispered prayer before the small sanctuary, long blond hair falling behind her. The windows were dark, reflecting the dozen fingers of candle flame glowing from their votive glasses. Aside from these, the sanctuary was simply an empty corner of the building. Seyha assumed the dented folding table, which normally served as an altar, must still be outside. Everything in the orphanage had multiple uses. There were no children sleeping along the floor at the moment, though the darkness outside implied a late hour. She'd forgotten many things about this place.

A large, rough crucifix hung on the wall above the nun. *Crucifix* was a loose term. The dying Jesus consisted of uneven paint strokes along the wood rather than a carved statuette nailed in place. Seyha found herself staring at the macabre artwork, remembering how it frightened her as a child. The eyes, slits of pain drawn with two loose whisks of the unknown artist's brush, stared down at her. Seeing it through adult eyes, Seyha realized she had every right to be frightened of the Jesus who watched them through this brushstroke agony. More threat than comfort in that face.

Sister Angelique continued whispering her vigil. Not knowing what else to do, Seyha stepped around the front pew then stopped, not wanting to close the remaining few feet to this woman who'd taken care of her for so long.

The nun stopped whispering, raised her head. "Pray with me, Doung Seyha." She then lowered her lips to the tips of her fingers, hands pressed together and the whispered breathing resumed.

Seyha did not want to pray. Pray to whom? The madman who'd abducted her inside their home, dragged her through this parade of torture and death? She'd been happy in her life with Bill, content to forget all of this. If God was love, why did he cause so much pain? Why did he let her family die? Why couldn't he leave her alone?

"So many questions," Angelique whispered.

The heat simmering inside her now spread through Seyha's arms and chest, twisted in her throat until the words it formed could not be contained. She gripped the side of the pew. The sacredness of this place, the darkened illusion of night and penitent flickering of candles restrained her voice to the nun's whispered volume, but the words themselves would not be held captive.

"You pray to a monster," she hissed. "You kneel and beg for succor, for.. for… love, from someone or some*thing* that cares nothing for you or these children. We're chess pieces crying and wailing while someone shoves us around the game board."

Surprisingly, the other woman smiled, almost laughed. She pressed her long calloused fingers tighter to her mouth. Through these fingers Angelique said, "So poetic, my little Seyha. Who was it that said suffering and anguish were fuel for the artist's heart?"

Seyha stepped forward and loomed over the woman. "I was fine, we were fine, before this, this..." she jerked her right arm around her, "... this *lunacy*. This evil game God's playing with us. That's not a God I will ever pray to."

Another quiet smile behind the fingers. "You were fine," Angelique said. It was not a question but a statement, an echo of her own hollow words. The nun slowly lowered her hands and got stiffly to her feet. Her face, its beauty accentuated by the soft red light of the votives, remained calm. Her blue eyes, their color washed to a pale hazel in the light, stared intently into Seyha's. "We both know, Doung Seyha, that you are not fine. You never have been."

She shouted, "Stop calling me that!" For a moment she feared waking the other children, then remembered they were not here. No rain-patter of breathing or small bodies hissing restlessly on their mats. They were alone.

Angelique put a long-fingered hand on Seyha's shoulder. She was not smiling, but the infuriating calm remained. "Seyha Watts, then," she said. She nodded to the place Seyha had been looking. "We have a new building, across the way. The dormitory is small, but compared to how crowded we'd been in this chapel, it's a *palace*. God provides."

"God kills. He could have saved my family!" When a tear fell down her face she hated herself for it. It wasn't real. *None* of this was. She knocked the woman's hand away. Angelique let the arm drop but her eyes never lost their intensity.

"God lets us choose whom we serve. Darkness or Light. Those who choose darkness hate those in the light. They are lost without the truth – truth which is both good and bad."

Seyha leaned closer. "That means nothing." Angelique allowed the advance, showed no fear.

"It means everything. It's not His job to make sure every person lives to be a hundred years old. We all die, when our time comes. This world is broken. Old age, fire, flood, bullets or simply *hate* may one day end our time here. The enemy's goal is to focus your heart only on its evil." She leaned closer. Seyha could smell the lingering spice from dinner on her breath. "You have to look past the hurt, past this *life*. Lies are fought only with truth. Lies always burn away in light."

Seyha leaned back and wrapped her arms around herself. She said, quieter only because of their proximity, "If this is the truth, I'll take the lies."

She saw Angelique's hand rush up a half-second before it landed, softly, on her cheek. Seyha winced reflexively. Only a rough, warm palm on her face. A paradox of speed and loving touch. Seyha had not practiced such restraint with Bill earlier. As with everything else lately, the memory of that slap spawned more self-loathing.

Angelique said, "You don't understand what's been happening, Seyha, do you?"

Seyha ground her teeth hard together. Her anger was

becoming saturated with some new, weaker emotion. Sorrow, so heavy and deep she wanted to scream. The woman's hand seemed to hold these emotions in check. For the moment. But she would not cry, would not break down.

The nun continued, "You're heart is hard. You've seen terrible things."

I will not listen. I will not let her manipulate me.

"But you've been given a blessing."

She wanted to run away, but the hand on her cheek... the hand...

"In a way, you could have rebuilt your family. Honored the one that had been lost to such evil, rebuilt it from ashes into new life."

Seyha closed her eyes. She needed to run but where was she going to go? There was nowhere, nowhere to run.

"You've dishonored your family," the hand pressed harder, fingers curling on her cheek, "dishonored your husband and the gift you'd been given," the fingers stretched and wrapped around the back of Seyha's head.

She summoned whatever anger remained and shot her arm up, knocking the woman's away again. She shouted something nonsensical and turned around, intending to run around the pews, hide as she had hidden as a child, until God or Satan gave up and sent her home. Her feet were leaden. Every step took more strength than she had left.

The voice behind her was sharper, harsher. "You do not even realize what I am, Doung Seyha Watts!" She was close. Seyha forced another step, then another. The corner of the pew looked a hundred miles away. She no longer cared where she would go, only *away, away.*

"Dark versus light. *Ruin* masked as blessing, joys of heaven disguised as pain by those trapped with you in the dark...."

Seyha fell to her knees, tried to crawl. Her hands were weighted, drawn into the floorboards. The woman's hoarse shouts crashed over her.

"...it can be joy, in this world and the next. Joy in acceptance of who you are and where you came from. Lies are nothing but *shit* flung into the face of God!"

"Get away from me! Get away from me!" Dozens of hands grabbed her head and arms, some painfully, pulling her in opposite directions. Nails and claws, digging into her skin. Wolves attacking, tearing her apart. Seyha screamed. They did not go away.

The nun was screaming now, fighting for Seyha's attention over a myriad of other voices joining in the chorus. Laughter, mutterings, giggled words, venomous accusations spit into her ear. Seyha knew she could go nowhere and be safe. More pinching and tearing of her skin, pulling it loose, flesh peeled from the bone. The nun's voice was a mixture of Angelique's and the demon of earlier, their combined weight on her back, pressing down.

"Even what you have done to your husband is not as terrible as the lies, the dishonor you have heaped on the pile of trash inside you. You are dying, Doung Seyha Watts!"

"Please..." she was crying, eyes squeezed closed, no longer trying to crawl, no longer caring that her arms and legs were only strips of muscle, her body a savage banquet. She sagged against the floor, then into it, then through it....

"If you will not take your medicine then it will be shoved down your throat." She grabbed Seyha's hair and pulled her head back, drawing her slowly back onto her knees using only the sheer pain of it. "Open your eyes!" The pain burned through her skull. She couldn't have opened her eyes if she wanted to. And she did *not* want to. She was being torn apart, devoured. To look would be to see her own death, bloody pieces of her body in the mouths of the wolves. It was too late for her, too late for anything except to die.

"Open..." the pain in her head exploded, "...your..." Seyha opened her mouth to scream, "...eyes!"

She did. Saw Bill's face staring at her across the living room from the same spot he'd been when the darkness had fallen over them. Her case of birth control pills was still held in his open palm, but he didn't seem to notice. His eyes were not quite focused on anything, lips moving as if in prayer.

She needed to go to him, fall to the floor and take the man she loved in her arms and tell him it was going to be all right. Everything was going to be all right.

He focused more intently on her and his lips pressed together. All of a sudden Seyha did not want to move, afraid of that stare. She knew what it meant. It was over, because now he knew everything.

*   *   *

Bill walked to the edge of the low concrete wall bordering the property of his boyhood home. Below him, the girl, Sally, stood on the narrow stretch of grass running between the base of the wall and the street.

She had just finished bowing in a child's curtsey, pulling one leg behind her like a dancer acknowledging the crowd. Bill was too tired to wonder what any of this meant or who she was supposed to be.

All he could offer her was an irritable "What?"

She stepped forward and scrambled up the wall, careful not to scratch her bare legs on the weather-worn concrete. At some point in the act of climbing, however, her outfit changed. The worn skirt became a pair of jeans and she now wore a light pink blouse, sleeveless and adorned with the logo of a fashion store Bill recognized but had never been inside of. Face scrubbed clean, hair showered, her skin wasn't as dark as he'd imagined a moment before, more olive. Asian, or something Mediterranean. These days, probably a blend of both. She looked older, too, or simply appeared that way with the new clothes and cleanup. A teenager, an age where the world before her was wide open with sunlight and possibility.

Standing straighter, she pulled a loose strand of dark hair from her face. The gesture was familiar. "Are you ok?" she asked him. No guile in the question, only a soft look and tone that was sincere, maybe a little concerned.

"Oh, please…" Bill said, not quite shouting the words but coming close, and turned away, walked a few paces away from… whatever this was. Still standing on the top of the wall, he stared up the road, wondering if any other humans existed in this place. Was this world real, or an illusion shoved into his mind only to be erased and redrawn at the whim of some celestial hand?

He waited. Nothing spoken from the girl behind him; no sudden touch of her hand. The constant background noise had probably been culled from years of ignored memories: hissing traffic, highway motorists wandering back and forth in the distance, random twitter of birds in the two maple trees rising from his yard. He thought about Gem's theory, that they had died when the world fell into darkness and were lost in some frozen limbo, maybe hell itself, fated to relive moments of their past again and again. No answers, only more questions. As he stood now in his old backyard, Seyha's case of pills in his pocket, Bill felt too drained and confused to be certain Gem had been wrong.

He finally turned around, bored with the waiting and with his own thoughts, finding solace in neither. The girl hadn't moved from her new position on top of the wall. She stared at him with the barest hint of a smile.

If nothing else, this new encounter might prove to be a distraction from the weight of realizing his family had been stolen from him. It was enough of a curiosity to bring him a few paces closer to her and ask, "Who are you, really?"

She looked down and away for a moment, considering the question, as if she did not *already* know what he would ask and have an answer ready. She looked up, more with her eyes than head, which still tilted towards the street below - both a shy and *sly* look. She reminded him of Seyha when she did that.

His stomach suddenly twisted.

"I'm nobody," she said then lifted her head, dissipating the image. "Just a secret. An unknown casualty of a mental war fought for decades."

Bill waited a beat, trying to ignore the rising fear in his gut, the certainty... but it could not be true. None of it could be. He cleared his throat, said, "What war?"

Sally was still offering that faint mist of a grin that nevertheless illuminated her face, and walked a step along the wall toward him. "Some wars are fought by just one person. Some are waged by millions in a world you can't see. Not yet, at least. Me," she put a long, thin hand over her chest, "I suppose I'm a victim of both." When Bill did not respond, she looked directly into his face, her own a mix of Seyha's and his... not Mediterranean, but a mix of Cambodian and his own, European-American genes. She continued, "You are a victim of these same wars."

His mind raced again through images of the pills, the scene at the church the day she taught in the kids' room, dinner at the restaurant after her miscarriage.

Bill opened his mouth, closed it, trying *not* to understand what she girl was saying because it took all of his remaining mental energy to stop the flood of images and conclusions and fears from driving him insane. From killing the last shreds of his love.

He put a hand on his stomach, reacting to the burning that grew worse with each image in his mind. He needed to go to the bathroom, needed to stop thinking.

Only a few minutes ago, he'd come to the conclusion, or hope, that Seyha might have only been afraid of the next pregnancy ending up like the first. Afraid of going through that pain again.

A consideration even now he dared not flick away too rashly. It *was* a lifeline. A desperate reach at something to cling to against what the truth might *really* be. The miscarriage....

Bill knew who this person was, knew what he was looking at... what was so patiently, gently staring back at him.

"Staring you in the face," the teenaged girl whispered.

His daughter.

The new smile that curved up along Sally's lips was slow and joyous even as her eyes fell with such sadness.

He had no daughter. When Seyha miscarried, they did not know what the sex was. It was too early in the first trimester.

No. She was simply afraid of going through that again. Starting taking pills, kept it a secret.

Afraid of becoming pregnant. Afraid of *ever* becoming pregnant.

She had miscarried.

His daughter's expression was soft and wide, one of love, true love, no judgment, some sorrow, too...

"No," he said.

...and pity. She began a slow, barely discernable shaking of her head. Denying his denial.

"She had a miscarriage."

She said nothing.

"Didn't she?" His question was a whisper that shouted in this abandoned place.

Her head stopped. Nothing to acknowledge or deny.

Seyha had been pregnant, but could not handle the idea of children.

She'd ended her pregnancy, and only *told* him she had miscarried.

"No."

Got a prescription and for the past nine years pretended she wanted exactly what Bill did. While they both moved along in life, disappointment returning every month when her period came, a little less each time, replaced by acceptance.

He barely said, "…can't be…."

His failed attempts at the "adoption" conversation, never understanding her reluctance, never pushing.

Never letting himself see.

Bill tried to talk, to argue against it. But he could not, because there was no argument.

His hand was open. The round plastic case was there, as it had been when the darkness engulfed them. He looked up and saw Seyha slumped prone on all fours on the living room carpet below the windows, the expression on her face almost feral.

He closed his fist around the case of pills.

Realizing where she was, and looking into Bill's eyes, Seyha's expression first changed to unblemished terror, locked in his stare. Then she sat back on her haunches, took in a long breath before letting it out and visibly calming. She never looked away as he walked towards her.

* * *

Joyce Lindu stood framed by the doorway to her daughter's bedroom, still unable to speak. Rebecca, holding the pajama top against her, sniffed loudly and said, "I'm sorry." She looked away, into the gloom of her bedroom. Her outline shook against the weak light. "It was my fault," she added, her voice wet and barely audible. "I'm sorry."

Now, as when this night happened, her daughter's words broke the paralysis holding Joyce in place. *My fault.* Hearing Bec take the blame for the actions of the monster Ray had become over the past few years was too much. Too much to accept, too much to hear. The room got darker. Joyce's eyes had closed to mere slits. Still not in control of her body, but somehow eager to follow it, even now, she felt herself turn away, back into the small kitchenette. Felt her thoughts as rocks falling to the bottom of a river. *Ray's fault. His fault. No more. No more.* Her hand on the handle of the knife, the largest, pulled it free. As she turned, Joyce heard the back door open but knew instinctively it had been Bec running outside. She knew where Ray had gone, where he always went to escape whatever emotional fire he'd set in the house. Not out to some bar like other beasts might go. Ray didn't have that much imagination, or energy. Downstairs, to the basement. He'd hunt through the small fridge they kept for parish supplies and forage like a raccoon through leftovers from the last church function. To him, leaving the house completely would be like admitting guilt, whatever he'd done.

Whatever he'd done. More rocks settling on the riverbed. *Too much. Has to stop.* When her thoughts turned towards Rebecca the confusion and hurt quickly pushed them away. Her daughter was only that, her daughter, someone to protect from the circling wolves. Joyce moved quietly but deliberately past the church pews, towards the main doors. The knife in her hand had no weight. Its smooth white handle was slick with sweat. She wiped her left hand against her bathrobe and moved the knife to it. She wiped the right in a similar fashion then opened the basement door, stepped downstairs, moved the knife back to the original hand.

Ray stood at the far end of the large basement room, leaning against the L-shaped counter which functioned as a serving space and delineated the kitchen's work area. He wore jeans, no socks and a white T-shirt with the cartoon character *Calvin* peeing against a truck tire. One of the many items no one in the congregation would ever suspect him of owning. She hated that shirt. She hated him.

Joyce didn't bother to hide the knife hanging tight-armed at her side as she crossed the room. In this moment, she did not feel like the helpless passenger she had been since the Darkness took over the house. She remembered this night, relived it almost every day, working always to change the events to something less terrible, knowing the exercise did nothing to change them. The memories had come a little less frequently lately, with a little less pain since time had a way of collecting other distractions and recriminations. Now, however, it was here again, actually *happening* again. All Joyce wanted to do was –

"Come to kill me, have you?" Ray said. When she first stepped into view she could see his face set, ready to deny everything, blame Bec or even Joyce herself, ready to look angry and hurt. It hadn't taken long to notice what she was holding. Now he stood straighter, defiant. He didn't believe she would do it, didn't imagine she had that much hate inside her.

Joyce didn't answer, only continued forward, faster, until there was an arm's length between them. Ray smirked, folded his large arms across his chest. "You don't really think – "

No, she realized now, *I hadn't thought.* Only acted. The scream which had been building inside her on the walk across the room found release at the same moment her arm shot up, shoving the blade under his folded arms. It slid smoothly into the flesh just under the ribcage. His arms shot out to his sides as if suddenly electrocuted. Eyes widened. She pulled the blade out, never looking away from his wide, stunned expression, even as his face folded in sudden pain at the knife's withdrawal, even as his eyes widened again in fear at what was actually happening. Something hot sprayed across Joyce's arm. She shoved the blade in again, then up. It hit something unyielding then scraped across it, the sound like fingernails on an underwater blackboard. Ray pressed himself back against the counter. His arms flailed, grabbing at her arms, her wrist, eyes still squeezed closed in agony. She turned and twisted the blade against the rib until it found another fleshy spot beneath, then pushed it all the way in again. All the while she continued screaming, shouting words which made no sense, spitting out every drop of hatred she tried so long to control.

Ray opened his eyes, slid down against the wall, pulling the knife and Joyce to the floor with him. She followed, never letting go, until she knelt before him. She fell silent, arm shaking, the blade vibrating against bone. Sitting on the floor, Ray looked at her, then smiled.

Blood poured over his bottom lip. Twin streams joined it from his nostrils. A small, struggling part of Joyce's brain tried to regain a thread of rational thought, insisted that this should not be happening.

Everything that had come before was painfully familiar, until now.

The smiling Ray struggled without any real vigor, as if play-acting for her benefit. His shoulders sagged, eyes still open but losing focus. The blood which had been pouring from his chest, soaking into his shirt and Joyce's robe, stopped flowing except what spilled from the entry wounds from simple gravity.

Joyce did not move. She waited to see what would happen next. What she would *do* next. None of this felt right. None of this gave her any satisfaction. It should have.

The dead Ray turned its head towards her, eyes still glazed and unseeing, and said, "I wonder why that is, Joyce, hmm?" A final pulse of blood dripped over his lip. He swallowed the rest. Joyce breathed in deeply and tried to back away, but Ray's hand grabbed her wrist and pressed the blade deeper into his chest. "This is what you wanted, wasn't it? This is what you dreamed of." He was looking sharply into her eyes now, fully conscious and alive. He forced her hand sideways, twisting the handle. He gave an *Oh* of pain that pulled his face sideways. "And," he gasped, "it became more than that. Self-delusion first, history later. Such is..." another twist, "our lot in life. Now you have your wish."

Joyce was shaking from a cold she didn't feel. Her voice was frightened and pathetically weak. "You're dead." She knew it wasn't true. She wanted it to be true, had almost made it so. He *should* be dead. This scene had played out so many times in her mind, the alternative to what actually did occur.

He stopped the pained act and looked at her blankly, no expression except a trace of tired impatience. "You wanted *this*," another quick jerk of her hand, "so much. So much easier to remember, that you murdered me, instead of... well, now, let's just replay this whole charade and see what *really* happened."

Again Joyce tried to pull away. The room dropped away, fell into a hole. No, she realized, they were both standing again.

Ray no longer had blood on his shirt. No blood *anywhere*. The tip of the blade was an inch from his chest, below one lone arm still crossed over his cartoon shirt. The other, his left, held her wrist. She had hesitated a second before thrusting the knife forward. Long enough for him to react. His grip tightened.

"I have to admit, Joyce," he said, voice deeper, gravelly, not coming from his mouth but playing from every corner of the room, "I didn't think you had it in you. I almost let you do it, too." He twisted his grip, pulling the knife up. The pain felt like cold metal shoved into her arm from elbow to shoulder.

This, now, was familiar. She cried out in pain, opened her hand, let the knife drop. She heard it clang to the floor. Ray stepped forward, his breath across her face. "You were going to kill me like a dog."

"You *are* a dog!" she cried, then and now.

He swung his free arm and hit her across the cheek with his palm. Everything flashed and went dark. Joyce came to her senses kneeling on all fours on the floor, facing away from Ray, back towards the steps leading into the church.

This is what happened, she remembered, trying to forget it all over again.

"Who's the dog now?" the demon shouted behind her. The sash of her bathrobe pulled free, but not before the knot first punched into her stomach as Ray yanked it upward from behind. It released with a hot zip of friction along her waist. She tried to crawl away, but he had a grip on the back of her robe.

"Bad dog," his voice whispered, husky, as if struggling

to breath.

She didn't turn around, knowing from the sounds of his belt what he was doing with his free hand. Her robe hung loose around her. She remembered the knife just before Ray kicked it across the floor. She watched it stop, spin a half turn, then the robe was pulled up and over her back. "I am your husband," he growled, pressing himself hard against her. She clenched her fists, stared at a broken piece of tile on the floor halfway across the room. It was too much even to see that so she closed her eyes, tried again to crawl away but her arms were caught tight in the robe which in turn was held tightly in his grip. She pretended he was her husband, the one she used to know, fought to imagine a happy moment from the past, something to get her though what was happening as he moved awkwardly but insistently against her. Because she was dry it hurt too much to ignore - to ignore the feeling that she was being turned inside out. Joyce screamed inside her mind, unable to let the sound free. She tried to separate herself from this frightened cow crouched on the floor, rip herself free of the flesh like she'd been able to do in the surreal church scene earlier. She could get the knife this time, kill Ray for real, kill him and defend the honor of the pathetic woman who gave up and did not do it herself. Joyce was not the same person now. Not anymore. Not *ever*. She had not given in like this. She didn't let him... not after what he'd....

She heard her other self sobbing and thinking, *I did not give in to this, I killed him, he's dead, this is a bad dream,* he *is a bad dream, he is dead. He is gone, I am weak. I protected my daughter I protected myself. I did not let him....*

She was trapped, feeling Ray, hearing her thoughts trying to blanket her mind from him, trying to change the world she was trapped in. Bec would be safe. Joyce screamed from her prison in the woman's mind, resigned to having to suffer through this moment as an outsider looking in.

Ray finished quickly, and pushed her forward. She sprawled on the floor, curled her legs up defensively. The pain was so intense, even now.

"Joyce!"

He'd left that night, packed random clothes, drove off and never came back. At least not while she or Bec were home. If he returned at all he would have found nothing left of his existence, everything bagged and trashed. His absence had become the only positive outcome from that night. Neither she nor Bec ever spoke about him again, at least to each other. In every way he really *was* dead to both of them.

"Joyce!" Gem's voice again.

She opened her eyes, curling tighter in a half circle, steeling herself to see Ray's face grimacing down at her, sated, victorious. But he was gone. Like a wounded deer on the side of the road she watched Gem run towards her, head turning side to side as if Ray had just vanished in thin air.

He probably had. This was a dream, after all.

"Joyce, what the hell was that? Where'd he go?"

The girl's face had an confused mixture of horror and rage. Joyce let herself be scooped up and tried to pull down the robe but now she was again wearing the outfit she'd worn to the Watts' house, a hundred years ago.

Gem said nothing else, only held her tighter. Joyce leaned against the girl, unable to summon the strength to sit up straight. The room melted away. Behind the basement waited the Watt's shiny white living room.

The kitchen wall was just as dark, as *gone*, as she remembered in those final moments before being snatched away. She couldn't talk or cry. She didn't want to do anything. Too much thinking had already been done, too little accomplished.

Before she could close her eyes and let the Darkness take her away for good, Bill Watts was suddenly standing on the floor a few feet away from them. Long streaks of tears lined his cheeks. He said nothing, not at first, only stared past the two of them towards the windows. His right hand was open, something plastic held in his palm.

He whispered something Joyce didn't understand, then after a few more seconds of his unwavering stare, a look that could have been sorrow, rage or relief, he stepped forward. Joyce turned her head to follow his gaze. Seyha knelt on the rug not far behind them, staring calmly back at her husband.

Third Night of Darkness

Seyha absently touched the back of her head to be sure no hair had been yanked from her scalp. The memory of the pain fell away, overshadowed by the end of her world walking towards her across the living room.

Joyce noted Seyha's presence only with a tired stare, before shuddering and wrapping her arms around herself. Gem's arms were also around her in a loose hug. "Thank you, Gem," she whispered. "I'm OK."

"I doubt you're OK," Gem said, "but..." She finally noticed Bill as he walked past her.

Seyha didn't have time for them. She couldn't let it happen like this. Sister Angelique told her she had a chance. Maybe she did. He was standing in front of her now.

Around them, the house renewed its creaking and moaning.

She stared at his open hand and the plastic case, before forcing herself to look up into his face. The face of the man she had married and to whom she'd promised love and devotion before God. She barely recognized him, so tightly twisted was his rage. He looked away for a moment, down at the pills in his hand. His expression oscillated through a dozen masks battling for control - anger, pain, disbelief - eyes puffed and squinting. He looked insane like this. Maybe he was. Driven mad, because of her.

He'd found the pills before the darkness came back, but even then hadn't looked this crazed.

What had he just seen? But she knew.

"How…. Why did…" He licked his lips between attempts. She barely heard him over the increasing turbulence in the walls and ceiling. The sound was probably only in her head, nothing but her blood racing to her brain.

He lifted his hand and tossed the pill case at her. The throw was awkward. It landed beside her. Distracted, Seyha didn't noticed him reaching down until her blouse was bunched into his fists and she was raised to her feet. His cheeks were red, pupils shaking, unsteady. She'd broken him. Seyha wanted to close her eyes when he killed her, but would not hide from it. He deserved that much.

Bill screamed the words, "How could you do that? Lie to me, take those pills and never tell me? Abort our child and pretend…." He got no further. Maybe speaking the words finally made it real to him. He shook her back and forth, ripping the blouse somewhere under her right armpit. He screamed, a long, raging howl into her face. Seyha's body was paralyzed with indecision and an odd, calm acceptance.

Beyond him, the far wall splintered. White dust sprayed from the crevice. A long, lightening-fracture raced along the ceiling towards them then split at the center of the room to continue into each corner. Directly above them, the living room ceiling bowed down, cracking, showering them with dust and plaster. Bill's eyes never left hers. He didn't notice what was happening, though he had finally stopped shaking her. He yelled something else Seyha could not understand. Maybe it was nonsense, or more of the same: more truth, lashed across her face in these final moments of life. Like the scene in the bathroom, his rage, finally released, was coming to life and tearing apart everything they'd built together.

More cracks in the ceiling and traveling down the walls around them. Joyce tried to wedge herself between her and

Bill, shouting for him to let go. He pushed her back with his shoulder, focused on Seyha again, but the moment had been broken. He tightened his grip on her shirt then tossed her aside with a grunt. She fell limply to the floor, rolled away, waiting for his shoe to kick into her ribs. It didn't come. Joyce stood in front of him, arms raised but always looking around at the crumbling house.

"Bill, look! Not now, whatever it is…"

Something massive retched behind Seyha. Still crouched on the rug, she turned in time to see the entrance to the hallway bend and buckle under the weight of an ink-black flood. The darkness reared back like a horse as it reached an invisible dam at the entrance to the dining area. When the flood rose up along the walls and ceiling of the hallway the wood and plaster there cracked and broke apart. From these cracks more darkness flowed, filling the entrance, devouring their home but still held back from the main part of the house even as the ceiling and walls everywhere continued to bulge and splinter.

"I'm sorry," Seyha whispered towards the scene. The light fixture above the dining table broke loose and crashed down. A shard of glass flitted free and bounced off the top of her head.

Someone grabbed the back of her shirt and pulled backward. Seyha obediently rose to her feet and turned, noting without emotion the remainder of the hallway collapse on itself, crushed underfoot by a monster stomping on the roof.

When Seyha realized that it was Gem holding her, she screamed and shoved the girl backwards.

*   *   *

Gem wasn't ready for that. The back of her legs hit the living room chair and she was suddenly sitting sideways in the cushions.

Seyha stood above her shouting, "Don't touch me!" Her eyes were wide. She'd finally gone nuts, apparently. Gem only had time to wonder how much of Bill's accusations were true when the house began to shake. She managed to half-fall out of the chair and get to her feet in time to see the kitchen wall collapse. Large, jagged chunks of it fell and were swallowed up in the black flow breaking free of its prison. The darkness moved out from the kitchen and hallway like magma.

Gem raised her arms to keep her balance as the floor slanted sideways, first left then right. Joyce lost her grip on the sleeve of Bill's shirt. He pulled free, taking a few steps towards the approaching flood before crumpling in a heap on the carpet beside a fallen dining room chair.

Mrs. Watts stepped over to her husband and knelt in front of him. Bill looked up at her, shouting something Gem couldn't hear. His wife's pleas were washed away in the roar of the collapsing house. The high-beamed ceiling over the dining room table, only a couple of feet away from them, groaned and bulged on one side, hanging like a balloon filling to the bursting point. Gem raised her arms to the side of her head, not wanting to –

"Gem!" Joyce's voice, then her hands, pulled her towards the center of the living room.

Gem shouted, "Don't leave me!" She spun in a half-circle to maintain her footing and grab hold of her.

Every window shattered. The sound was of a million people screaming. Blackness poured unfettered from outside, slowly like molasses down the walls and across the floor. Gem looked past Joyce's shoulder to see the Watts shouting at each other, oblivious to their own impending destruction. The ceiling over the dining room table finally burst and drowned that section of room, and the Watts, in black. She screamed, unable to hear herself. Joyce wrapped both arms tightly around her.

The ceiling above *them* now groaned as it had done over the dining room. Both women looked up as it tore open. A waterfall of darkness rained down.

Gem closed her eyes, feeling Joyce covering her as much as possible. The darkness washed over them with a roar, burying Joyce's scream, Gem's scream, the snapping and crushing of the house. The darkness *removed* her. Everything was erased. Everything was lost.

Light exploded into their world so brightly it burned through Gem's closed lids. She continued screaming, pressing against Joyce's chest, waiting for the flames to peel her skin away. In her ear, Joyce shouted prayers. Her lips moved against Gem's head with every word. Trembling, holding her tighter. The light was so bright....

Joyce's trembling stopped.

Gem felt the light, its heat on her back. It didn't get any hotter. It *would*, though. She knew it would, and the last thing she wanted to do was open her eyes and see it happen.

"Gem?" Joyce whispered. She felt the woman's chin move to the top of her head as she looked around. When she said her name again, her tone was more awe-struck than panicked. "Gem..."

Gem peeked. The room was flooded with daylight. She squinted against the glare streaming through the living room windows.

Into the Light

Eliot Davidson whooped with delight as his friend Carl caught the football with a desperate, backward dive. Carl hit the ground, did a perfect roll and stood, ball raised triumphantly. He didn't notice the grass-stained scrape along his right arm, and Eliot wasn't going to tell him. Not after such an incredible catch. It wasn't like there was any blood or anything.

The windows of the Watts' house flickered. Eliot looked right but saw nothing different. Maybe someone closed the shades for a second. He looked away. Didn't want it to look like he was spying. His buddy's return toss was too wide to catch. Eliot could have made a diving attempt of his own, but remembered Carl's arm. The ball hit the ground and bounced into his own yard. Eliot scrambled after it, wishing Gem would get her butt outside so he could ask her how the house looked. Besides, the first kick-off of the pre-season was going to happen in less than ten minutes.

*   *   *

They held each other close, breathing hard. Joyce's heart hammered so wildly she worried it wasn't going to slow down. She took a deep breath, felt Gem move with it. Slowly, deliberately, she let the air out.

Daylight outside, shining with such intensity she wanted to kiss the windows. She watched Gem's brother laugh and stagger back to his spot beside the house.

Gem's brother....

"Gem," she whispered again. This time the girl moved away, just a little, not letting go completely. She looked over at Bill and Seyha Watts. They knelt on the floor where they'd been before the darkness washed over them. Bill was staring at the floor. Had he even noticed what happened? Seyha, like Joyce and Gem, looked around at the kitchen, the dining table, the ceiling. Nothing broken. Everything gloriously illuminated by the sun and the colors cast through the alternating stained glass.

With a thick voice Gem finally answered. "What?"

Joyce released one arm from around her and pointed to the window. The arm felt heavy, like it was asleep. "Your brother's still outside...?"

Gem turned, but the boy twisted into a myriad of colored shapes as he moved in front of the stained glass. Then he ran backwards to make a new catch and tripped, landing only inches from the road.

Gem had been turning, following his progress. She backed into Joyce but said nothing.

Joyce put a hand on the girl's shoulder and forced her attention back to the Watts. Bill wiped his face with the back of one arm, finally looking at his surroundings. Now it was Seyha's turn to stare down at a spot in front of her knees. What had she done, Joyce wondered? Bill had screamed something earlier but Joyce was too dazed to understand what he'd said. What had he seen that so destroyed him now?

Bill looked at his wife. A renewed sobbing started but he cleared his throat and said, "How could you have done something so... so... without talking to me?"

He gripped the arm of the dining room chair beside him, began to pull himself up. He didn't have the energy to rise all the way, only lean against it. Joyce didn't understand what he was saying, but didn't think it was time to get involved in the discussion. Not yet, at least.

She *wanted* to get the hell out of this house, so much so that she almost grabbed Gem's hand and ran for the door.

Instead, she took a deep breath in through her nose and closed her eyes, forced herself to be patient, to wait, let the air out past trembling lips. The sudden darkness behind her lids was too frightening. She opened them again and looked outside at the beautiful day.

* * *

Seyha stared at the floor. She did not reply to Bill's question. Now and then a shiver ran through her, sometimes so violent she feared having a seizure. The room was bright. Daylight. There were shadows again, reaching under the windows and across the floor. Bill's shadow touched her right knee.

The nightmare was over. At least for Joyce and Gem. Seyha wished they would leave so Bill could kill her and end this misery. She hitched back a sob. She would not cry. She deserved no pity and wanted none.

"Seyha!" Bill snapped. "Look at me!" She did. He looked away, squinted up at Joyce through his tears. "Do you know what this... this...." He stopped, half-forming the next word. Sister Angelique's statement came back to her. *You don't understand what's been happening....*

She understood now. Her life, *their* life, had been a fabrication. A lie she tried to protect with so much wasted energy. Now Bill hated her and she deserved it. He reached out, grabbed her wrist and squeezed. Seyha looked into his eyes, afraid to see the disgust burning across his face but willing herself not to turn away from it.

He said, "Why?"

Answer him, she thought. *Even if you don't* know *the answer completely.*

His hand shook as the grip on her wrist tightened. He wanted to hurt her, but his fingers relaxed, slid away – never to touch her again, she knew.

We both know, Doung Seyha, Angelique had said, *that you are not fine. That you never have been fine.*

Bill fell back on his haunches, mouth open either to speak or scream, then simply crawled away in a lopsided crabwalk, so desperately he wanted to get away from her.

"I'm sorry," she said at last. "I was afraid...."

He mouthed the word, *afraid?*, but had no voice. Like in the visions, in the nightmares which had blended with the real world and destroyed everything.

Two hands, gentle, on her shoulders. Seyha tried to shake them off, but they held tight. Joyce's voice, "Seyha, you two have a lot to discuss, but we need to get outside."

Bill shouted, "We have nothing to discuss!"

"Come on, Seyha. Stand up. You too, Bill."

"And you kept telling me we would keep trying. Every time, you were popping one of those.. *things* in your mouth! Every day after you killed our daughter..." He staggered to his feet as if drunk, looked around the house. "God!" Seyha didn't know if he was talking to her or actually speaking to God, blaming him for her sins.

A sudden kindle of hope flared, but she mentally snuffed it out. It was far too late for redemption.

She allowed Joyce's help as she stood. Seyha assumed she looked much like Bill in this moment, unable to stand without someone holding her. The windows, so clear, so bright outside. They were free. They could escape. Where would she go? No freer than when the darkness had swallowed them. Less so, now.

The truth will set you free.
The truth had killed her.
Lies had killed her.
"I'm sorry," she whispered, to no one in particular.
They were moving towards the front door.
You've dishonored your family, dishonored your husband, the nun spoke in her head. Seyha feared that voice would stay inside her forever.

*　　*　　*

As Joyce ushered Mrs. Watts towards the front door, Gem kept one fist curled around the priest's sleeve. Afraid an invisible hand might pull her back, trap her here forever. She'd never see her family again. The closer they came to the door, the more this certainty grew.

"Gem, don't push," Joyce muttered over her shoulder.

"Sorry… hurry….."

Bill Watts walked zombie-like beside her. The guy was completely miserable. Gem was afraid to look at him. She'd heard enough to know she didn't want to hear any more. She'd seen too many secrets already, theirs, Joyce's….

When Joyce released one of Seyha's shoulders and opened the front doors, Gem moaned out of desperate hope. *Almost there, almost there….* Her vision blurred. She was crying… again. She hadn't sprouted this many tears her whole life.

As soon as she followed Joyce over the threshold and into freedom, Gem knew she'd be completely nuts in a few days. Inside, they *had* to cope, had no choice. Now, with fragrant summer cut-grass-normal air filling her lungs, she'd be free to start drooling, drawing on her bedroom walls with a crayon between her toes.

Gem turned and held the screen door for Bill Watts.

His eyes were red and swollen, face wet. He sniffed, took the door and absently muttered, "Thanks."

Gem didn't know what to say. She walked down the steps and turned her face to the warmth of the sun. It felt *so good* she wanted to scream. Grass pressed beneath her feet. She looked down. After having been attacked by a demon, impaled through the stomach, and taken on a trip to hell itself, her socks were still in pretty decent shape.

*   *   *

Bill made it outside as far as the bottom step. The neighborhood was bright with the sun burning overhead. How long they'd been inside, or how they might cope with what just happened, held no weight to him. The houses along the street looked alien and cold. He stood on the bottom step, trying not to look at Seyha being led along the walk towards the driveway. She was struggling to free herself of Joyce's grip. They were outside, back to *reality*. What could he do now? Where would he go?

Who is your life, William Watts?

"Leave me alone," he whispered, and sat heavily on the porch. His head was filled with sand. He rested it on his palms, elbows propped on his knees. He stared between them at a crack in the walkway. Tufts of grass forced themselves into the sunlight. His mind raced with thoughts which never made a connection, barely alighting on his brain before another pushed it aside.

Snippets of conversation, talk of children....

Could he get an annulment from the church?

He was the one always talking about a family. Seyha never said....

Did he *want* a divorce? Did he really want to lose her?

Sally at the side of the road, looking so strong and

beautiful, Seyha in the children's liturgy...

The laughter, mocking him, *I've got a secret* its tone said.

Nightmares upon nightmares. Everything spinning. How could anyone deal with this much insanity and betrayal? Seyha. Who *was* she, really, if she could do this?

Seyha, his life....

His blindness....

Opening the drawer, pulling too hard. No, that wasn't right. It had fallen in the vision, not when he'd opened it.

What vision?

He squinted. Was he so mad with misery he was hallucinating? The darkness. Like a dream, fading with morning. Bill struggled to remember the thread...

He remembered the small plastic container of pills. That memory was clear, unmistakable. Seyha's startled confession when he'd confronted her. She'd barely spoken, so *did* she confess? Other events... coming forward, fading, slipping from his mind, or changing into something else.

*   *   *

Joyce noticed it, too, a sudden confusion about what had just happened. She finally released Seyha, asked if she was OK. Of course she wasn't, but Joyce's main concern was to get the woman to focus. What just happened was...

Confusion. Joyce looked at the door through which they'd emerged. Bill sat sullenly on the stoop, face hidden behind his hands. Past him, the screen door was closed, dark beyond. Hard to see anything, except the hint of a white wall.

She was forgetting. Joyce blinked, tried to recapture it, save it. The horror inside, the dreams, the jungle, Ray. Something about Ray. A flash of him, in the basement. In the basement where he'd raped her. Her chest tightened.

Gem mentioned she'd seen Ray recently. When had she said that? Ray was dead. No, Ray wasn't dead, except in her own childish fantasies. Not anymore. Coming back here had been a mistake, too much lingering emotion, memories – true memories – rushing in. There was more, dissipating like a dream in the sun. She fought to hold on.

No, Lord. Don't let me forget anything. Bad as it was, it was a miracle. Even if it might not have come from you, what we witnessed was a miracle in every sense. In a way a blessing...

A blessing of the new home. And an unfortunate accident involving the wrong dresser drawer pulled open, Bill too excited about showing off his handiwork.

The drawer falling to the floor, spilling its contents. Something he saw on the floor starting them down this -

"No!" She shouted the word and looked up. "That's not what happened. I want to remember!"

Everyone looked at her, Bill with an equally confused expression.

Why she had yelled? The Watts were a strong couple, they'd survive this, with God's help.

"No, *please*," she said again, looking up again at the blue sky. "I want to remember." Something cleared in Joyce's mind, like ears popping during an airplane's descent, then a calm certainty, the last of her memory drifting away, then just as gently returned to her. A gift, not a curse. She looked over at Gem. The girl stood on the grass in her socks, staring back and forth between them and her brother's curious stare from the next yard. Joyce still remembered everything, the nightmares, reliving that final night with Ray. She'd hold on to it, she'd remember. *Thinking against the tide*, an expression heard long ago, somewhere. Looking at Gem's confused face, Joyce understood that *this* one needed to let go of the whole experience. How could someone her age live normally after what happened? How would *she*?

"Gem..."

The girl met her halfway. They took each other's hands.

"I'm forgetting," Gem said. "How can I forget..." Joyce gripped her hands tighter.

"It's OK, Gem. Let it go...."

"I won't forget," Gem said, but her wavering expression said otherwise. "I don't know how – "

Her face cleared of expression, smooth as only a sixteen year-old's could be, then gave the Watts a sideways glance.

"I should be going. I doubt the neighbors want me hanging around."

Joyce exhaled, tried not to look as relieved as she felt. She gave her a light pat on the shoulder, then let her hand linger. "Gem, it would be best if you kept what happened – with the Watts, I mean – between us. It's too personal."

"No problem." Gem raised one hand in a mock Scout salute. "Can't exactly say I understand everything. Except..." The confusion flared one last time, then was gone. "Well, no, never mind. None of my business. I was nice seeing you again, Joyce."

Joyce kept her hand on Gem's shoulder. "The parish in Westminster is only ten minutes away. Do you have a driver's license?"

Gem nodded, then blushed. "You're still there?"

Joyce smiled, let her hand drop. "For now. Come and visit."

"Maybe," Gem said, a little too quickly. She added, "But, I mean, didn't you say you were going to South America, or something?" She squinted as if the sun was in her eyes. "Maybe not. Don't remember you actually *saying* that, though, now that I think..."

"You know," she interrupted, "I think I might have. But I'll be around for a while. We can talk about it sometime."

Gem looked down. "OK."

Joyce looked back at the Watts. A leaden sorrow crept into her. She thought of Ray, and would probably never *stop* thinking of him now, wondering too late if it really was wise to hold on to what happened today. She looked into the doorway, knowing that she would never return here. Too many memories, even before the Darkness came. The house had no qualms about sharing its burden, given the chance. At the moment this couple's problems needed to be more important than her own.

Seyha knelt on the grass, ten feet from her husband. She faced him, head bowed like his was. Neither spoke. Joyce caught Bill sneaking a peak at his wife through his hands before staring back down at his feet. Right now they needed her, for no other reason than to be reminded there would always be at least one mediator to help them recover. After that, it was up to them. Considering the magnitude of Bill's reaction to whatever he had discovered, Joyce prayed the damage *could* be repaired. Since the dawn of time, marriages had been destroyed for much less.

Gem began walking away. "Bye," she said. "Good luck with – " She nodded towards Bill and Seyha.

Joyce nodded absently, then crossed the lawn and knelt between the couple.

*　　*　　*

Gem opened the front door of her house. Eliot had followed her across the lawn and stood on the bottom porch step. He whined, "Come on, Gem! Tell something! What was it like inside?" His friend ignored both of them, focusing instead on a nasty scrape along his arm.

Gem paused, one foot over the threshold, and tried to decide what morsel to toss his way. She shrugged and said, "Dark. It was dark."

"That's it?"

For the moment it was, Gem decided, and stepped inside. She climbed the stairs and bypassed her room. She had an overpowering urge to find her father and give him a hug.

Epilogue

Thirteen Years Later

Every pew of Saint Cecelia's Episcopal church was filled. Though many people were regulars, the first few rows had been reserved for guests. Mark Camez, Bishop of Central Massachusetts, bishops of most every other New England diocese, representatives of the central Episcopal office and various local selectmen.

Joyce Lindu lay silent before the altar, her sermons and quiet conversations never to be heard again. For many, those had ended eleven years earlier on the Sunday she said goodbye to the parish and moved to a mission village in Papua New Guinea. Instead of a usual wake, Bishop Camez requested this open casket memorial service the night before the funeral. Because of the time it took to bring her body home from PNG, the casket was closed. No final glimpses of her face, but at least she'd come home. That was closure enough for most people.

The woman at the podium, one of many offering remembrances, hesitated as she gathered her index cards in front of her. She tried not to look at the coffin beside her, lest a new surge of emotion rob her of these last few minutes with her friend. By any standard, the woman preparing to speak would be considered beautiful. Late twenties, medium height with thick blonde hair draped across the shoulders of her business suit – her *only* suit, though she wouldn't admit that to anyone. Gem looked up from the podium and smiled. Even now, the expression was easy for her when she thought of Joyce. She said as much to the sea of faces as a way of beginning.

"Even growing up next door," she continued, "I never really knew her. Ironically, we became friends after she moved away, when we started the first of many long talks after she'd come back to the neighborhood for a visit." She hesitated, scratched a nonexistent itch at the back of her head, a habit she'd developed years ago whenever she was stuck for words. "I can't tell you exactly what we'd talked about then, only that I was this brat of a kid. Thought I knew everything. She could have answered whatever questions I had and moved on. But she didn't. She cared – about me; about everyone." Gem looked down at her notes, but the words were blurry.

I won't cry, she thought. It was a mantra she'd repeated from the moment she'd been called up to speak. Unable to read her notes, knowing her time to explain what this woman meant to her was short, she looked up and took a breath. The corners of her mouth trembled.

"I can't read my notes," she finally admitted, one tear dripping onto the cards. At least her voice was calm, and that gave her strength to improvise. "My tiny problems weren't anything compared with what the folks she served for the last eleven years had to deal with. They needed, well, they needed *everything*, and looked to Joyce as a friend, someone who really wanted to help. So many," she waved a hand in the air, brushing away the thought. "Enough of you already mentioned her mission work down south. That's what she called it. *Down South*." A few light murmurs of appreciation from the crowd.

Gem paused. Suddenly whatever notes she had didn't matter. She'd understood more about the woman than she could ever say up here, anyway. After the embarrassing fiasco in the Watts' house years before, she and Joyce spoke often, especially after Gem began attending church. The woman would only need to make a remark or minor reference to her past, and more details would fill Gem's head, more than Joyce had ever told her. They joked about some psychic connection between them. Maybe there was. Gem could never explain it any other way. Over time, Joyce told her everything, about her daughter, and Ray. Gem told her about the episode with Mister Lindu before the Watts bought the place. When she did, Joyce took the news as if she'd already known about it. That psychic connection again.

Most of these people had no idea how bad the woman's life had been with her husband. No sense shattering their illusions now.

She had to say *something*. Gem didn't dare look over at her husband. She could throw up on the altar right now and Paul would probably think it was cute. She'd give him a whack on the arm later, just in case.

"If she hadn't gone away," she said, struggling to get this last thought out, "if she'd stayed right here, she would have been a great pastor, somewhere. She'd already proven it. She was *good* at it. But she had to leave, and I'm glad she had the guts to do it." She cleared her throat. "I think she was glad, too" She tapped the unread index cards against the podium and added, "Thanks," before walking uncertainly around the platform.

Paul got up from their pew, four rows behind the reserved area, and met her at the edge of the sanctuary railing. She leaned into him, more enthralled with her husband now than the day she'd first gotten up the nerve to ask him on their first date. That hadn't been long after she'd become a regular at Saint Cecelia's. To this day, Paul refused any other explanation for her sudden attendance than his casual invitation the night he helped carry the altar out of the old church. Gem didn't remember what they'd said that night, but he insisted it was true, and she didn't argue. Sounded romantic enough to be a Paul-thing to do.

Rebecca Lindu reached out from her seat in the front row as Gem passed, gave her hand a gentle squeeze. She'd been the one to put her on the list of speakers. Gem hoped she hadn't messed up too badly. Bec's friend LeAnn sat close beside her, holding her other hand.

Gem smiled but stayed close to Paul since his arm was the only thing holding her up at the moment. As they reached their seat, she noticed a familiar face in the last row, shrouded in long, stringy hair. For a second she thought it was Eliot wearing one of his old Halloween costumes. Then, between unwashed strands of gray falling in random directions over the face, Ray Lindu's eyes met hers. Paul guided her to the right, away from the nightmare flash of memory. Maybe that's all it was, a memory. Ray hadn't come back. Not since that day in the pre-Watts church. She looked over her shoulder, trying to appear casual, but couldn't see past so many heads and faces.

The rest of the memorial service was a blur. Gem lost herself in the scent of Paul's musky cologne and her father's constant fidgeting on the other side of her. Eliot would have also come but had been called into the office. Her brother worked too much. Gem kept trying to set him up with Amy Gilbert from church, get a feminine influence to settle his type-A-ness.

Not long after Gem began coming here she'd taken a chance and invited the family to join her. Surprisingly, Eliot agreed. But then, he'd been watching his sister's "new thing" for a while, treating it with the cautious indifference they'd both developed for the various fads their mother would get into. Her father had only nodded, told her he *couldn't think of a reason why not*, and that was the end of the discussion. After his first after-service coffee hour, he never missed another. He talked and mingled with everyone with such an enthusiasm, Gem wondered why she'd ever worried about broaching the subject before. It didn't take long to understand. She never claimed any deep knowledge of the human psyche, but her Dad was easier to read than a Dr. Seuss book.

The man had been lonely. Aside from a family which overlooked him as much as they, themselves, felt ignored, his only company had been the disembodied voices hissing from that damned radio. Gem found herself inexplicably terrified when her father headed up to the attic. She'd had some vivid nightmares about that room years before. The phobia faded as her father dived headlong into *his* new thing, joining as many boards and committees at the church as possible. His time upstairs became an exception rather than a rule. Now and then the nightmares returned, but Gem was never one to have normal dreams, anyway.

She leaned toward him and whispered, "I think I saw Mister Lindu in the back."

Jim Davidson's brows furrowed as he looked around, having no better luck seeing anything than she had. He turned back around and whispered, "You sure? I'd heard he died a while back."

Gem felt a flash of shame at the joy that news offered. Just a flash, though, fading a notch when her father added, "But I could be wrong. I can ask. You'd think he'd be up front if he was around, though…."

Gem shrugged, not thinking that *at all*. "You're probably right."

When they stood for the final hymn, she cringed at a sudden jolt of pain in her chest.

Paul stopped singing, bent to her ear. "Feeding time?"

"Almost. The service is pretty much done. I can wait."

Paul laughed. "Yea, but can Connor? He's probably screaming in Nana's arms right now."

Gem leaned a playful nudge his way. "I left a bottle. He'll be fine." Of course, that depended on whether Nana remembered to take the cover off before putting it in the microwave. Technology was never Deanna Davidson's strong point. Gem wondered if the twins went to bed on time. If not, they'd be wild in the morning. *Sarah and Sean.* Paul came up with those names. Gem had argued against the alliteration, but in the end she had to concede it was nowhere near as bad as her new *Mary Poppinsish* name "Gem Giroux" since marrying Paul.

Her mother still showed no interest in church, and still sometimes disappeared at night, but not as often. At least this provided them with a babysitter. If nothing else, the woman noticed her family more now that she was a grandmother. Family dinners became more frequent. Mom would sometimes ask about Saint Cecelia's and catch up on news of people whom she'd probably never end up meeting.

At the end of the service, they followed the procession down the center aisle towards the exit. Gem tried unsuccessfully to spot Mister Lindu again as the threesome reached an impromptu receiving line at the doors. Bishop Camez excused himself from the line and stepped outside with them. "Thanks so much for coming."

"Our pleasure," her father said, offering him a quick, perfunctory handshake.

"I won't hold you up." The bishop handed Gem a piece of white notebook paper, folded twice. Both sides were covered with pen scratching. "From Bill Watts. He feels bad about not being here, but, obviously it can't be helped." He moved back up the steps to stand with the others, talking over his shoulder. "He sent it to me originally, but he asks about you and said I could share it. I've already read it, so you can keep that if you'd like. I made a copy." His attention was then captured by Phyllis Cowles, an elderly woman who latched onto his arm and spoke quietly into his ear.

Gem waved the paper between her fingers in a silent thank-you then shrugged her coat tighter against the chill. They could read it on the drive home.

*   *   *

The Sisters of Compassion compound was situated twenty miles southeast of Rayong, near Thailand's southernmost border with Cambodia. The orphanage was accessible via a rutted path branching a kilometer and a half from the main road. Its home for the past forty-eight years, the facility benefited recently by a long-awaited affiliation with the Maryknoll monastic order. Even so, the few buildings were humble and in constant need of attention.

Bill Watts pulled his white button shirt away from the sweat on his chest. This early in the morning the temperature still reached twenty-seven degrees Celsius, the air saturated with humidity. It would be worse by lunch, when the children would have their naps in the relative cool of the dormitory. The sisters cared for eleven residents these days. Currently, only ten sat at the table enjoying breakfast. Bowls were tipped at the edge of the long table, spoons tapping out the meal's usual rhythm. Bill smiled. These kids loved to eat.

Four-year-old Sovann, whose stomach seemed never to fill, held up his depleted bowl and asked with as much charm as he could muster – which was considerable, "*Ow kinyum sum wunteptip, Pappa?"*

Though he'd visited this tiny place for the past nine years, staying four months at a time, Bill still hadn't gotten used to speaking the language. The sounds were too unnatural on his tongue. He understood the words well enough, although it didn't take a linguistic genius to understand the meaning of an empty bowl held aloft by a boy who looked more and more well-fed since he arrived six months ago.

Bill looked across the table to the gray-haired nun trying to separate two others fighting over a spoon. Kalliyan had dropped hers on the ground and immediately grabbed her younger brother's, insisting the dirty one was his.

"Sister, do we have enough for seconds?" Questions like this were always spoken in English. Older children usually understood them, but the practice tended to prevent an empty-bowl-stampede if the answer was "yes."

Sister Angelique calmed the siblings down with slaps on the shoulders and a few harshly-spoken words. She reached over and tilted the main serving bowl. Her hair was dry silver, the long tail along her back tied with a blue ribbon. She claimed to be only fifty-six years old, but the deep wrinkles and spotted skin on her arms and neck implied otherwise. Of course, serving in such harsh environments could age a person quickly.

She tipped the bowl this way and that, careful to neither shake nor nod her head and risk revealing her answer to the increasing number of children holding up their bowls. "Let the birthday girl have hers first, then we'll see how much is left."

One of the older girls, an eleven-year old fluent in English, lowered her bowl with a disappointed clunk. Little Sovann looked at Bill for confirmation. Bill raised one finger in a gesture the children had quickly learned meant "Wait, I need to check something," in non-verbal *Papa-speak*. He turned from the table and walked to the chapel across the quad, slapping at the few mosquitoes for whom the heat hadn't yet become unbearable.

The chapel's inner door was open. The outer, a long screen framed one-by-twos, was closed against the insects but allowed in whatever breeze might show itself to pass through. He held up his hands and pressed his nose to the screen, wanting to gauge the situation inside.

Seyha sat cross-legged on the floor in front of the sanctuary. On her lap sat the "birthday girl." Her official name was Mary. One year ago she'd been left on the road leading into the compound, hands and feet bound with twine to prevent her from escaping the large wicker basket. Sister had guessed the girl's age at two when they found her, dehydrated and wailing in fear. With no other information to go by, today became Mary's birthday. Seyha always spent time alone with each child on "their day," this rare moment one of two gifts his wife would give. The second was whatever she could buy or make during the year. In this case, the faceless, hand-stitched doll Mary now clutched in her arms. Bill had offered more than once to bring a case of dolls back from the States, but Seyha had begged him not to. As usual, she never explained why.

Bill watched "Mama Seyha" and the girl with a mixture of love and pain. After all these years, Seyha never overcame her reluctance to bring children of her own into the world. A world which, always and forever, would be a dark and dangerous place to her. Not until the day she announced her plans to join the Sisters of Compassion as a lay worker, with no prior discussion of her plans with Bill, did Seyha's paralyzing phobia of children find some relief. That had been ten years ago. The three years before that had been the worst of Bill's life. In those early months his initial anger had been so insatiable he worried both for his own sanity, and Seyha's. They had separated for a time. Bill spent so much money on hotel bills he once considered leasing an apartment, but doing so felt too permanent.

He eventually moved back home. Divorce was never more than an itch he would scratch in the back of his mind, one that returned in exceptionally low moments. They always had a chance, if he included God in his decisions and Seyha in his prayers. Joyce Lindu had a lot to do with that. She'd been an unfortunate bystander on that infamous day of the home blessing when he discovered the pills, and all of Seyha's secrets. The priest visited often, kept them talking. She never came into the house, even on cold days they talked only on the porch, but she remained a personal representation of Bill's faith, shaken as it had become. Always, Joyce's words, her interest in their problems and simple presence gave him a spark of hope for the future. But only him.

In those first years, after so much darkness had crept into their life, Seyha withdrew into herself. Even Joyce gave up trying to reach her. Seyha said a lot of strange things in those days. Early on she'd apologized for slapping him, and when Bill told her she'd never done such a thing Seyha began to protest, then raised her fingers to her mouth. *You don't remember*, she'd said. When he asked, *Remember what?* she never explained, only fell back into her usual silence.

But Seyha *had* been coming to grips, in her own way. During later, less cryptic conversations, she offered snippets of memory to him. From these Bill had been able to infer other details, filling in the blanks as if he'd known them already and simply needed reminding. Perhaps she'd already chosen her eventual course of action, and was spoon-feeding him the reasons in her own, indecipherable way. Regardless, she eventually decided the only course open to her.

So came the day when Bill arrived home to Seyha waiting with two suitcases packed and a one-way airline ticket to Phnom Penh International airport tucked in her purse. She tried to explain how she felt, that this was the only way she could come to grips with her life, with *their* life. Seyha had never felt at ease in their new house, in the lingering silences and hurt. The latter he almost could understand. But coming to grips with their marriage by traveling to the opposite side of the planet....

He saw her departure as giving up. She was running away forever. He shouted. She cried.

She left.

That night Bill left the house for the last time, unable to be in any room for more than a few moments. He returned to the hotel, eventually located a one-room apartment over Mrs. Torgersen's garage in Hillcrest, found tenants to rent the house. Two years ago when the tenants moved out, Bill sold the place. He could have gotten a better price for it, but he liked the new owners, kept in touch with them. He never visited the house again. Too much hurt lingering in its rooms.

"*Kinyum klein,*" Mary muttered, leaning back against Seyha. The girl hugged her new doll tightly against her chest.

Seyha leaned in close, noticed Bill at the door and gave him a quiet smile as she whispered to the girl, "*Mog nais, nyum mahop bega bruk.*" At the mention of breakfast Mary leapt from Seyha's lap as if burned. She looked worried. When she saw Bill peering in at her the girl shouted, "*Min mahop nasal te?*"

Bill nodded and said in English, "Yes, ma'am. More than enough. We're saving a bowl just for you!"

When she hesitated, Bill smiled and added in Khmer, "*Bat*," then backed away a second before Mary slammed through the door and ran towards the table, doll in tow. Seeing her, the other children raised their own bowls with renewed earnest.

Seyha stepped out and let the screen close behind her. She stood close enough to Bill so their arms touched as she watched the girl clamber onto the bench.

These moments, touching in unspoken acceptance, confirmed for Bill that he'd made the right decision. A decision made six months after his wife left, after dreaming of standing at this very screen door, the hot night filled with bugs biting his face and neck. In the dream he'd knocked on the door and Seyha answered, her face washed featureless by the overhead moon. She did not smile but Bill somehow understood that she was overjoyed to see him. She stepped back into the gloom, reaching to hold the door open. Waiting for him to follow. He woke up.

Later, walking across town, unseen by sleeping neighborhoods, Bill understood his choice. That morning and every morning since, he accepted this would be their life. Four months every year he came to this place, to this woman and her new, old world. Maybe this time he'd finally sell the business and come back here to stay forever. He still prayed that the scars inside his wife would heal. That she could some day face the world outside of this small compound. Whether those prayers were heard, or would ever be answered, time would tell.

The distant bickering of the children over breakfast's remainders punctuated the silence between them. Seyha slipped her hand into Bill's. The two were content with each other's company and the beautiful chaos of their adopted family. In that moment, Bill and Seyha Watts were as close to happy as they would ever be. And it was enough.

*   *   *

Gem drove while Paul read Bill Watts' letter aloud, holding the paper under the map light. A foot of heavy March snow had fallen two days earlier, and the back roads retained a thin coat of drift and frozen slush. Gem took her time cruising into Ledgewood. Her father listened contentedly from the back seat, offering comments and praising the Watts for their work.

Gem made one final turn. Her parents' house was dark, its façade illuminated by an old-style lantern mounted beside the driveway. Gem turned into the driveway of the house next door.

Two years ago, Bill Watts had pulled them aside during coffee hour and casually mentioned his plans to sell the place. They'd still been in the apartment in Worcester, but had been thinking, wistfully, about finding a bigger place for the twins. The price he gave them was ridiculously low, and for a brief moment Gem had become a teenager again, picturing herself standing in the old church. They made the offer the next day, signed the Purchase and Sales agreement two days after that. If the house had hit the market at that price it would have been only a blink on some realtor's chart, but the Girouxs had gotten it. Sometimes Gem wondered if Bill had singled them out specifically, deliberately holding off putting it up for sale publicly until he'd offered it to them. He'd been eager, almost *relieved*, when they said yes.

In the letter Paul was reading, Bill reminded them that the Internet wasn't a commodity where they were, and he'd hoped to "kill two birds with one stone" by including them and Mark Camez on the same letter. He asked after the house and if they still planned to add the second story above the bedrooms. If so, he suggested they get on his crew's schedule soon. He was still considering staying overseas when the building season rolled around. *One day*, he wrote, *I may stay here for good.*

"He's right, you know."

"Yea," she said, not convinced. Even with Bill subcontracting the work, they'd have to take a second mortgage to cover the expense. They never talked of selling, however, nor buying a bigger house. From the moment they moved in, the place felt more like home to Gem than her old house next door. The Lindus and Watts had nothing but bad luck there, but *their* life would be different.

The house had nothing to do with it.

She killed the engine, letting the yard fall back into darkness.

In the house the foyer light was off but through the front windows came the glow of a single lamp further inside the living room. Deanna Davidson preferred the dark. Gem, on the other hand, kept as many lights shining as possible when she was home. Paul had long forsaken his routine of turning them off behind her, and she'd stopped trying to understand the need to see into every corner.

The front door opened as they headed up the front walk. Connor slept contentedly in the crook of his Nana's left arm, absently raising his chubby fists against the sudden cold. Deanna lifted him to her face in a quiet hug, the gold loop of her earring dangling over his face like a tiny mobile.

"He was hungry so I used the bottle," she said. "Not the whole thing. I assumed you'd need to feed him when you got here." She backed up to allow them room to enter. Gem lifted Connor and held him against her own cheek, hoping the act would wake him a little. His small fingers grabbed her lip, but his eyes remained closed.

Her father asked, "You ready to head next door?"

Deanna grabbed her coat off the old pew and draped it over her shoulders. "Not to worry," she said with a grin. "You won't miss your beloved Ten O'clock News." She kissed Paul on the cheek, did likewise to Gem and added, "S & S went to bed about twenty minutes ago, no problems."

Gem inwardly groaned. Considering their usual bedtime was two hours ago, she wasn't surprised they went to bed without complaining.

With a final wave to his in-laws, Paul closed the door and bent down to kiss the baby on the forehead. He whispered, "Wake up and be hungry, little guy." He put a hand softly on his wife's cheek and gave her a short but wondrous kiss. As they moved deeper into the house, Gem began turning on the lights.

About the Author

Dan's previous novels include *Margaret's Ark* and the Bram Stoker Award finalist *Solomon's Grave*, as well as the horror novel *Destroyer of Worlds*, under the pseudonym G. Daniel Gunn. His short fiction has been published in a variety of professional magazines and anthologies over the years, including *Cemetery Dance*, *Shroud Magazine*, *Apex Digest*, *Coach's Midnight Diner* and more.